Simon's Jubilee Game

BY JOHN A. REID

Book cover and all interior page design by John A. Reid

iUniverse LLC

Bloomington

Simon's Jubilee Game

This is a work of fiction. All of the characters, names, incidents, organizations, and dialogue in this novel are either the products of the author's imagination or are used fictitiously.

iUniverse books may be ordered through booksellers or by contacting:

iUniverse
1663 Liberty Drive
Bloomington, IN 47403
www.iuniverse.com
1-800-Authors (1-800-288-4677)

Because of the dynamic nature of the Internet, any Web addresses or links contained in this book may have changed since publication and may no longer be valid. The views expressed in this work are solely those of the author and do not necessarily reflect the views of the publisher, and the publisher hereby disclaims any responsibility for them.

Any people depicted in stock imagery provided by Thinkstock are models, and such images are being used for illustrative purposes only.

Certain stock imagery © Thinkstock.

ISBN: 978-1-4502-9346-4 (sc)
ISBN: 978-1-4502-9347-1 (hc)

Library of Congress Control Number: 2011901158

Printed in the United States of America

iUniverse rev. date: 7/8/2013

PART ONE

Simon decided to begin his jubilee game in 1920s America because it had been there and at that time he'd experienced the first major change in his life. He then whirled his thoughts into vivitime, which immediately caused him to almost forget that he was at the beginning of his game.

CHAPTER ONE

Lynn and her two sons hadn't spoken for over two minutes as they waited for Harold to stop reading something else in the previous day's newspaper before they could start eating breakfast.

Harold closed the newspaper, folded it, and then instead of placing it on the dining room table, he threw it across the room as his wife, Lynn, frowned. He then leaned forward in his chair, put his elbows on the table, and after resting his chin on his folded hands, he stared across the table at his youngest son, Gary.

"Ken told me you stole some coins from his coin collection, and that you spent them," said Harold.

"That's a lie!" Gary shouted at his elder brother.

"You did so!" exclaimed Ken.

"Shut up! Both of you! Go to your room, Gary."

"Yes, dad," he said while getting up from the table, and then he left the dining room.

"Harold, please don't get upset," said Lynn. "I know that Gary doesn't lie, and I know he'd never steal. Maybe Ken put his coins in another drawer, and now he forgets he did that."

"If Ken said Gary stole the coins, then I believe him. Are you calling my eldest son a liar?" Harold asked his wife.

"No, I said he might've misplaced some of his coins."

"How could I do that?" asked Ken. "I keep them all in a jar at the back of my top dresser drawer and Gary's the only one besides you and dad who know that."

"Why don't you count them again? Maybe you..."

"Shut up, Lynn! He told you that Gary stole them, and that's good enough for me!" shouted Harold, getting up from the table.

"Where are you going?" she asked him.

"To teach your son not to steal."

"Kick the heck out of him, dad."

"Harold! Please don't! Have your breakfast while I look for the coins. They could've fallen inside the drawer."

"Yeah, right," said Harold, walking away.

Gary had walked into the bedroom he shared with his elder brother, and then he'd lain face down on the bed to wait for his father to come upstairs to discipline him.

He hadn't stolen his brother's coins, but Ken always accused him of doing something bad almost every other day. Gary had never been able to understand why his father disliked him, and yet he favored Ken to the point of adulation.

Ken had never been liked by any of the boys in school because he was mean and a tattletale, and Gary felt sure that Ken was as ugly on the inside as he was on the outside.

When he heard his father coming upstairs, Gary stopped thinking about Ken and quickly sat up on his bed while worrying that his father was going to beat him. His heart leapt when the door burst open and slammed against the wall, then a moment later, Gary heard his mother's voice.

"Before you strike *him*, strike *me*," said Lynn.

"This is between father and son! The boy's constantly in trouble, and talking to him obviously hasn't worked! Now get the hell out of here!"

"Please punish me, instead, because it's my fault for not adequately teaching him right from wrong."

"How dare you interfere with the way I raise my sons?"

"But you can't prove there are coins missing from Ken's collection, so, you don't have the right to punish Gary. I respect your superior intelligence, and I know I'm merely a woman, but I'm also a mother, and as such, I have a duty to protect my children. I know I deserve to be slapped hard by you when I've made a mistake, but Gary's just a small child. Please, Harold, think of the damage you could do to him while you're so angry."

"If you ever interfere again, I'll do more than slap you! I'll beat you black and blue!" Harold exclaimed as he glared at her.

"Oh, I know that, dear, and I'd deserve it, but you know this is the first time I've overstepped my position as your inferior, and I only did it to protect our son. I fully agree with your method of discipline, but not until he's another year older. Please."

"Fine. You hear that, Gary? Your mother said I can discipline you *my* way in another year! And by God I'll make sure you never get into trouble again! Is that understood?"

"Yes, dad."

"Your father's very angry with you, Gary. He's the master of this house, and I want you to remember that. You must respect everything he tells you. I want you to pay close attention to the way I respect your father, and the way he beats me or slaps my face very hard when I've been stupid enough to do something wrong. If he makes *me* cry, then just think of how much more *you'll* cry when you misbehave badly and he has to beat *you*. Well, Gary? Do you understand everything I've just told you? And will you pay close attention to the way he disciplines me?"

"I will, mom."

"You'd better!" shouted Harold.

"Oh, thank you for sparing our son, dear. I'm so sorry that this incident has disturbed you, and I promise I'll search this house from top to bottom for those coins. If I can't find them, I'll do my very best to try soothing dear Ken by buying him a new shirt that

he can choose, as well as a big sundae and a milkshake whenever he wants," said Lynn, forcing a smile.

"Well, that's the least you can do to make him feel better, but Gary's not to have any treats. Is that understood?"

"Yes, of course, dear. No treats for Gary. Not until we solve the mystery of Ken's missing coins. If we can't find them, then I'll buy Ken five more coins from the numismatist."

"From the new Miss who?" asked Harold.

"That's the man who owns that old coin shop on Lohman Street, dear. That's what they call people who study coins from all over the world."

"Oh, yes. I knew that, but it'd slipped my mind," he lied.

"Of course it did, dear, but that's because you always have so much on your mind. It's such a burden to be a man and have so many decisions to make, such as who to invite to dinner and to business lunches, too, of course. You're out there meeting very important people, and you have to be on your best behavior at all times when you're having lunch with them at the club, and well, just being polite at the office all day, every day. I'm so thankful you don't have to *work* on top of all that, dear. Men have so much to think about, and more women should appreciate that, so, I know how difficult it is for you to come home and then have to face a family problem."

"Hmmm, yes, you're right, and some people in this house should realize that, especially the boy I'm looking at right now. It's about time Gary learned how to behave, instead of stealing and

lying all the time, so, he's not to get any weekly allowance, either. Is that understood?"

"Yes, Harold, dear," she replied.

"I hope you *do* understand because if I find out that you're giving Gary even one penny of allowance this week, then I'll beat you senseless. I'm holding you completely responsible for anything else Gary does wrong. Is that understood?"

"Yes, dear," replied Lynn. "It's completely understood. Thank you for your great patience and generosity."

"If you don't want me to slap your mother around, then stay out of trouble. Is that understood?"

"Yes, dad. I promise."

"Yeah, well, we'll see about that," said Harold.

"Now go have your breakfast, dear, and we'll be downstairs right after I make sure that Gary knows you meant every word you said to him."

Harold swore as he left the room, then after he slammed the door shut, Lynn leaned back against it, crossed her arms, and scowled as she said: "To make your father feel pleased, I'll take Ken for a sundae and a milkshake after school, but you won't be coming with us. Is that understood?"

"Yes, mom."

"Good. I'll give you some money to have a sundae and a milkshake somewhere else with your friends. But don't you dare tell Ken. Is that understood?"

"Yes, mom," replied Gary, trying not to giggle.

"I know you didn't steal any coins, and that you never, ever would. Is that understood?"

"Yes, mom."

"And I know that you'd never lie or do anything bad. Is that understood?"

"Yes, mom."

"Good! Now look very sad when you come back downstairs, and while you're having breakfast, and then after your father leaves for work, and Ken leaves for school, you can be your old smiley self again when *you* leave for school a few minutes after him. Is that understood?"

"Yes, mom," he said as he smiled.

"Now pretend you're so sad, and then we'll go back downstairs. Okay?"

"Okay. I will," said Gary, then he frowned and pouted before saying: "Do I look sad now?"

"Yes, you sure do. Now let's go downstairs and you keep trying to look sad."

"I can do that. Mom? I love you."

"And I love *you*, sweetheart."

Late that evening, Lynn sat at her dressing table, then she pulled off her wig, and ruffled her very short, dark brown hair. A month after they'd married, Harold had told her that he preferred blondes, and he'd demanded that she bleach her hair. Lynn had

realized that she had to obey her husband's demands or else he'd become very angry.

After bleaching her hair once a month for three months, her scalp had become rather dry and sore, therefore, she'd bought a blonde wig, and then cut off almost all of her own hair. She'd then spent many hours developing the best way to apply a paste of talcum powder tinted the same color as her skin to cover her dark eyebrows.

After the paste dried, she would carefully color her stiffened eyebrows with a light brown crayon, hence, everyone she and Harold had met since the time they'd married and moved to this part of the country, thought that Lynn was a natural blonde.

To add to that illusion, Harold had bought her big eyeglasses with tortoise shell frames that hid her supposedly pale brown eyebrows. Lynn felt thankful that Harold had bought nonprescription glasses because she had worried that prescription glasses would cause her to suffer constant eyestrain.

Harold was jealous of any man looking at her, therefore, he'd insisted that she never wear any makeup other than what was necessary to lighten her eyebrows, but he was greatly annoyed because Lynn was still a very lovely woman without makeup.

In an attempt to soothe her husband's insecurity about her facial features, as well as her beautiful figure, Lynn had begun wearing loose-fitting, conservative clothing, although she'd never been able to understand why Harold felt so insecure because she would never think of cheating on him.

Her adoptive father had been a close friend of Harold's father, and she'd married at sixteen years old to appease her father whom had felt that Harold would be an excellent husband for her because he had a good position in his father's company. Lynn had often wondered if she would've been forced into marrying Harold had she not been adopted.

Harold's dislike for his youngest son had started when Gary had been a toddler, but he'd adored his firstborn son from the moment Ken had been born.

He felt pleased that Ken resembled him, and had Harold's small eyes, equine nose, and thin, wide lips, as well as a rather small chin. Harold had always been obese, just like all members of his family, and Ken seemed to have inherited the same genetic trait as the rest of the Creighton family.

Gary, however, had taken after his mother's side of the family. Lynn's male relatives were admired for their rather handsome facial features, and by the time Gary was four years old, Lynn had realized that he'd be much more handsome than any of the males she'd seen in her real family.

She had spent several years searching for her real family, but after finding them, Lynn had felt disheartened when they ignored her. She didn't care that her real family refused to accept or acknowledge her, because she had more important concerns, which were mostly regarding Harold.

She hadn't known when she'd married him that he was quite jealous and possessive with a bad temper, nor had she known that

he'd take out his rage by physically abusing her on occasion. Lynn knew that Harold would eventually start beating Gary so hard that he'd end up in hospital.

Gary was now eight years old, and already taller and stronger than Ken whom was three years his senior, and one of the reasons for the difference in their physical structures was that Gary had always loved participating in every sport he took an interest in.

Ken had always been moody, cruel, and a snide troublemaker, therefore, he only had one friend whom had similar personality traits, whereas Gary had always been quite popular, with many friends. Ken had never fared well in school, and because Gary was a brilliant student, it gave Harold more reason to dislike him.

Every other weekend, Harold would take Ken camping in a forest, far from the city, and they'd hunt and fish together, while Gary was left at home.

Lynn had often pleaded with her husband to take Gary with him on those camping trips, but Harold had always refused. She now planned to make certain that Harold would again refuse to take Gary with him on the next camping trip.

She smiled slightly at Harold as she entered the bedroom, and began walking to the bed, then she stopped, pressed her hands against her stomach, bent over and groaned loudly, and then after leaning slowly back up, she frowned while uttering: "Uhnnn! Uhhhh-huh. Ohhhh, God."

"Damn it! You're having your period again!"

"I...ohhhhhh...I'm...Yes. Mmnnff!"

"I'm not listening to your moaning and groaning all God damned night! I'm sleeping in the guest room!"

"I'm so sorry, dear. I just...Uh! Unff!" Lynn groaned loudly.

"One of these days, I'll make Gary groan even *louder* than you! He's a thief *and* a liar!"

"I was so...So sure he hadn't done it. Maybe if you'd be nicer to him. Ohhhnff! I...I don't think my menstrual cramps have ever been this strong. I think that if...If you took him camping with you, Gary would...Ohh, that last cramp felt like a knife going through me. You've got Friday and...Ohhh, the pain. And Monday off, too. Four whole days, so, if Gary would...Unff! Sorry, the cramps are...Unnf! Gary would love to go camping with you for the next four days," said Lynn, frowning as she gasped and moaned.

"He's not coming with us this time, either, because I'm not going to waste my time trying to teach him how to fish or anything else, and that's that."

"But Gary tries so...Ohhhh! That cramp was even worse than the others. He tries so hard to please you. He...He's even helping me...Hnnnff! Helping me do housework. I appreciate even a bit of help because I do all the shopping. All...All the budgeting. And writing cheques for everything we need, too. I...I...Ohhh, these cramps hurt so much. Hmmnnff! I really appreciate Gary's help. If I'm always doing so many things for *you*, it would be so nice if you'd do just one thing for *me*, and that'd be to take Gary on a

camping trip. But you're right, as usual. Gary would be a burden to both you and Ken if you took him camping with you. He'd want to climb trees, and run through the woods, and swim, and all sorts of things like that, but you and Ken would find that annoying while you two are sitting somewhere, fishing. Ohhh! Hmmmffff! That cramp almost made me faint. But maybe if you *did* take Gary camping with you sometime, he might learn to sit quietly and fish with you and Ken. You *could* think about taking him with you in the morning. Gary would like that."

"Damn it! I've already told you that I won't *ever* take him camping with me, so, stop nagging, you idiot!"

"Yes, dear. Sorry, dear. It's just that I thought you might do me this one, small favor because to please you, I take on so many other responsibilities besides all the household duties. I do all your bookkeeping, handle all our finances, and I also do all the budgeting for your business, as well as here at home, too. I've always told you what to invest in, too. Why do other businessmen have accountants and secretaries, whereas I have to do so much for you, as well as being a wife and mother?"

"Why should I waste money?"

"Speaking of money, I do all the banking, too."

"Damn it, woman! Will you stop whining? Goodbye!"

"Harold, wait! I'm sorry, dear! I'll sleep in the guest room!"

"And hear you bitch about *that* for weeks? Certainly not!"

He walked out of the bedroom, slammed the door shut, then moments later, Lynn smiled as she reclined on the bed, thinking

about Harold and Ken leaving early the following morning for their camping trip.

For the past seven years she'd found Harold to be quite repugnant, and she had learned ways to avoid sexual contact with him. One of those ways was to feign very painful menstrual cramps several times per month.

CHAPTER TWO

Gary awoke very early the next morning, looked across the room and saw Ken packing his suitcase. He watched his elder brother finish packing, then leave the bedroom, and then Gary got out of bed and went down the hall to the bathroom while wishing that he could go camping with his father and brother.

Lynn was pouring another cup of coffee for Harold when Gary entered the kitchen.

"Good morning!" exclaimed Gary, smiling.

"Good morning," said Lynn, winking and smiling at him.

"I counted my coins, so, if there's even one missing, I'm telling dad, and you'll get what you got yesterday," Ken told him.

"Hmmmm," murmured Gary.

"Hurry up, Kenny. I want to leave in half an hour or less."

"Okay, dad."

"Four days this time, huh?" asked Gary.

"Damn it! Don't *you* start whining! Your mother did enough of that last night!" exclaimed Harold, glaring at Gary.

"I'm so sorry, dear," said Lynn, frowning.

"Well, you're not as sorry as *I* am," Harold retorted.

"Yes, I know how you feel, dear, and I hope that this little vacation away from the office will soothe you. I'm so pleased that you decided to go camping for four days this time because it'll do you the world of good."

"Hmmm, I'm sure it will," said Harold. "I need a rest."

"Mr. Thomas is getting a new car, dad," said Gary.

"Are you telling me that my car is too old?"

"No! I didn't meant that! Honest!" cried Gary. "I just meant that he's getting a new car, that's all."

"Hmmm, I see," said Harold. "I'll have to ask him what make of car he's getting. Good for him, and the car industry. Yes, sir-ree, I'll bet in ten years, everyone on this street will have a car."

"Oh? Do you really think so, dear?" asked Lynn.

"Yes, I certainly do. People are talking about the nineteen-thirties as being the richest decade in over a hundred years, and I can see my assets increasing more than tenfold."

"We...Oh, sorry, I meant, *you've* invested so cleverly, dear. Not many men had the good sense to put their money into the automobile market, and into every new radio station. Why, I'm

always so surprised at how lucky we've been with stocks and bonds, and that's because you're so clever, Harold, dear."

"You're darn tootin' I am. Pretty soon, we'll not only have one of the biggest houses in the city, we'll also have a huge country estate. Household staff for all our needs, and..."

"If we'll have all the household staff we need, dear, then does that mean you'll also be hiring business staff to take care of all the finances, too?" Lynn asked him.

"Of course it does, woman. You've performed adequately, but with a much larger income base through my new enterprises, I'll need smart, competent, professional *men* who understand the workings of high finance."

"Well, you seemed to have been pleased with my capabilities, so far, dear. I mean, I've always been the one to decide what you should invest in, and I've always done all the banking and all the household duties, and that's certainly helped us...I mean, helped *you* acquire quite an impressive fortune, considering most other people we know. And even though we've got far more money than everyone else in this neighborhood, as well as most of your business acquaintances, we still don't have even *one* maid."

"I don't believe in flaunting what I have, and I never have, but yes, things'll change when much bigger money starts rolling in. They'll *have* to change because then we'll be rubbing elbows with heads of state and all kinds of high society people, so, there'll have to be proper, well-trained household staff to set up all the parties we'll be having for those types of people."

"Oh, that'll be wonderful," said Lynn, smiling. "Well, we've certainly led quite a frugal existence up to now. I'm sure that no one within ten blocks of this neighborhood would know that you've amassed so much money and other fine assets through your brilliant business tactics, dear. Why, I'm always astonished by how your mind works."

"Most people are. Yes, sir-ree, in a few years, I'll have three or four cars, and I might even buy my own private plane. I can afford it *now*, but I'm waiting until I land another ten or so lucrative contracts, and they'll be landing on my desk as soon as we hit the thirties. That's when I'll be able to retire, and loll around in my gigantic swimming pool on my country estate, and have two or three servants waiting on me hand and foot at the pool. Once in a while, I'll have one of my chauffeurs drive me into the city to check up on all the bosses of all my employees, then trips every two weeks or so to Europe. Yes, sir-ree, I'll be buying all the latest gadgets and anything else that strikes my fancy. You'll see."

"Hah! But you're like Scrooge!" cried Ken as he laughed.

"Well, that's because we may have more money than many other people around here, but I don't and never have believed in wasting it," said Harold, smiling.

"No, you certainly haven't done that, dear. Not ever. You've got well over two hundred thousand dollars in the bank, but no one knows that," Lynn said as she smiled sweetly at Harold.

"Maybe they don't know now, but in a few years, they'll know I've got a lot more than I've got right now."

"Hmmm, sometimes I get worried because of the way you invest your money," said Lynn. "You know, like the times when I take almost all your money out of the bank for you so that you can pay cash for a new company."

"Have I been wrong yet?" Harold asked, glaring at her.

"Oh, no, you haven't, at all, dear. No, and I put back almost double in the bank after you've invested in whatever I've suggested that you should invest in. It's just that I worry what would happen if one of my...Oops! I mean, if one of *your* investment choices turned out to be the wrong decision."

"Hah! You just keep your nose in the books, and let *me* worry about the outcome of the investments. I'm a hell of a lot smarter than you think I am. The worst thing in finance is a woman poking her nose in and offering her stupid opinion. That's why men are the business leaders of the world. A woman's function is to look good for her husband. Chatting to the other wives of successful men, and knowing how to set a table, as well as how to run the house and the staff in it."

"I hope I can prove to be the best wife for you when you start making so many millions of dollars per year, dear."

"Yeah, well, thank God you've got class and beauty, even though you don't have the brains of a man. Finish your milk, son, and let's get on our way," said Harold, smiling at Ken.

"Gee, I'm the only one who won't be at school today and I don't have to go to school on Monday, either, and I bet all the other kids are really jealous," said Ken, grinning.

"I'm not going to school, either, because mom told the teachers that she wanted them to let you and me be away from school on Friday and Monday, too," said Gary.

"You shouldn't be off school because you're not doing anything special today or on Monday, either, but I'm going camping with dad and you can't come with us again. I bet you're really jealous and I'm glad you are."

"Stop talking to him, Kenny, because we're leaving right now, so, say goodbye to them if you want to," said Harold.

"What time will you be returning home, dear?" asked Lynn.

"Probably around midnight on Monday, but if it gets too late, we'll be home early Tuesday morning."

"Four whole days. How nice," she said, smiling.

"So, um, have a good time," said Gary.

"We always have a good time when we go camping," Ken told him, then he snickered.

"Bye, dear," said Lynn, smiling.

"Bye, dad. Bye, Kenny," Gary said as they left the house.

Lynn and Gary stood out on the front porch, waving at them as Harold drove away down the street.

"My! Leaving so early! Five-thirty in the morning. I'm sure they'll have a wonderful time, too," said Lynn.

"Kenny keeps telling me that they always have a real nice time when they go camping. Gee, it sure would be swell to go camping

for all that time. They always go away for Saturdays and Sundays, but this time, they'll be going for four whole days. Boy, is Kenny ever lucky," said Gary, pouting.

"Hmmm, I've got to go to the bank as soon as it opens at ten, and I also have something nice planned for us to do."

"You do?"

"I sure do, honey. I've decided that we're going to take a little trip to see some of your father's relatives. We'll be staying overnight, so, you hurry and pack, all right? And make sure you pack your favorite things so that you can show them off to everyone, all right?"

"Okay, mom. Are we taking the train?"

"Yes, we are. I packed my suitcases yesterday, so, we'll leave for the train station as soon as you finish packing."

"But you have to go to the bank."

"Yes, but first, we'll go to the train station to check-in our suitcases at the baggage counter, then we'll have breakfast at a restaurant. After that, you can sit in the lobby of the bank and look at magazines until I'm finished banking," said Lynn as she looked into a mirror and patted her wig. "How does that sound?"

"Swell! Hey, mom? There's a park right beside the train station, and it's got some real neat rides there, so, I can hang around there 'til you come back from the bank. Okay?"

"Oh yes, I forgot about that little amusement park. It opens at nine every morning when the commuter trains start running. That's a much better idea, but don't wander away from there until I come

back from the bank. Okay?"

"I won't. Does dad know we're going?"

"Oh, no, he doesn't know that because he would never approve of me spending money in a nice restaurant and taking the train out of the city to visit relatives," said Lynn, smiling.

"Well, he sure spends money on Kenny and himself."

"Yes, he enjoys doing that. He told me that he's thinking of buying a big cabin to stay in for their trips. Why, he could afford to buy a hotel out in the woods with all the money he's saved up in the bank. He's so frugal. But then he's a man and the master of this house and his office, so, I'd never ask him why he's so frugal. I think it's wonderful how I can depend on him for always being the same way, and never wavering. Yes, and so steadfast in his decisions to have this or that for lunch with his business associates. But as I said, he's a man, so, as a woman, I have no right to even suggest that he try ordering something else that I think he might enjoy having for lunch. All I've ever done is tell him what to invest in, and that's made him so happy because he's made so much money. Of course, he's never acknowledged the fact that my suggestions have made him a wealthy man, but I'm sure that one day soon, he'll realize that, although I'm sure that even then, he won't thank me. Now you go upstairs and pack. Hurry now, because I'd like to leave here before it gets too light out. I don't want to get caught in all the morning rush hour traffic, so, we have to leave the house in about twenty minutes."

"Wow! You're really tops! I'll hurry, mom!"

Gary felt so pleased that he would be going on a train to visit relatives outside the city, and he hoped that he'd be able to go fishing and swimming.

They left the house, and walked to the end of the street to take a bus to the train station, then Gary felt excited while watching all the people carrying suitcases as they hurried to take a train, or to greet someone getting off a train.

Lynn bought the tickets, checked their suitcases in at the baggage counter, and then she took him to a restaurant close to the train station, and they had breakfast.

After they'd eaten, Lynn had almost two hours to wait before the bank opened, so, she hired a cab to take them down to the waterfront, and then they went on an hour-long tour of the waterfront on a ferry.

They rode in a cab from the waterfront to the front gates of the children's amusement park beside the train station, then Lynn stayed with Gary until it was time for her to leave for the bank.

She then gave him a dollar to pay for the Ferris wheel and other rides, then made him promise to stay inside the park until she returned in slightly over half an hour. After saying goodbye to her, Gary ran over to join several other children who were also waiting to take a train ride out of the city.

Although the Ferris wheel wasn't very high, Gary could see for many city blocks, and he became more excited each time he was taken up to the highest point of the Ferris wheel where he could see trains chugging in and out of the station.

CHAPTER THREE

Lynn arrived at the bank, and was greeted with smiles by the bank employees as she walked to the reception desk, and then asked to speak to the bank manager.

The manager, Mr. Sym, was told that Lynn was in the bank, so, he quickly tidied his desk, combed his hair, straightened his tie, then hurried out of his office to escort her inside.

His secretary took the vase of flowers off her desk, rushed into his office, and placed the vase on the desk near the chair where Lynn would be seated.

Lynn sat in Mr. Sym's office, and agreed with him when he said that Harold had always surprised him with investment ideas that other bank clients would deem foolhardy, but Harold's business investments had always proved to be quite successful.

"Yes, he's quite the unpredictable entrepreneur," said Lynn.

"And a highly successful one whom I greatly admire."

"As well do I, sir."

"Clever man, however, I must confess that I doubted his business acumen when I first became aware of his, shall we say, investment adventures. That was a little over eight years ago, when he had become one of our nicest and most preferred customers. Back then, he withdrew almost all his savings to buy your first home and the small building his office was in, and that venture was surprisingly successful. Two years after that, he'd insisted on

paying cash for your second and larger home, as well as paying cash for the office building next door to the one he'd bought two years previously. Those investments were quite successful, too."

"Yes, he certainly knew what he was doing. Harold's never believed in mortgage payments, nor in car payments, so, that's why he paid cash again for his latest new car. Harold's never believed in paying interest on a loan," Lynn said, smiling.

She felt it best not to tell Mr. Sym that it had really been through her clever thinking that Harold had acquired every penny he now had in the bank, so, she simply continued smiling.

The bank manager winked at her and said that quite a few people referred to Harold as the stingiest man they'd ever known because he lived on such a tight budget.

"I've heard several people refer to him as that," said Lynn.

"Ah, but one has to admit that your husband is a wise man, and he's never spent his money foolishly. He's made many sound investments in automotive manufacturing companies, as well as other fast-growing businesses, and I'm more than certain that his next business venture will be quite successful, as usual. And, as usual, he never discloses the details of a new venture until after he asks you to make an almost complete withdrawal of his savings, However, I'm always quite able to accommodate his sudden requests within half an hour."

"It's Harold's way, which brings me to the reason I've dropped by to see you today. Now I expect what I have to say to be kept in the strictest confidence."

"Oh, most definitely, Mrs. Creighton. As you know, I've never disclosed anything of a private nature concerning you or your husband, and certainly nothing of your husband's investment plans because I know too well that it could jeopardize his plans if other investors knew he was about to take on another lucrative business. No, never a word from me, Mrs. Creighton. No one would ever know that you were in my office to discuss another new business venture of your husband's. I, as always, will simply tell other businessmen clients of this bank that you came in to review Mr. Creighton's account. Nothing else, I assure you. Are you here for that reason, ma'am?"

"Yes, I am. You see, my husband is very excited about this new plan he's thought of, and it's to do with..." Lynn began explaining that Harold had devised another business plan that would be highly successful. Mr. Sym's eyes widened as she told him that Harold's plan, as usual, had to kept in the utmost secrecy for perhaps a month before he felt it was time to reveal his latest very successful business venture.

Mr. Sym excused himself, left the office, then told his employees that he would personally fulfill Mrs. Creighton's request. He then asked an employee to brew fresh coffee for Lynn, and then Mr. Sym told another employee to rush out and buy pastries to be served with the coffee.

Fifteen minutes later, Lynn put down her coffee cup when Mr. Sym told her that everything was in order, and that he was just as excited as Harold about the new business venture, then Lynn

smiled as she said: "You know, Mr. Sym, there was a time when I doubted Harold's unpredictable way of doing business, but now I truly admire his clever business sense."

"Well, women don't have that sense of forging new frontiers in the business world. But that's not to say that women don't serve a truly great and wonderful purpose, because without them, we wouldn't have future presidents and leading businessmen here and everywhere else in the world," he said while smiling.

"Why, Harold told me the very same thing this morning. That's why he's a business leader, and you are, as well. I'm rather impressed by your success, too, sir. Commanding a large bank such as this, and being able to give the best advice to all of your clients. Decisions, decisions, decisions. I know that I certainly couldn't think of sound advice to give someone about finance and loans and mortgages, and all. It's always a pleasure visiting you, and I always feel more than satisfied and relieved after I've spoken with you. Excellent service at all times. My, such constant professionalism. I know that this new venture of Harold's will greatly surprise me again, but of course, not *you*, because you have the same sort of mind as my Harold."

"Thank you, Mrs. Creighton. Your husband is a wise investor and all my clients agree because he's done quite well, especially in the past five years. Yes, quite well indeed."

"Thank you, sir, and yes, he certainly has done quite well, but he's so secretive. He won't tell me very much about the huge factory he's buying," said Lynn, smiling.

"Factory?"

"Oh! I wasn't supposed to mention that. Oh, dear."

"I won't breathe a word, Mrs. Creighton. I'll bet he has a few partners on *this* venture, if it's a very large factory."

"Well, no partners, yet, but he told me there's a huge...No, I won't say anything more," she said, giggling.

"And I won't ask," he replied, winking at her, as he grinned.

"Oh, but I'm sure he'll tell you much more when he comes in to see you on Wednesday afternoon. Well, now I suppose I'd better be on my way. Hmmm, I wonder which hotel Harold chose to stay at when he arrived in...Oops! I almost said more than I should."

Mr. Sym smiled at her as he picked up the phone on his desk, and told his secretary: "Miss Wharton. Please bring that canvas package to me, now. Thank you. My secretary's bringing in the canvas package now, Mrs. Creighton, and then you can put it in your bag before you leave my office."

"Oh, my, yes, I'll certainly do that. I feel a little nervous about carrying one hundred and eighty-five thousand dollars in cash on my person. Why, our lovely new house is the nicest on the block, and it cost us a little over twelve thousand dollars, so, I'm slightly intimidated with all this money in my bag. But men are so much braver, and that's why no amount of money bothers them, and they know more about business matters than we ladies do. For instance, my Harold told me that by nineteen-thirty, the economy of this country is going to take great leaps. It's astounding how men are able to predict the future like that. Oh, would you have someone

call me a cab, please? I can get right into that instead of waiting on the street until one comes along."

"Certainly, Mrs. Creighton. I'd intended to do that, anyway. That'll be all, Miss Wharton. Please have Mr. Lawson hail a cab for Mrs. Creighton, immediately."

"Yes, sir," said Miss Wharton, hurrying away.

"Now don't you worry, Mrs. Creighton. There are many cabs on this street, so, you won't have long to wait. Less than a few moments. Guaranteed."

"Oh, thank you, sir. This is so kind of you. Hmmm, is the large, canvas case noticeable in my big handbag?" asked Lynn.

"No, it's not, so, there's no need to worry."

The phone rang again, and Mr. Sym answered it, then smiled as he said: "Yes? Thank you, Mr. Lawson. We have a cab waiting for you now, Mrs. Creighton. It's been so nice seeing you again. I admire a woman who can rear a family and be her husband's private secretary at the same time. Even do all his banking."

"I think Harold has an allergy to banks because I've always done all the banking. But you do see him occasionally at the club, don't you?"

"Yes, I do, and sometimes once a month. I hope I'll see him at the club a week from next Friday when my wife and I have dinner there, but if not, then I'll look forward to seeing him here at the bank on Wednesday afternoon."

"I hope you won't be too disappointed if he asks me to drop by here in his stead," said Lynn, smiling.

"Oh, I'm used to that by now, and I expected that I'd be seeing you instead of him on Wednesday, anyway."

"I've got oodles of things to do, so, I might not be in 'til oh, perhaps Thursday. No, Friday? Or maybe on the following Monday or Tuesday. Hmmm, oh, well, sometime next week or the week after that, and that's only if Harold doesn't come see you before I do. Oh, I wonder if he'll be back within the next two weeks? He's so busy doing...Oops! There I go again. He told me not to say a word about his new business venture. Anyway, if he isn't back home in the next two weeks, then I'll be here at your bank one day next week or the week after that because we're so busy right now with this clever, as usual, new business venture of his. My Harold's always so busy earning a much more than decent living for us. God bless him. I'm so lucky to be his wife."

"Yes, I imagine you are. Goodbye, Mrs. Creighton, and please congratulate your husband for me."

"Oh, I certainly will. Thank you, and goodbye, Mr. Sym."

Lynn was escorted out of the bank, and then Mr. Lawson held the cab door open for her as she smiled and thanked him before the cab whisked her away to the train station.

She got out of the cab a block away from the train station, then Lynn walked to the amusement park, and beckoned Gary, and then he held her hand as they walked past the train station.

"Where are we going?" Gary asked her.

"There's a row of shops down the block, and I want to do some quick shopping. I've decided that instead of waiting in line to get a table in the train's dining room, we'll have lunch and dinner in our compartment. Okay, honey?"

"Yeah, that'll be fun."

"I'll buy a big picnic hamper and we'll fill it with food and sweets, too. Hmmm, there's a big deli up ahead. I'll have them make up lots of sandwiches, and then we'll choose some of their pastries. After we place our order, I'll ask them where the nearest store is that sells picnic hampers and linen napkins," said Lynn.

"Won't it be really heavy when there's bottles in it?"

"No, it won't, sweetheart, because I'll have the porter bring all our beverages to the compartment, and every time the train stops at a station, we can get off, and buy an ice cream treat."

"Yeah? Boy, this is going to be even better than the camping trip that dad and Kenny went on."

"I'm sure it will be, honey. Very sure."

Lynn went into the delicatessen, ordered a variety of sandwiches and pastries, then asked where she could buy a picnic hamper. After buying a picnic hamper at a store farther down the street, she and Gary went to another store to buy a few new clothing items, and a baseball cap for Gary, which he loved.

They then returned to the delicatessen and had the hamper filled before they walked to the train station, then Gary was elated when Lynn and a porter helped him board the train, and then the porter led them to their private compartment.

After they were seated in their train compartment, Lynn took off her tortoise shell-framed eyeglasses, then broke them in half before putting them in her handbag.

"Gee, you look a lot different after you take off your glasses."

"And they're staying off," said Lynn, smiling. "I don't really need to wear glasses, but your father thought I looked prettier with glasses, so, he asked me to wear them all the time. The next time I see him, I'll tell him that instead of wearing glasses, I'll change my hairstyle in a way that'll make me look prettier."

"I think you look a lot prettier now that you took them off."

"Aw, thank you, Gary. That's a very nice compliment."

Lynn opened two soft drink bottles, then put straws in them, and then she asked Gary to sit beside her while she told him about a game they would play during their train trip.

"There are at least four or five other children your age on this train, so, you can play in the aisles with them as long as you make sure you don't cause too much noise, all right?" said Lynn.

"Yeah, I know. So, what kind of game are we going to play?"

"It's called 'Secret Agent,' and we'll play it right up to the time we get to where we're going."

"Oh, yeah? That'll be fun," said Gary.

"I think so, too, but no one but us will know we're playing the game, and we'll have secret code names, all right? I'll play Miss Elizabeth O'Donnel, and I'll pretend I'm your governess, and

we're on our way back to a big city after I took you to visit your relatives. But we won't tell anyone where your relatives live, or what big city we're supposed to be going to. That'll be part of our game, and if you want, you can tell the other children that you're going to whatever city you decide to tell them, and you make up a name for a city where you were supposed to be visiting relatives. Oh, and you'll have to have a secret name, too, same as me. Hmmm, let me see. What names can we think of? Oh, I know. I'll call you, Master Robert Bellamy. How does that sound?"

"Yeah, I like that name. It's easy to remember, too."

"I'm glad you like it, Robert," she said, smiling.

"I like it a lot, Miss O'Donnel," said Gary, then he giggled.

"I used that name when I bought the tickets, just to start the game off, so, unless you tell someone our real names, no one'll know about the secret agent game that we're playing."

"When will the train start going?" asked Gary.

"In about two minutes."

"Yeah? Oh, boy!"

"Now don't forget when you're playing on the train, not to tell the other children that we're spies for the government."

"Nope, I won't forget. I can be just like a spy, but nobody'll ever know I'm a spy. You wait and see."

"Oh, I know you can play a spy very well, honey, because you're the smartest boy I know anywhere, so, I bet everyone'll believe you," said Lynn, smiling.

Three minutes later, Gary heard a whistle blow, and then he

laughed when he felt the train shift forward, and then start slowly rolling along the tracks.

The train picked up speed after leaving the city limits, and within five minutes, Gary felt so excited as he looked out the train window at the rural scenery.

By late afternoon, they'd traveled over three hundred miles, however, Gary had been too busy playing cards with his mother, and meeting other kids on the train to notice how long they'd been traveling.

The train stopped at another station where they had a snack in a restaurant, then boarded a different train.

"How many more trains are we going to be going on?"

"I'll tell you that when the president sends me a secret message. That's part of the game," said Lynn, winking at him.

"I really like this game, and none of the other kids on that other train even knew I was playing it with you, and they all believed me when I told them my name is Robert, too."

"I knew you were a very good actor. There's going to be another stop at a station, after we're on this train for a few hours, and it'll be enough time for us to have a nice hot dinner, and we'll buy some ice cream that you can have when we get back on the train. All right?"

"Oh, yeah! That'll be super-duper!" Gary happily exclaimed.

At the next scheduled stop, they had dinner in a restaurant close to the train station, and then Gary climbed back on the train while holding a double-dip ice cream cone.

Lynn asked the porter to make up their beds at seven o'clock, and although Gary protested at first when his mother told him to get ready for bed, he'd been up so early that day, that he fell asleep just after Lynn kissed him goodnight.

The following morning, Gary helped his mother carry their suitcases off the second train and onto a third train, and he was finding the secret agent game to be so much fun. He excitedly nudged Lynn and told her to look out the window when he saw the ocean, then he gawked at her when she told him they were going to take a trip on a very big boat.

"Yeah? Oh, boy! I'll bet Ken'll be really jealous when I tell him I was on a really big boat! What do you think they're doing right now?"

"Well, I imagine they're just waking up, and they're going to heat up a can of beans on the campfire for their breakfast."

"They told me they don't take eggs with them because they don't stay fresh while they're camping. But *we* can have eggs for breakfast every morning and we're going to lots of different places on the train," said Gary.

"Yes, but in about half an hour, we'll be off the train and then getting onto a big boat."

"Will we see any whales?"

"Maybe. Sometimes you can see dolphins out in the water."

"Oh, yeah? I drew some pictures of a dolphin in school, and the teacher put one of them up on the wall. Dolphins like to jump way up out of the water, and they like to play with people, too. That's what my teacher told me."

"I've heard that they do," said Lynn, smiling. "Here, let me fold that shirt for you, honey. We're almost finished packing our suitcases, so, you go to the bathroom."

"I already did before."

"That was almost two hours ago, so, go see if you have to go again. Oh, and if there's a long lineup, then come back here, and we'll go to a washroom in the station when we get off the train."

"Okay. I'll hurry, mom."

Gary left their train compartment, and as he hurried down the aisle, he wondered how long he'd have to wait to use the bathroom because there were two adults waiting outside the door.

He looked out the train window as he waited to use the bathroom, then after entering it, Gary soon learned that he didn't have to urinate. He pulled a little paper cup out of the dispenser on the wall by the sink, and after filling the cup with water, he began drinking as he looked into the mirror above the sink and he decided to make his hair look a bit neater.

He took his comb out of his pocket, and then as Gary looked into the mirror while combing his hair, he smiled as he thought

about how wonderful it was being on the train and playing his mother's secret agent game.

His reflection faded because of a sudden light in the mirror, then Gary saw a nude man seated in a chair in a small room, and his arms were lifted out to his sides while syringes imbedded in his wrists and neck were filling with blood.

A moment later, the light went off in that small room, then Gary's could see his reflection clearer. He felt sure that it was a two-way mirror, and that somebody in the train compartment behind the bathroom had turned on a light to look into the mirror, and when that person had seen him, he or she had quickly turned off the light.

Gary presumed that all bathrooms on trains had two-way mirrors, then he slid his comb back into his pocket, left the bathroom, and when he returned to his compartment, he smiled at his mother while saying: "I didn't have to pee, mom."

"Oh, okay. Sit down here beside me. The train'll be stopping in just a few minutes, and then we'll take a cab to the docks."

A week before they'd left home, Lynn had reserved a very nice accommodation aboard ship. When they arrived at the docks, Gary felt excited as he looked around at the huge crowds of people waving to passengers who were already on the ship.

After he and Lynn had boarded the ship and put their suitcases in their cabin, they took a long walk along the deck. Just before it

was time to have dinner, Gary was astonished when Lynn opened one of the suitcases, and removed new clothing that she'd bought the week before they'd left home.

They took baths before dressing in their new clothes to wear for dinner, and Gary felt both pleased and proud when they left for the dining room because Lynn was wearing a lovely, full-length gown, and he had on a tuxedo.

When they'd been at sea for a week, Gary wondered how angry his father would be because they'd been away from home for so long. He stopped worrying about that when Lynn assured him that he'd never have to worry about Harold getting angry with him again. Gary loved his mother, and trusted her implicitly, so, he felt pleased that he'd never have to fear his father again.

CHAPTER FOUR

The ship docked in England, and then while they were having dinner in a fine restaurant, Lynn told him that they were going on another rail trip.

They left the restaurant, and Lynn hired a taxi to take them to the train station, as Gary felt excited while looking forward to another fun adventure.

The train left London, then passed by small cities and towns, and then even smaller towns until they got off the train at noon the following day in the southern part of England.

Lynn hailed a cab, then as she spoke to the driver, Gary looked around at people walking to and from the train station, and then he got into the taxi with his mother.

"It won't be long now," said Lynn. "I'm glad you slept so well on the train last night."

"We sure have come a long way," said Gary, smiling.

"Have you had fun?"

"Oh, yeah! Lots and lots of fun! Where's this taxi going?"

"Right downtown, honey."

"Are we going to buy some more new clothes?"

"No, we're going to a real estate office to look for a nice house to buy because we'll be staying here for quite some time."

"We will? Oh, boy! Then we'll have our *own* place instead of a hotel, right?"

"That's right, honey. But first we'll have lunch."

"Sssssst. Mom," whispered Gary after he leaned close to her.

"Yes?"

"Are we still playing the secret agent game?"

"Yes, we are, so, we'll keep having secret names, and we won't tell anyone where we really come from. We'll just say we come from Chicago, and we'll keep playing our secret agent game until I tell you it's over. All right?" she whispered.

"Yeah, okay. So, we'll have more secret names?"

"Yes, we will, but later today, after I choose a nice house for us to live in, I'll tell you a big secret about the next part of the game. The next secret is the biggest and most important one of all the other secrets," whispered Lynn.

"Gee! That sounds like a really, really big secret."

"It sure is, and I bet you can keep this next secret, too, because you're so smart."

Gary giggled and looked out the cab window at the streets and people they passed on the way to the restaurant, and he felt very excited about playing more of his mother's secret agent game.

They had lunch before going to a real estate company where Gary sat in the reception lounge, looking through magazines while his mother spoke with the owner.

Lynn looked through a portfolio of homes for sale, then after pointing out her selections, they were driven out of town and

shown the prospective properties.

She made her decision, and then later that day, Gary felt pleased with the house they would be moving into because it was close to the ocean and he could play on the beach.

After buying the house, which was partially furnished, Lynn bought a car in town. She then shopped for groceries and other necessary items before driving back to the house to prepare their first dinner in England.

They had dinner out on the veranda while talking about the trips they'd taken on trains and the ocean liner. After they'd had dessert, Lynn poured him another glass of milk and a cup of tea for herself, then she told him that she would now explain the final part of the secret agent game, which held the biggest secret.

"This is the end of the game, and from now on, I want you to play the part of a whole new person, and I will, too."

"For how long?" Gary asked her.

"Forever, honey."

"Yeah? What about Kenny and dad? Will they have the same last names as us?"

"No, they won't. Gary, what would you think if we never went back home?"

"Never?"

"Not ever."

"I don't know. I mean, they don't like me, and if I'm going to be here with you all the time from now on, I'd really like that. Dad and Kenny are always real mean to me, and they don't want me to

be with them, ever, and I always get blamed for things I didn't do because Kenny always lies and tells dad I did bad things. Dad said he's going to start hitting me really hard, too, and I don't want him to do that. But I'm sure he will because Kenny'll just keep telling him I stole his things and all kinds of other stuff to get me in trouble. He lies all the time about everything, and he tattles on all the other kids, too, and so that's why he doesn't have any friends at school or anywhere. I don't know why he's so mean to everyone. He always picks on kids who are a lot smaller than him, too, and that's why everyone calls him a big, fat bully. I guess he's going to keep doing that, and dad'll keep on believing Kenny's lies. That's why I like being way over here with you, okay? And this place is a lot better than back home, too."

"I had a feeling you'd agree to living here, but it means that you can never tell anyone you meet what your name was before we came here."

"I won't ever tell, mom. I promise."

"If people ever find out what our other names used to be, then your dad and Ken will know where we are, and then they'll come over here, and tell us that we have to go back home."

"Yeah, I bet they will, too, so, I'll make real sure I never tell anyone. Not ever. That way, they'll never know we're here. Have you thought up a new name for me and for you?"

"Yes, I have, sweetheart. A long time ago, too. When I knew I was going to have another baby, I chose a name for you, but your father wouldn't let me call you by that name, so, *he* chose 'Gary.'

I've always felt that the name *I* chose for you, was the best one, and that's the name I'd like you to use now, and I'll be using the name that I've always wanted to be called, too, and that'll be, 'Miranda,' and *your* name will be, 'Simon,' " said Lynn, smiling.

"I really like those names, and I like my new name best of all."

"I'm so glad you do. And our last names'll be, Hayworth."

"Simon Hayworth. Yeah, that's a super name. I like your name, too, mom. Miranda. Miranda and Simon Hayworth. Yeah, they're a lot better than our other names."

"Now I'll show you something else."

Lynn raised her right hand, pulled off her blonde wig, and then Gary's eyes widened.

"Wow! Your hair's black like mine, too!"

"Yes, it is, but your father wanted me to have blonde hair. I began bleaching my hair to make it blonde, then my scalp began breaking out in terrible rashes, so, I had to wear a blonde wig."

"Yeah? Are you going to stop wearing that wig now?"

"Yes, I sure am because I never liked wearing wigs. I've been letting my real hair grow for a few months, so, very soon, it'll be much longer."

"But the man who sold us the house and the people where we bought the groceries saw you wearing that blonde wig."

"That's okay, because many women wear a wig when their hair is messy, and they have to go to town or to a party in a hurry. Besides, we probably won't be seeing that real estate man again because he lives so far away from us. Even if he *did* see us again,

I'm sure he either won't remember that I had blonde hair, or if he asks why my hair is a different color, then I'll tell him what I just told you. That my hair was a mess and so I put on a wig to see him at his office."

"I like you much better with black hair like me."

"Why, thank you, Simon."

"You're welcome, Miranda. Oh, but I'll keep calling you 'mom' and the grownups can call you Miranda."

"We'll be used to our new names very soon, too."

"Yeah, I know we will," Simon said, smiling broadly.

Lynn tucked him into bed for the night, then she went back downstairs, poured a coffee and a liqueur, and then she sat out on the veranda. She thought about her furtive trip to England, buying a house while using the name Miranda Hayworth, and about shopping for new furniture in the next few days.

Lynn then felt so pleased that Gary would be much happier here, and then she sighed and smiled as she looked at the view from her veranda.

From the time she'd been ten years old, Lynn had taken a keen interest in her adoptive father's conversations regarding business methods he'd used to acquire his constantly growing wealth.

He had thought it would be another wise business decision to have Lynn marry the son of one of his business associates, then

soon after marrying Harold, she began making financial investment suggestions to him that proved to be quite lucrative.

Harold had then begun to rely on Lynn for all future business investment decisions, hence, she felt that all the money they'd acquired during their marriage was rightfully hers.

She had earned that money while continually tolerating both verbal and physical abuse from Harold and he had also threatened to start abusing Gary.

She realized, however, that until she felt sure that she couldn't be found by any investigators hired by Harold, she had to live a modest lifestyle.

She loved both of her sons, and she often wept when thinking about Ken, whom she'd most likely never see again. Lynn had had to make the agonizing choice of giving up Ken for the safety and well-being of Gary, as well as herself.

Harold had conditioned Ken to disrespect her, and because of that, Lynn felt certain that with the love and much attention Ken received from his father and grandparents, that he'd soon stop grieving over the loss of his mother.

CHAPTER FIVE

During the first year of Lynn's residency near the small town, Lynn had established the reputation of being a pleasant and very beautiful young widow with a son. When her hair had grown longer, Lynn loved the feel of fresh air blowing through her natural, wavy, dark brown hair again.

Not wanting to attract too much attention to herself, Lynn dressed in the same fashion as other women in town with less means than herself, and living two miles out of town helped to assure her new identity.

She'd opened all three bank accounts using the name, Miranda Hayworth, because she'd paid for new identification papers for herself and Gary while back in the U.S.A.

She hired a woman to care for Simon whenever she traveled to London and other large cities for weekend visits. After a few months of weekend visits to large cities, Miranda was delightfully surprised when she met Noel Baldry in London, and fell in love with him.

Whenever she and Noel visited his friends, Miranda noticed that he was fond of children, then after inviting him to her home on several occasions, she felt quite pleased when he and Simon became fast friends.

She married Noel a year later, with Simon's blessing, and then realizing how much Miranda and Simon loved the area they lived

in, Noel bought a large old estate eight miles from the home that Miranda had bought when she had arrived in England.

Noel was a thirty-five-year-old successful barrister, therefore, Miranda didn't have to spend any of her savings. His wealthy family's wedding gift to him and Miranda was a month in Hawaii. Simon loved taking his first airplane trip, and the trips around the Hawaiian Islands.

Twice each year, Miranda and Noel took two-week vacations to many different countries, accompanied by Simon and a friend of his choosing, as well as either a niece or nephew of Noel's.

Simon had many friends, so, he'd put their names in a hat during a party, and then the boy or girl whose name was drawn would be the next of Simon's friends to go on a two-week vacation with him.

By the time Simon was ten years old, he'd almost forgotten about his home back in America, and his former name seemed like a distant memory.

A few months before his fourteenth birthday, his stepfather renovated the stables, and bought four horses, one of which was given to Simon, and from then on, he loved riding every day, and going on two to sometimes three-day camping and fishing trips with his friends and his stepfather.

Harold had predicted a great economic surge in the 1930s, however, that decade became known as The Great Depression.

Unemployment soared along with much social unrest. Miranda then realized that if she hadn't left Harold when she did, she would've been financially destitute because he would have kept an even tighter grip and a more watchful eye on his assets.

Noel lost a large percentage of his business, but he was still financially sound, and Miranda admired his dedication to offer his legal services pro bono to people with overwhelming debts.

Miranda and Noel also worked together to ease the financial burdens of their neighbors by hiring them on a temporary basis, paying them a quite substantial wage, then replacing them after a few months to hire new staff.

Noel would hire men to build an addition to the house, then he'd hire other men to tear down the new addition and rebuild it. Miranda often visited families to assess their situation, then she and Noel would surreptitiously return to their homes late at night with gifts of food, new clothes, and an envelope containing cash to pay for household expenses and any medical expenses.

Miranda and Noel smiled when they began hearing rumors among their neighbors of a mysterious and benevolent creature similar to Father Christmas whom arrived unseen during the night with big bags of gifts.

PART TWO

CHAPTER SIX

Simon whirled his thoughts forward to a month after his eighteenth birthday while knowing he'd have to concentrate very hard on his jubilee game fun so that he wouldn't veer into the awful tragedy he had suffered a few months after that birthday.

One sunny afternoon, he rode his horse to the top of a high hill, then he dismounted and stood looking out over the landscape. He then raised his arms high above his head, closed his eyes, and laughed as he began turning in circles, faster and faster while loving the feeling of dizziness.

He opened his eyes again, and then laughed as he fell to the ground and rolled over and over in the grass while his horse whinnied and nodded its head at seeing Simon taking such pleasure in a wonderful summer's day.

Simon laid on his back, smiling while looking up at the slowly drifting clouds that were creating what he imagined were fantasy ghost shapes of memories.

He then thought about the time when he and his mother had played the secret agent game while leaving America to live in England, and then he grinned while thinking of his jubilee game

that he'd devised as a celebration of his life with the person whom he loved so much.

His thoughts were interrupted when he was asked: "Is the coffee too strong?"

"Mmmm? Oh, no, it's perfect," replied Simon.

"I thought it might be because you took a sip of it, then you frowned while looking into your cup."

"I was just thinking about something that happened in my past. I wasn't sure if I'd had a particular experience blended in with an experience I'd had at another time."

"Don't dwell on that, and get on with the next part of your past. Incidentally, in our reality, almost a day has passed, so, you must be over halfway through this amusing jubilee game you insisted on playing."

"Yeah, you're right, I am, but I'm not always completely sure of what point I'm at in the game when I go so deep into it."

"I warned you that would probably happen sometimes."

"Yeah, but there's other things that I hadn't expected to happen. Like for instance, I often have bizarre dreams, then I wonder if I'm really asleep or awake. Some of those dreams, or whatever, scare the hell out of me, but they vanish fast."

"Be careful, Simon. I worry that while you're playing in the past, you might let your mind drift too close to that senseless, horrific tragedy you suffered."

"Don't worry. I'll concentrate on ending my game before that happens. Hmmm, considering how fast time passes in my game,

compared to real time, it means I should be ending my game sometime after we have lunch tomorrow, so, in about half an hour, you'll start playing the game with me."

"That's good, because the only time we've been able to have a decent conversation with you is during meals. We're ready to play whenever you want us to start, so, get on with your game."

"Okay, I'm going into...mmmmm," murmured Simon while his thoughts whirled back into his game.

CHAPTER SEVEN

Simon started packing for a camping trip that he'd been looking forward to for weeks, and because of his excited anticipation of leaving the next morning to spend two days camping and fishing with his two best friends and his stepfather, he found it difficult to sleep that night.

It seemed like hours had passed since he'd gone to bed, and he felt certain that he would never feel drowsy, and then moments after thinking that, he fell sound asleep.

He dreamed that he got out of bed, walked over to the window, opened it wide, then suddenly felt himself lifting off the floor, and then he began floating out of the window.

After rising high above the trees, Simon swooped down close to the road, and as he glided through the darkness, he peered into bushes where various sizes of luminous eyes stared back at him, then he alit on the road and began strolling along it.

Every few moments brilliant flashes of both forked and sheet lightning lit the landscape, and each time Simon could see that on both sides of the road, for what appeared to be many miles ahead and behind him, nude people were suspended upside down from the tops of very tall, stainless steel poles.

All those people had long, narrow, rubber tubes attached to syringes imbedded at both sides of their necks, as well as in their wrists, and inner thighs while blood flowed down through all the tubes and out into very big, carved crystal goblets on the ground at the base of each tall, steel pole.

Some of the hanging people were staring at him while moaning, and Simon thought that was ridiculous because they must see that he didn't have a ladder to climb to unhook them from the poles.

After lightning stopped flashing, it was again a very dark night, and Simon thought it was odd how the road, which had previously been level, was now slanting steeply downward, and the farther he walked down the road, it was getting so dark that he couldn't see his hands in front of his face.

He suddenly tripped over something in the dark, then gasped as he began falling forward while desperately reaching out into the darkness, hoping to find something to grab onto to break his fall.

Moments later, he alit on his feet, then winced from a sudden bright light, and then cupping his hands above his eyes, he saw that the light was emanating from a shimmering, lime green sun.

Massive white clouds rapidly crowded together to block the sun, causing an eerie glow around him, then Simon saw that he was standing alone on a beach, looking out at gigantic waves suspended in midair above a motionless black sea.

He looked up at the sky and saw a dark red cloth slowly undulating as it drifted in his direction. He instinctively raised his arms, and the cloth very slowly fluttered down to him, and as it draped itself around him, he felt thrilling sensations all over his nude body.

Simon gathered the cloth closer around his body, then he began walking along the shore without leaving footprints in the bright red sand. He heard someone calling his name, then looking around to determine where the voice was coming from, he saw his stepfather standing by a small campfire, and a few of his friends seated around it.

Noel asked him if he'd managed to catch any fish for their dinner, and then feeling something heavy in his hands, Simon looked down and saw that he was holding a solid block of black water, with the heads and tails of fish sticking out of it.

He tossed the block of fish to Noel, who tossed it into the fire, then as the black block sizzled, the fish began to wriggle free of it and swim in circles above the flames.

Smoke from the campfire clouded his vision, and when it

cleared, he found himself amidst a crowd of whispering people standing near the tall, open gates of an amusement park. Simon pushed his way through the crowd, went up to the ticket booth, and then found that it was empty because the park had closed for the season.

He turned around and saw that all the people had vanished, and he was alone again on the vast, deserted beach of the motionless black ocean.

He then saw someone run along the beach, then go through a door at the side of a huge house, and then presuming that he'd just seen Noel or one of his friends go inside the house, he hurried over to it.

Simon opened the side door of the house, stepped inside, and when the door slammed shut behind him, he couldn't see anything in the blackness surrounding him. A flash of light appeared from a sudden crack in what Simon presumed was a wall of the room, and it lit up a screeching bird that was hovering close to his face.

He crouched down in the very dark room, holding up his hands to fend off the rapidly fluttering bird, then suddenly, he was sitting in a deck chair on a beach, and a nude, obese woman wearing a motorcycle helmet was seated on a bench beside him.

He couldn't see her face through the big, mirrored visor of her helmet, but he felt sure that she was smiling as she nudged him, and handed him a banana. Simon thanked her, and began peeling the banana while looking around at the many different shapes and sizes of tombstones standing at various angles on the beach.

He turned his head to speak to his quite overweight companion in the motorcycle helmet, and saw that she was now lying on her back in an open coffin a short distance across the beach from him.

He then saw ten, gray-fleshed people dressed in gaudily colored clothing, struggling to drag coffins along the beach. They were followed by a group of laughing children, seated astride three enormous, yellow and white striped lizards on leashes, and four of the children were riding two, gigantic crocodiles.

The very long, thin, luminous purple tongues of the lizards kept flicking at the eyes of the crocodiles that would in turn hiss and viciously snap at the lizards while the children giggled and laughed. Simon wished that the children didn't have to be there on the beach, but he felt so pleased that the adults were, and that they looked so unhappy.

The adults stopped dragging the coffins, and began slowly moving toward the children, so, Simon got up out of his chair. When he took a step forward, his leg felt slightly heavier, then he looked down and saw that he was clad in glossy black armor.

A sudden rush of wind caused his long, gold and black-striped cape to billow as he took a few more steps toward the adults at the same time the children ran to him. He removed his golden-plumed, black metal helmet as the children cowered close behind him, then suddenly, Simon was standing close in front of the adults, and the children were far behind him.

He quickly picked up adults, snapped their backs, necks, arms and legs, jammed them down inside coffins, and after slamming

the lids closed, he hurled the coffins one at a time out of sight amid the huge, petrified waves of the black ocean. Simon then walked back to the children and smiled while telling them they could now resume playing with their lizards and crocodiles.

Moments after the children and their pets had disappeared around a curve in the beach, Simon saw a misshapen, white object far down the beach, moving in his direction, and when it was nearer, he thought that it looked similar to a massive, distorted white spider with bright blue splotches on its body.

He watched the slow progress of the distorted, white shape, then as he began walking toward it, he saw that it was a colossal piece of white driftwood with glowing, pale blue chunks of human bodies and entrails snagged in its twisted, sharp branches.

Simon grimaced while looking at the gory driftwood, and as he backed away from it, the driftwood began tumbling faster toward him, so, he turned around and began running along the beach.

He had to stop running, then start struggling forward as quickly as he could because with every step he took, his feet sank deeper into the carmine red sand. Simon flapped his arms until he lifted himself off the beach, then he kept flapping his arms until he was high above the rapidly tumbling, gruesome driftwood.

He looked down through the gathering dark yellow clouds and saw that the red beach that had been littered with tombstones, and children playing with their crocodiles and lizards had vanished.

The black ocean was no longer there, either, and Simon was astonished to see that he was now floating outside his bedroom

window, looking in at himself lying in bed. He tried to open the window, but it wouldn't budge, then after giving it one more upward yank, his fingers slipped off the window, and he started falling backward.

Simon twisted himself around to look below and he saw that he was plummeting toward the large piece of white driftwood that had suddenly reappeared, and he felt sure that at any moment he'd be skewered onto some of the sharp, twisted branches.

He waved his arms around frantically, trying to slow his rapid descent, then seeing how close he was getting to the driftwood, he squeezed his eyes shut while clenching his teeth.

He opened his eyes again when he felt his feet gently touch the ground, and then Simon saw that he was standing in waist-high grass that glistened with dew in the moonlight.

He looked around at the pale blue and pink mountains surrounding the valley he was standing in, then he panicked when the valley and mountains suddenly tilted sharply. Within seconds, he and the entire landscape began sliding rapidly down into what appeared to be endless, deep magenta space.

His horse, Blaze, appeared at the top of the tilted landscape, and then began trotting and often skidding down the steep incline until stopping beside him, then Simon leapt up onto Blaze's back, and then Blaze began struggling back up the tilted landscape.

After reaching the top, they teetered on the edge of the landscape where Simon could only see endless dark clouds, then

his heart leapt and his horse whinnied when they suddenly toppled off the edge, and began falling through the clouds.

The dense cloud mass whisked away, then Simon saw that they had come to a stop halfway up the staircase of his home, so, he began goading Blaze to climb to the top of the stairs.

He pulled harder on the white reins as they became shorter and thicker until they formed his pillow again, and then he hugged it, and fell into another bewildering dream.

He awoke early the following morning, and during breakfast, his dreams from the previous night lingered like fading, magical mists, and Simon found it slightly difficult to stay awake.

"Thanks, Fiona," said Noel, smiling, as the most recent housekeeper refilled his cup with coffee.

"Ahhh-hmmm," murmured Simon as he yawned.

"Oh-oh. I hope you don't fall asleep on your horse and fall off. On second thought, perhaps you should go back to bed, and we'll leave later this afternoon," said Noel, smiling.

"No! I'm wide awake! Besides, I've got everything packed."

"What time are your friends arriving?"

"They'll be here in less than an hour," replied Simon.

"Good morning," said Miranda, walking into the kitchen.

"What are you doing out of bed?" Noel asked her.

"Well, if Fiona is up when she should still be asleep, then so should I. Fiona, you needn't have gotten out of bed to make breakfast for these two early birds."

"Oh, it's no bother, whatsoever. I wanted to make sure they had a proper breakfast."

"You're too sweet for your own good. You go back to bed and I'll take the helm. Oh, and the other reason I'm up, is that I've decided to go camping with you men," said Miranda.

"Yeah? That's super!" cried Simon.

"Now we're *really* going to have fun," said Noel, grinning.

"Oh, you think so, huh? But first, I need a coffee. Thanks, Fiona. Oh, and because I'm going camping, too, then you go home whenever you want."

"Thank you so much, Miranda. You're such a dear. I'm up and dressed now, so, I'll get on my way."

"By the way, I packed a few boxes with things I can't use. I seemed to have over-shopped again. There's a few dozen tins of vegetables, and an assortment of preserves, tea, coffee, ham, and other things. I feel so embarrassed because I buy too much when so many other people can't afford to buy enough food for one, decent meal. Simon, would you please carry out the boxes for Fiona, and put them in the car? Thanks, honey."

"All those groceries are for me?" cried Fiona. "Oh, Miranda, thank you. You always say you make a mistake shopping, but I don't believe it for a minute. You and Noel pay me far more than you should, too."

"But she *does* over-shop, Fiona," said Noel. "Miranda's so empty-headed that she has no idea how to shop, nor how to cook, so, we have to hire someone to prepare all our meals for us."

"A likely story, indeed," said Fiona, smiling. "Don't you think for one minute that everyone around here doesn't know you're creating unnecessary work for them to do on the house just to pay them a very good salary. You're a pair of angels. Both of you."

"Why, I have no idea what you're talking about, Fiona. But thank you for tolerating our stupidity," said Noel. "Simon, I'll help you carry some of the boxes out to the car, and then we'll drive Fiona home. Hurry up. We have to leave soon."

"All that food! There's not enough words to tell you how grateful I am," said Fiona.

"I'm the one who should be grateful. You're helping me get rid of all the excess food that keeps piling up," said Miranda.

"Oh, you know that's not true. Thank you so much."

"You're welcome. But I'm sure you won't be thanking me when I have to let you go at the end of the month because I'm not satisfied with your work," said Miranda, suppressing a smile.

"Oh, I know. You've let me go twice now, but that's just to give someone else the opportunity to earn money. You hire us for two or three months, let us go, and then rehire us again. I'm onto your game, young lady."

"It's not a game, Fiona. I'm just a very confused woman. Now off you go, and we'll see you late Sunday afternoon."

"All right, I'm going. God bless you. I hope you and your family have a wonderful time. Goodbye, dear."

"Goodbye, Fiona. Give my love to your family."

Fiona had tears in her eyes as she hugged Miranda before she left the house. Simon accompanied Noel as he drove Fiona home, then he and his stepfather carried the four, large, cardboard boxes of canned goods, and other food supplies as well as toiletries into Fiona's home.

When Noel and Simon returned home, Noel went to talk to the men he'd hired recently. He crossed his arms as he stared at the house, then he told them that he wasn't satisfied with the new addition, so, he wanted it torn down and rebuilt.

The men grinned because they knew that the addition had been rebuilt several times already, and that the work was simply an excuse for Noel to pay them a generous salary.

Three other men arrived to tend the many vegetable gardens, and besides being paid for their work in the gardens, they were always told they could help themselves to as many vegetables as they needed to feed their families.

Noel and Simon went back inside the house and saw that Miranda had changed out of her dressing gown and she was sitting at the kitchen table, reading the newspaper.

"Are you sure you want to come with us, Miranda? Because we'll be venturing into an area that we've stayed away from before. It's really quite dangerous because there are dozens of dinosaurs and saber tooth tigers," said Noel. "Not only will there be those hazards, but many others. For instance, at one moment

you think you're walking along a path, and then suddenly you realize that path is really a gigantic, poisonous snake."

"Yeah, mom, and there's huge birds with long fangs and claws, and those birds are big enough to grab you and your horse, and then fly off with you to their nest where they'll eat you."

"Oh? So, if I hadn't gotten out of bed, you would've awakened me to ask if I'd come along to protect you from all those horrors. A woman's work is never done. I have to take care of my men, all the time."

"Oh, thank you, love. Now Simon and I'll be able to enjoy the camping trip with you protecting us," said Noel, smiling.

"Mom? You can carry the big net, and then who knows? Maybe you'll catch a dinosaur."

"Can you imagine trying to cook it? We'd have to use over a hundred loaves of bread to make the stuffing, and then we'd have to use shovels to stuff that dinosaur before putting it in the oven."

"Yeah, and then we'd have to use the garden hose to baste it. Oh, I just thought. Are you hungry? I'll make you some scrambled eggs and bacon," said Simon.

"No thanks, honey. I had breakfast while you and Noel were taking Mrs. Boyd home. Am I the only woman going with you?"

"Nope. Jennifer's coming, too."

"Good. Then you'll *really* be safe from monsters. Just how far will we be going?"

"Last time we went all the way up to Lydford Gorge, but this time we're going up around the Erne River," Noel told her.

"That sounds like fun. Well, I'm almost ready to go. I'm just going to look for my camera and film, so, I'll meet you at the stables in about ten minutes."

"You don't have to hurry, mom, because Colin and Jennifer aren't going to be here for maybe half an hour."

"Oh, then that means I can have another cup of coffee."

Simon's best friends, Jennifer and Colin, arrived on schedule, then they left for their camping trip. Colin and Jennifer had their own horses, and Noel had used one of his other horses to carry most of the camping supplies.

They rode along an area near the river until noon, and then after stopping for a picnic lunch, they discussed their plans for the afternoon. Noel unfolded two big maps, and spread them out on the ground in front of them.

"Now on each of these maps, I've marked the area we're in and where we'll end up for the night," said Noel. "I thought it'd be fun if we separated into two groups, and the first group arriving at this spot here on the map will put one of these flags in the ground. After we all meet up, we can try our luck at catching some nice big fish for our dinner. So, how should we decide on groups? Ladies in one, and men in the other?"

"How about adults versus teens?" suggested Jennifer.

"Yeah! That's a good idea! But maybe it wouldn't be fair because we can move faster than you old folks," said Simon.

"Ahhh, now that sounds like a definite challenge. What do you think, Noel?" asked Miranda.

"Hmmm, well, it may be unfair because whenever we're not riding, we can take longer strides than these little children. After all, they're only in their teens, so, they're not fully developed yet, physically *or* mentally," he said, winking at her.

"Hah! It's a bet, then!" cried Colin, laughing.

"All right, it's settled. Adults versus teens. Now do you have your dinosaur nets?" asked Miranda.

"Yup. And all kinds of other weapons," replied Simon.

"Fine. We'll part at the next bridge, then Mrs. Baldry and I will travel the other side of the river. And remember, go slowly on foot, leading your horse if a fog settles in for a while. You know how fast they appear," Noel told them.

"We'll be careful. Let's get started," said Jennifer.

They followed winding bridle paths, passing hikers along the way, then almost an hour later, they had ridden up to the top of a hill, and then after they stopped to look out over the landscape, Colin said: "You can see for miles and miles."

"It's very beautiful," said Jennifer, smiling. "Oh, look over there. See all the sheep?"

"Yeah, and some ponies, too. So many little roads running through that area. I guess each one of them leads to a farm or to one of the villages around here. Hey, do you see that little road

way down there? The one that goes past those huge boulders and then it goes into the forest like some of the other little roads? See the one I mean?" asked Simon.

"Hmmm, past the...Oh, now I see it. It looks like it goes around to where we're headed," said Colin.

"Why don't we cut through that part of the forest over there, then over the fields to that small road? I'm sure we could get there long before my parents if we did that," Simon suggested to them.

"Hmmm, well, I don't know about that. There mightn't be a path through that part of the forest," said Colin. "Although, I suppose we *could* find another way around to that road. It'd take us a bit longer, though."

"Yeah, it might," said Simon. "But I'm sure that by going that way, we'll make better time. Do you want to try it, Jenny?"

"Sure," she replied. "There's a stream through the trees over there, and another one over there, so, we just have to follow those streams to where they come out on the other side."

"Why don't we split up?" asked Simon. "Two of us follow one stream and one of us the other one? And we can make it a contest, okay? The first ones to get to the field on the other side of the forest gets a...hmmm, how about say...I know. The winner gets half a crown. How about that idea?"

"What if two of us win?" Jennifer asked him.

"I've already thought of that," replied Simon. "If you two win, I'll pay you both, but if *I* win, then you wouldn't have to pay me

because I get a bigger weekly allowance than you."

"So true, so, I won't argue with you if you want to lose a bet with us," said Colin, then he laughed. "All right then, Jenny and I'll pair up and you go separately."

"Which stream do you want to take, Simon?" asked Jennifer.

"That one over there."

"Fine by me," said Colin, smirking. "It looks like it's going through the densest part of the forest. You sure you don't want to change your mind?"

"Nope. I'm sure that it'll be easy to follow that stream because usually trees don't grow right close to a river."

"You'd better hope they don't, or else Jenny and I'll win the bet, then we'd have to wait an hour or so before you make your way out of the trees. So, ready to go?"

"Yup. Let's ride down there, and after I get to the stream I chose, I'll wave at you, then we can start off at the same time."

"It should take us about half an hour to go through that area of the forest to get to that other road over there," said Jennifer.

"Maybe a bit longer," said Simon, smiling. "We're high above the trees so we can't see how many twists and turns those two streams make. This is a really good idea because we'll beat my parents for sure. I should've made a bet with my mom. A big one. Hey, maybe they'll run into a fog and we won't, and then for sure we'll win."

They rode down the hill, then after reaching the first stream,

Simon told his friends: "Wait 'til I wave at you, all right? Then we'll start off at the same time like we planned."

"Hurry now. We're waiting," said Colin, then he laughed.

"Good luck. Oops! I shouldn't wish you that if Colin and I want to win the bet," said Jennifer, laughing.

"Bye! See you soon!" Simon shouted as he rode off, grinning, then after reaching the next stream, he stopped, looked back at Jennifer and Colin and waved before the three of them began slowly riding their horses into the forest.

He felt rather pleased to find that the narrow trail he was following alongside the stream seemed to head straight in the direction he wanted to go, which meant that he'd win the bet he had made with Colin and Jennifer.

Simon rode for another few minutes before the trail became narrower, so, he had to slow his pace. He rounded a large area of big bushes, and then saw that he'd reached a part of the woods where there was much more open ground, and although the trees and bushes were spaced much farther apart, the tops of the trees intertwined, so, it was quite dark in some areas.

Simon had neared areas that had first looked impassable until he'd reached them, therefore, he felt sure that by keeping close to the stream, he wouldn't lose his direction, even if he came across areas of the forest that were darker than the one he'd now started riding through.

When he came upon an area with trees growing much closer on each side of the path, he dismounted, then began leading his horse while looking at the great amount of ivy growing up the thick tree trunks and into the branches.

The trees looked as though they'd been formed out of ivy because it covered them like a thick blanket, and he felt it was almost like walking along a narrow hall with very high walls made of ivy.

He looked at the high, dense growth of ivy to his left, and Simon noticed that at intervals, there were green and brown mottled shapes amongst the heavy growth of ivy.

He stopped walking to look closer at those odd-looking shapes, then he realized that they were either the large, stone slabs of a very old building, or a high, stone wall, and then he started talking to his horse.

"They're maybe parts of an old stone wall that bordered what used to be somebody's farm. Right, Blaze? I bet that at one time there weren't this many trees and bushes, and farmers used to be able to grow things on this land. Well, the land near here, anyway."

He continued talking to Blaze while following the stream, and Simon felt sure that he would reach the other side of the forest in about half an hour if they kept walking at the same pace.

"It sure gets very dark in places, doesn't it, Blaze? If elves lived around here, I bet you'd see little tables under the trees, with little lamps on them. Maybe teapots and cups and saucers, too.

Hey, maybe elves have got little horses to ride, too, so, if we see some of those little horses, then you can talk to them while I talk to the elves. Wouldn't that be fun?"

Five minutes later, he could see more light through the trees ahead of him, and soon sunlight was streaming down on them when they'd reached a more open part of the forest. After walking a little farther, he looked over to his left, and he was surprised to see more of the high stone wall above the bushes.

He left Blaze standing by the stream, and went over to have a closer look at what appeared to be a huge, broken piece of the wall, and then after passing under low-hanging tree branches, his eyes widened when he saw that area of the wall wasn't broken, after all, and he wondered how much longer it was.

Simon was intrigued by the obviously ancient wall, then he walked back to his horse, took the reins again, and resumed leading Blaze along the side of the stream while taking glances over at the high stone wall.

Several more minutes passed by, then he caught a glimpse of a turret on the wall, and it was then that he realized that the high wall surrounded a castle, or the ruins of one.

He tied the reins to a tree branch, patted Blaze, and then made his way up the slight incline to see if there was a crack in the stone wall that was wide enough to peer through it to the other side.

Simon walked along the wall, hoping to find a wide crack in it, then he noticed a small shield carved into the wall. The large,

entwined initials carved into the shield were so ornate that he couldn't read them, but because there was a crown above the initials, he assumed that it was the crest of a wealthy person whom had once owned the land that the very old stone wall had been built around.

He walked farther along the wall to see if there were more shields carved into it, then he saw a massive amount of ivy forming an arch slightly higher than the wall.

Simon felt the urge to satisfy his curiosity by finding out what that arch might be, so, he pushed his way through big bushes to get closer to the wall, then after yanking ivy vines away from the wall, he was surprised to see a very old pair of tall, iron gates almost completely covered in ivy.

He yanked ivy vines away from the gates until he was able to look through part of the ornate, wrought iron bars, and he saw a mostly weed-covered, flagstone path leading away from the gates and into a huge growth of tall bushes.

Simon presumed that the path continued on to perhaps the ruins of an ancient castle, but it was too dark to see more of the old property because of the shade from so many trees standing close together, with thick growths of ivy spreading up and over them like an immense, green roof.

He began calculating the time from when he'd started out, to the time he estimated that he would reach the other side of the forest, and then he decided that he could spare about twenty

minutes looking around the old property, and still be able to win his bet with Jennifer and Colin.

He climbed over the iron gates, then he began walking along the old, flagstone path. Less than a minute later, Simon could see much more light beyond the trees and high bushes, and he felt sure that there was a large, open area ahead of him.

He made his way around huge trees and very big bushes while hoping he'd see the partial ruins of a wonderful old castle on the open area of the property.

He'd just squeezed through another mass of high, thick bushes, when he almost lost his balance, then he stumbled out onto what appeared to have once been a small, circular patio with three, curved, stone benches around the perimeter of it, and a broken stone fountain at the center of the patio.

Simon saw the beginning of another path, so, he pushed his way through more bushes to see where it led. He'd almost reached the other side of the bushes, then he stopped when he saw the side of a massive house.

With the very high walls surrounding him while he stood amidst many tall trees, Simon felt as though he were standing inside an immense, dark church, instead of a heavily shadowed garden, or what had once been a garden.

He began making his way toward the enormous house, which was brightly lit by sunshine, so, he knew there were less trees in that area. Simon broke through another mass of high bushes, and

when he could see much more of the house, he saw that the windows were sparkling clean, and there were geraniums, petunias, and other flowers in window boxes.

He realized that people were presently living in the house, therefore, there must be a road leading to it. Now all he had to do was find a way to get to that road while leading his horse along the stream, close to the long, high stone wall of the property.

But before he could go back to get Blaze, he had to walk alongside the high, stone wall to the front of the enormous old house to see if he could lead Blaze up onto the road.

He stepped out from the bushes and onto an immense, well-groomed lawn, and he felt certain that if the owners of the house saw him, they wouldn't mind him trespassing on their property.

Nearing the house, he looked quickly to his right when he detected a movement, and then he caught a brief glimpse of someone whom had just walked through a large, broken part of the high, stone wall.

He started hurrying to the opening in the wall to ask the person if the path alongside the stream continued all the way to the road. Simon reached the opening in the wall, and saw that past the rubble of broken wall strewn on the ground, there was an incline leading down to the stream.

He realized that the stream was a deeper in this area because there were little rapids. He began walking down the incline, then stopped when he saw the back of a man whom was seated on a big

boulder that stood near the stream. The man had a thick growth of black, curly hair, and he had on a loose-fitting, white shirt, tan-colored pants, and there was a dark, emerald green jacket laying beside him on the boulder.

When the man sensed someone behind him, he turned around, and then Simon saw that it was a young man, wearing a pair of dark green sunglasses with pale brown frames, and he estimated him to be about nineteen or twenty years old.

He felt both relieved and quite pleased when the young man smiled and waved at him, so, Simon walked over to him.

"Hello. I saw you from an upstairs window, climbing over those old gates at the far end of the property, but I wasn't sure if you'd climb back over the gates."

"Oh, hi. I'm Simon."

"My name is, Wystan. What brings you this way?"

"I'm heading in *that* direction with my horse. There's a road where I'm meeting my friends. Could you tell me how I can get to the road that leads to this house?"

"Yes, and it's only a short distance from here. Walk back to your horse by way of this stream, and lead him along the side of it 'til you reach the road."

"Thanks," said Simon, smiling. "Have you lived here long?"

"Excuse me. Hello, Morag. This is Simon."

Simon quickly turned his head to look in the direction that Wystan was looking, and he saw a beautiful blonde young woman

smiling at him. She was wearing an ankle-length, white dress that had a small pale blue, yellow, and pink floral pattern. Her dress was similar to several dresses Simon had seen his mother wearing when she relaxed on the patio beside the pool.

He realized that the very pretty young woman was around the same age as himself, and he presumed that she was Wystan's sister. Morag smiled as she said: "We don't often have guests jumping over the back fence."

"Oh, um, no. I just told Wystan that I was looking for the road that runs along the front of your house."

"He's meeting his friends," Wystan told her.

"Oh? And *where*, pray tell, is *that*?" she asked, smiling.

"About a hundred meters that way. Maybe more."

"I told him to keep following the stream and he'd come to the road," said Wystan, then he looked at Simon and said: "If your friends followed the other stream, which I imagine they did, that one has many more curves to it, so, I'm sure it'll take them perhaps twice as long to reach the road."

"Yes, even longer, I'd say." said Morag. "Wystan, fetch his horse, and tether him. You'll have time for a cold drink, Simon, and still be at your meeting place before your friends reach it."

"Oh, okay. Thanks," said Simon, smiling at her.

"I'll be back in five minutes," Wystan told them, then he began walking along the edge of the river to get Simon's horse.

As Simon sat at a large, white, ornate wrought iron table, waiting for Morag to return with the cold drinks, he looked around at the lawn and gardens, and saw a small easel standing beside one of the large, oval flower beds, and he could see a partly open portfolio leaning against the easel.

He walked over to the easel, picked up a small stack of the watercolors, and smiled when he saw that most of them were depictions of various areas of the property, and about a dozen of the watercolors were portraits of Wystan and Morag seated on the lawn or at the patio table.

He looked through a few more of the watercolors before he walked back to the table and sat down just as Wystan walked back through the huge opening in the broken wall, and then he sat at the table with Simon.

When Wystan removed his sunglasses and smiled at him, Simon was mesmerized by his startling green eyes, then moments later, he quickly looked away from Wystan, and said: "You sure don't need to wear sunglasses when you're at the back of your property because there's so much shade in some places from so many trees and high bushes."

"Yes, I should get rid of most of that wild growth, but with all these big lawns and gardens to tend, I find there's not much incentive do that," Wystan said with a broad smile.

"I guess not. I mean, yeah, I'll bet it takes a lot of time to keep this part here looking as nice as it is now."

"It takes much effort at first, but it's easier to tend for the rest of the summer. Hmmm, I detect a slight trace of an accent other than of this country."

"I used to live in America before we moved here."

"Ah, I see. One or both of your parents must be rather handsome because you are strikingly so," said Wystan, smiling.

"Oh? You think so?" Simon said as he blushed a little.

"Most certainly. You must have many young women vying for your attentions."

"Um, thanks. You're very handsome. Really. And Morag is very beautiful."

"Yes, isn't she?"

"I'm eighteen, and I guess she's around the same age as me."

"She's slightly past eighteen years old."

"Oh? Oh, here she comes now."

"Would you please excuse me? I'll have my cold drink in the house. Please come by to visit us again, very soon," said Wystan.

"Sure, thanks, I'd like to do that. Bye."

"Goodbye, Simon."

Morag smiled as she handed him a glass of lemonade, then she sat down at the table.

"Wystan's very nice," said Simon.

"Yes, I think he is, too. It's so nice having a surprise visitor. You must have had a difficult time getting over those old gates at the back of the property."

"Naw, it was easy. Wystan was just going to go for a swim down by the stream when I got here. Do you swim there, too?"

"No, and neither does Wystan. He was just going to walk back to the house to change into his bathing suit when you saw him. We have a freshwater pool on the other side of those hedges."

"Oh, yeah? I didn't see your pool because I came around the other way," said Simon.

"With so many bushes where you came through, and then tall hedges here and there, it must look like a maze to a stranger."

"Yeah, it does in places, but I was really surprised when I saw how very nice it is at this part of the property. Lots of big flower gardens and lawns. Oh, and I looked at some of those watercolors over there. They're really very nice. Which one of you did them?"

"*I* did. You liked them?"

"Yes, I did. I noticed that you had some drawings and watercolors of Wystan and of yourself, too."

"My struggling aspiration to be a portrait painter, someday. If anyone saw me sitting in front of a mirror while sketching myself, they'd think I was rather vain, but I'm really not. I'm just trying to develop my skill at portraiture. Wystan won't sit still for a long time, so, I have to draw myself most of the time."

"I think you're a very good artist because the portraits and paintings of flowers are quite realistic," said Simon.

"Why, thank you. I find flowers much easier to draw because they don't change the expression on their faces, whereas people

look different with every mood, and there's also many ways a person smiles. I start drawing Wystan, then after awhile, I look up, and he's sticking his tongue out at me, or else he's scrunching up his nose, and doing all sorts of funny things."

"Well, I suppose it's hard to sit in one position for a long time, and try to keep the same facial expression."

"It has more to do with Wystan's sense of humor. If you weren't on your way to meet your friends, I would liked to have painted a portrait of you."

"I would've liked that, and I would've tried to keep the same facial expression while you painted me. Um, I've really liked meeting you, and I'd like to see you again sometime."

"I've enjoyed meeting you, too," said Morag, smiling.

"I'm on a camping trip for two days with my parents and my friends, and I'd like to see you soon after that."

"I'll look forward to that. How about the day after your camping trip? I'd prepare lunch for us. Would you like that?"

"Yeah, I sure would. I'll plan to get here around noon, okay? I live about a three-hour ride from here, so, I could leave home at nine, then I could leave here an hour or so after we have lunch."

"You must live quite a distance from here. Would your parents approve of you coming all this way?"

"Of course. I'm not *that* young. I was eighteen last month."

"Oh, I didn't mean that. It's just that I thought perhaps they might be worried about you because there's sometimes sudden

fogs throughout this part of the country, and you could easily lose your way."

"Naw, I know my way here now, so, I know I couldn't get lost. So, um, like I just told you, I just turned eighteen, and Wystan said you're a bit past your eighteenth birthday."

"Yes, I was eighteen in March, and I'm two years younger than Wystan, but I do hope you don't feel that a few months age difference between you and I would matter."

"Oh, no, it wouldn't. So, um, this was part of an old castle before, wasn't it?"

"Yes, it was. The walls are original, and much of the house, or what's left of the castle, but I think the newer part was built within the past thirty years. I can take you on a tour sometime."

"I'd really like that. Well, I'm sorry, but I'd better get on my way to meet up with Jenny and Colin," said Simon, smiling.

"This was fun."

"For sure. Okay, bye. Thanks for the lemonade."

"You're most welcome. I'll walk with you to your horse."

While walking from the garden, then through the broken wall to the stream, Simon kept taking side glances at her, and he loved the way her hair glistened in the sunlight, and her dress slightly billowed with every slight breeze.

He untethered Blaze, then smiled and said: "So, um, I guess it looks clear enough to get through to the road."

"Yes, all the way there," said Morag, smiling.

"I'm really glad I met you, and it was so nice of you to give me a glass of lemonade, and talking, and, um, everything else."

"I had a nice time, too. You seem very nice."

"So do you. Well, so, um, I'll be back tomorrow for lunch like I said, so, I'll get on my way now. I had a great time here. So, I just go right along the stream past those trees, and then I'll be at the road. Right?"

"Yes, just past those next big trees, you'll see the bridge, and I'm sure you can walk under it with your horse. But if not, you can lead him around the side of the bridge, and it won't be difficult getting up onto the road because it's just a small hill up to it."

"Yeah? Okay, so, I'll see you in a few days."

"Bye, Simon."

"Bye, Morag."

He felt his heart beating faster from gazing at her lovely features and wonderful smile. Simon decided that he'd tell his mother and Noel about Morag and Wystan, but not Colin or Jennifer because they'd tell his other male friends that he'd met a very beautiful girl, and Simon felt certain that they, and especially Colin, would want to meet Morag, too.

Simon preferred instead to spend much more time with her until hopefully they became close friends, or even more, and then he'd introduce Colin and his other friends to Morag. A few of his friends had girlfriends, but Simon knew that if he had Morag for a girlfriend, then his friends would be astonished.

He grinned and kept turning around to wave at Morag as he led his horse along the side of the stream that flowed toward the old stone bridge, and then reaching it, he found that the short tunnel below it was just high enough to clear Blaze's head.

He came out the other side of the bridge, and made his way up the hill to the road, mounted his horse, and began riding in the direction he was supposed to meet his friends.

He knew that he could find his way back to the enormous house, and he felt quite pleased when he arrived at the spot where he'd planned to meet Colin and Jennifer. Almost fifteen minutes later, Simon saw them riding along the road toward him.

"When did you get here?" asked Jennifer.

"About fifteen minutes ago," replied Simon, grinning.

"Clever beggar," said Colin, smirking. "We would've won but we came across some fog and lots of bushes that we had to walk our horses around. Did you have much of a problem?"

"A bit," replied Simon. "But there was a good path most of the way, and bushes blocked my way only in a few places. Most of the time, I found it wasn't too difficult to follow the stream, but I sure wouldn't want to go that way again."

"Neither would we. It's quite dark in places, and because of that, the ground was a bit mucky for walking. Not enough sun to dry it out from the last time it rained. So, now that you've won the bet, we owe you," said Colin, smiling.

"Naw, I told you that you didn't have to pay me if I won

because I get a big, weekly allowance, and besides, I didn't have as much problem as you did, and if I had, then you and Jenny would've been here long before me. Anyway, now that we're here, do you see what I mean? This road goes straight over to that hill, and on the other side of it is where we're supposed to meet up with my parents, so, I bet we get there long before them," said Simon.

"I think so, too," said Jennifer. "There's cyclists and other people on foot up ahead, so, there must be a village nearby."

"It must be back that way, beyond those hills because there's no village close to where we're meeting them," said Colin.

"Yes, I suppose so," said Jennifer. "I'm getting thirsty. We finished our bottles of lemonade."

"I've got lots left. Here, have a good, long drink of it," Simon said, handing his thermos bottle to her.

"Thanks. Oh, you hardly drank any of it," she said.

They reached the prearranged meeting place, then twenty minutes later Jennifer, Colin and Simon began laughing as they watched Miranda and Noel riding toward them.

Simon enjoyed the camping trip, but he was at his happiest whenever he recalled Morag, and he excitedly looked forward to seeing her again. He didn't tell anyone that he'd met her and Wystan, however, when they returned home from the camping trip, he told his mother about meeting them, and that Morag had invited him to lunch the following day.

When he awoke in the morning, he immediately began thinking of how wonderful it was going to be having lunch with Morag and Wystan.

After breakfast, Simon felt very excited as he prepared to leave for their home, and Miranda smiled as she listened to him still happily talking about Morag and Wystan.

"Where did you say they live?" asked Miranda.

"Just a bit past where we left you and dad, after we'd made the bet to see who could get to that spot we met, first."

"I see. Well, I've packed some fruit and I gift-wrapped a box of assorted fancy biscuits you can give to them."

"You did? Aw, thanks, mom."

Simon opened one of the paper bags Miranda had placed by his big, brown leather saddlebag, then he took out the box of biscuits she'd wrapped, and then he grinned.

"You wrapped this really nice, mom. Thanks so much."

"You're welcome. Are you just about ready to go?"

"Yeah, I think I've got everything packed. Oh, I almost forgot to tell you that I told Morag I'd stay just over an hour so that I'll be back here by about four or a little bit later."

"You can stay longer than that, honey, because we won't be having dinner 'til after six."

"Yeah? Brilliant! She's really nice. She's so pretty, too."

"Yes, so you've told me a dozen or so times since we arrived back home yesterday," she said, smiling.

"Okay, I'm going now. Bye."

"Bye. Have a nice time."

"That's for sure!" exclaimed Simon as he rushed away.

Miranda smiled as she watched him hurrying away to the stables, and she knew that Simon had his first big crush on a girl.

CHAPTER EIGHT

Simon made much better time returning to Morag and Wystan's home, and he knew that once he saw the small stream that widened and deepened as it flowed near their house, then he could walk the rest of the way, leading his horse.

He was walking along the side of the stream when he saw slight flashes of white amidst the foliage ahead of him, then a moment later, he noticed it was somebody wearing white clothes, and walking toward him.

Simon grinned after he passed by more big bushes and saw Wystan waving and smiling at him. He was dressed in a white shirt and pants, and he had on a pair of white shoes, and Simon thought the white clothing accented Wystan's white teeth, his black hair and his golden tan.

Seeing Wystan with his loose-fitting shirt open to the waist, Simon realized that he'd been exercising with barbells three or

four times a week for several years because his chest and abdominal muscles were very well-developed.

"Hello again. I was sure you'd be here soon, so, I decided to meet you partway," said Wystan, smiling.

"Hi. I got here faster this time because I'm more familiar with the ground running alongside the stream, so, it made it easier to lead Blaze here."

"I realized that. Morag has lunch ready."

"Will you be swimming with us?" asked Simon.

"No, I won't. I have some work to do in the house, so, I'll be having lunch there, instead."

"Oh, okay. Sure is a really nice day, isn't it?"

"Yes, it is, so, I'm sure you'll enjoy your afternoon."

Simon's smile broadened when he saw Morag's head and shoulders above the top of a long hedge as she walked alongside it on her way to the patio.

"There's Morag, now. She's going to the patio," said Simon.

"Before you join her, I'll show you an essential room just inside the house."

"Sure, okay, thanks."

Simon followed him into the house, then he glanced around the large room they'd entered before Wystan opened the door to a small bathroom, and then Simon grinned and said: "Yeah, this is an essential room, all right."

"Yes, this *is* rather handy when one is pressed for time. Of

course, there's no need to use any of the bathrooms in the house, because you can simply take a stroll past the patio to the bushes and trees where you can water a bush or tree in privacy. I do that quite often," said Wystan, grinning.

"Now I know what's made them grow so high. Oh, I meant to ask you something. Way back on the property, about halfway to those old iron gates I climbed over, I saw a small structure made out of stone blocks, and it was built against the east wall. It looked sort of like one of those old sentry posts, but because it's the same color stone as the wall, it's hard to notice it at first. Was it originally like a guard house for the castle?" asked Simon.

"No, it wasn't, and from what I've researched about this old estate, nobody was supposed to notice that small structure you thought was a guard house. Apparently, to hide it even more, tall-growing hedges were planted close to it. It's sealed shut now, but at one time it was the entrance to a tunnel that led back to the basement of the castle. I imagine it served as an escape route in case of a fire, or as a means of eluding enemy soldiers."

"Wow! There's so much exciting history to this place."

"Yes, indeed. Well, I'll leave you now and get at my work. I hope you enjoy your lunch on the patio," said Wystan, smiling.

"Thanks, I will," said Simon, then after saying goodbye to Wystan, he hurried out of the house, ran to the patio, then slowed his pace before walking around the hedges to sit at the patio table with Morag whom had made a nice salad and a few sandwiches.

"That looks very nice. I like the way you've decorated the plates with sprigs of parsley, and the way you've cut those tomatoes to look like flowers," said Simon.

"Thank you. I hope you like the taste even more."

"I'm sure I will."

Simon smiled at her as he picked up a sandwich, then as he took a bite of it, he noticed that Morag hadn't taken a sandwich, so, he wondered if he should've waited until they had said grace.

"Sorry. Did you want to say grace, first?" he asked.

"No, please go ahead and eat. I kept tasting the salmon salad as I prepared it for the sandwiches, and I ate an apple, too, before I brought the lunch tray here to the patio. But I'll have some salad with you a little later. I hope you like the sandwiches."

"Mmmmmm, this tastes delicious," said Simon, smiling.

"This is ice cold tea I poured in our glasses, and there's mixed berry juices in it."

"Oh? Mmmm-hmmm, the tea is delicious, too. Everything's just perfect. Thanks for inviting me. Oh! I almost forgot!"

Simon opened his leather saddlebag and took out the gift for her, as well as the large package of assorted fresh fruit.

"These are for you," said Simon as he handed her the gifts.

Morag opened the gift-wrapped box of fancy biscuits first, then she smiled and exclaimed: "Oh, how lovely! How sweet of you! Some people say that very handsome boys are too conceited to be generous, except to themselves, but *you're* not conceited. Thanks

ever so, Simon. Oh, what pretty biscuits! I love the shapes. Mmmmm, and many of them are covered in so much chocolate. This is so surprising, but you needn't have brought me a gift."

"I really wanted to," said Simon, grinning.

He'd blushed when Morag had told him that he was very handsome, and he planned to make certain to not only tell her several times how beautiful she was, but to also bring her an even nicer gift the next time she invited him to her home, and Simon hoped that would be very soon.

As Morag talked, Simon watched her form each word with her lovely mouth, and at times he lost track of what she was saying. She stood up to remove the dishes after their lunch, and then Simon gaped at her body.

The hem of the yellow dress Morag was wearing hung just below her hips, and during lunch, there'd been a round vase of flowers blocking his view of the bodice of her dress, which he now noticed exposed a generous amount of her cleavage.

"I'll take these dishes inside, and then we'll have a swim."

"Yeah, sure, okay," said Simon, watching her walk away.

Now he had a rather hard problem that had arisen in his trousers while he'd been gazing at her beautiful face and body, and he hoped that his embarrassing problem would soften before he undressed down to his bathing suit.

Simon walked around the hedges and saw the freshwater pool, which was fed by water pouring out of the mouth of a large, stone lion's head attached to the high stone wall.

He then recalled that when he'd been leading his horse alongside the stream, he had seen a rivulet running down the slope at one part of the high, vine-covered wall, and he realized that the rivulet had been water draining from the base of the pool.

He undressed quickly, and before he could sit in a deck chair to hide his erection that had made a rather obvious bulge in his bathing suit, Wystan walked onto the patio.

"Hmmm, I see that old Mother Nature blessed you with quite a sizable genital gift," said Wystan, then he laughed.

"Oh, no! Now I feel so embarrassed!"

"There's no need to feel that way because it's a natural reaction, considering this heat and the sudden removal of your clothes. Temperature change. It happens to me all the time."

"So, um, you're staying?" asked Simon.

"No, I just returned to get this book. Incidentally, the water's rather cold, so, it'll take a little while to get used to. The sun might've heated that end of the pool by now. Goodbye again, and enjoy yourself."

"Thanks, I know I will. Bye, Wystan."

Simon felt relieved that the cool water softened his erection, and as Wystan had told him, the water in the shallower area of the pool had been slightly warmed by the sunlight.

Morag appeared from around the hedges, and Simon smiled as she walked quickly toward him, then she astonished him by diving into the pool wearing her very short, yellow dress. She resurfaced and laughed as she splashed water at him.

88

"You swim in that dress?" said Simon.

"I thought I would, because it's just as brief as a swimsuit."

"I guess so. It'll dry fast, too, because it's made of light material," said Simon. "Um, I usually don't go swimming 'til an hour after I eat, but I guess it's okay to do it in a pool. Swim, I mean. The water's really cold at first, huh?"

"Yes, it is, but I find it so refreshing. I brought a big, big towel for us to lie on," said Morag, smiling at him.

They talked and laughed as they swam in the pool for almost half an hour before climbing out, then they rushed to the large towel and laid on it. Simon then stifled a moan when he noticed that the water had made her dress almost completely transparent in areas, and one of those areas was over her breasts.

He felt certain that for the rest of his visit with her, he'd have to lie on his stomach to hide his erection, and then sometime later, he would have to make sure that Morag didn't see him stand up to put his clothes back on.

A few minutes later, Morag turned over onto her side, facing him, and propped herself up on her elbow, then she smiled as she said to him: "You certainly must be rather active in sports because you have a remarkable physique. Such big biceps and chest, and legs, and...Well, everything."

"Oh, um, thanks. I guess that's because I play rugby and just about every other sport you can think of, and I've also been lifting

weights four or five times a week since the time I was thirteen years old. You've got a very nice figure. I really mean that."

"Thank you," said Morag. "Hmmm, yes, very few young men are as well-developed as you. Wystan has a marvelous physique, too. He's really quite muscular."

"I sort of thought he was because when his shirt was open, I could see that his torso...Or I mean, like his chest and his stomach muscles were very well-developed, so, considering that, I guessed that the rest of his body was just as muscular."

"Yes, it is, and that's because he lifts big barbells and other types of heavy weights almost every day."

"I was sure that he must lift weights a lot. I didn't know he had hair on his chest, either. What I mean is that his chest hair wasn't noticeable 'til I was standing closer to him. Before that, it sort of looked like his chest and stomach muscles were shaded by the sides of his open shirt," said Simon.

"Yes, it looks as though a light breeze had dusted very short hair over his chest and stomach, but the hair becomes more noticeable when it forms a little, black line down the middle of his stomach. It's almost as if someone had taken a black crayon, and sketched in that tiny line of hair dividing his stomach muscles, but there I go again; always the artist. Perhaps you'll have hair on *your* chest, too, when you're a little older. That's if other men in your family have hair on their chests, too," said Morag, smiling.

"I haven't met any of my uncles, so, I wouldn't know if any of them have hairy chests."

"I see. Well, it wouldn't matter to me if you never grow hair on your chest, because I think men look wonderful, either way. I'm so pleased you came to visit, and I wish I could see you every day."

"Just ask me. I'll come here anytime."

"And I'd like you to do that, but unfortunately, I only came here to visit for a week from my home near Hathersage, and now I'll be leaving at four this afternoon."

"Oh? Aw, darn. Will you be back here again?" asked Simon.

"I'm not quite sure. You see, I was only supposed to spend a week here, and then a few weeks at our cottage. But I'm hoping to persuade my parents to let me stay *here*, instead, because my little cousins will be at the cottage, and they can often be very annoying. It'd be wonderful seeing you again when I return because I enjoy your company very much. I haven't seen or met anyone as pleasant as you, or quite as handsome. Wystan told me that he'd invited you for a tour of the house, and I'm certain you'll become good friends. I do hope I can come back here to stay for at least a few more weeks because I really like it here. This old relic of a house has been in the family for many generations and Wystan comes here to ensure the house and gardens are tended. I love coming here with him, and now that I've met you, I know I'll enjoy my visits even more. I wish we had a telephone here so that we could keep in touch *that* way, but every week or so, it'd be nice if you came by to see if I've returned, and if I have, then we can have lunch and go swimming. You could even take me for rides on your horse."

"Yeah, I'd really like that."

"You really would? I'm so glad. We'll have so much fun together, just like today. Mmmmm, this is so relaxing, isn't it?"

"Uh, sure," replied Simon, wishing his erection would soften.

Wystan smiled as he brought a tray of cold drinks, then he sat at the patio table and watched them frolicking in the pool. Morag rushed away after saying that she'd be back in a few minutes, then Simon got out of the pool, and sat the table with Wystan.

"You've certainly brightened her day. I've never seen her so happy," said Wystan. "Morag told me that she finds you to be quite charming *and* rather attractive."

"She said that? I think she's very nice. Very beautiful, too."

"While you were playing in the pool, I paid a visit to Blaze, and fed him an apple and a few carrots," said Wystan.

"You did? Thanks. That was very nice of you."

"It was a pleasure, because he's a fine horse."

They continued talking until Morag walked back onto the patio, wearing a lovely pink and yellow-striped dress.

"Ah, Morag. Ready to leave now?" Wystan asked her.

"Yes, the car's waiting out front. Thanks for one of the nicest afternoons I've had in so very long, Simon."

"I had a wonderful time, too," he told her.

"I wish I didn't have to rush away," she said.

"Enough of this nonsense!" exclaimed Wystan as he smiled broadly. "Simon, kiss her cheek. I know Morag would greatly appreciate it."

"Um, sure," said Simon, then he walked over to her, kissed her cheek, and then Morag ran her fingers through his hair.

"I'm sorry I have to go, Simon. Keep watching for me? I'll look for you every day when I return," she said.

"I hope you come back real soon, and I'll come by here all the time to ask Wystan when you're due back."

"Thank you," said Morag. "I don't want to say goodbye at the car. I'd rather say goodbye here where we played."

"You run on ahead, then, and I'll keep Simon company. Give my regards to the family," said Wystan.

"I will. Well, goodbye, Simon."

"Bye. Come back real soon, okay?"

"I have good reason to, now," said Morag, smiling. "All right, I'm going. Bye again."

"Goodbye. Have a pleasant trip," said Wystan.

Morag kissed Simon's cheek, then Wystan's, and then she hurried away.

"I'm really going to miss her," said Simon.

"Not to worry. I'll let you know when I expect her back. How about a change of venue? Come with me, and I'll show you through the house."

"Sure, I'd like that. Just give me a minute to get dressed."

"Oh, just bring your clothes along with you. You can dress in the house."

"Okay," said Simon, feeling disappointed because Morag had left for perhaps almost two weeks before he'd see her again.

They entered the house, and after walking down a very long corridor, and then through a pair of tall doors, Simon was surprised by how large the first room was, then he followed Wystan through two other huge rooms, and he realized that this part of the house had originally been the castle.

He was shown through six more big rooms as they walked along a wide hall that took them back in the direction they'd entered the grand old house, and then they stopped in a large, elegant living room.

Wystan explained that the electricity had been turned off in most of the old part house because of the cost, so, after Simon was dressed, Wystan lit a candelabrum to take with them as they walked up a very wide, long staircase to the second floor.

"Jeez. This house is like a huge old hotel with lots of antiques everywhere in it," said Simon.

"A large portion at the west end of the house is in ruins. It needs much restoration, however, with such economic hardship throughout the country, we'll have to delay most of the major repairs for a while."

"I can understand you wanting to wait to do that. It's really terrible knowing there are so many thousands of people out of work all over the country and abroad, but my family's doing well because we're financially stable."

"Our family is also doing well, but it'd be folly to undertake renovations on this house for now, considering that the future is still financially uncertain."

"Yeah, I see your point," said Simon. "When renovations *can* be done on this house, I bet it'll look spectacular. Morag told me that you don't live here all the time."

"No, I don't. I occasionally come by to take care of the house. Make sure it hasn't been vandalized or burglarized. Although, a burglar would have difficulty breaking in because there are iron gratings on every window and door. It's also set back a fair distance from the road, and there are trees and high bushes blocking most of the view of the front of the house, so, it's not immediately noticeable to passersby."

"Yeah, I know because when I was on the road, I could only see a bit of the roof," said Simon, as he looked at all the big, gold-framed paintings lining each side of the second floor hallway, then he grinned and said: "That's a portrait of Morag. It's really nice, and quite big, too."

"The house is filled with family portraits."

"This is sort of like walking through your family photograph album. We've got a few paintings of our family, too. My mother

and I posed for an artist about ten years ago, and then we sat for another painting of the three of us at Christmas, four years ago."

"Now that's a Christmas gift you'll always cherish, however, my family is much different from yours. As you can see, none of us were nude whilst having our portraits painted," said Wystan.

"Hah! I'll bet if you turned these paintings over, I'd see the naked backs of your family," said Simon, then he laughed.

"Ah, you've discovered one of our family secrets."

"Yeah, and there's probably a lot more secrets. Hmmm, that's a beautiful staircase over there."

"Yes, but it's rarely used. You see, almost the entire upper floor is closed in this area because most of the roof has fallen in. The rooms are empty, except for birds and squirrels, so, it's now their home until repairs are completed. This hall leads us back to the center of the house where my bedroom is situated."

They walked to the center of the house, then up a great, curved staircase to the second floor, and after walking almost to the end of an elegant, wide hall, Wystan opened two tall and very ornately carved, wooden doors, which led into his bedroom.

Simon was rather impressed by the grandeur of the room, which was the size of three large bedrooms in his own home, and the room was lit by five tall windows at one end of it, and in the center of the windows, there was a pair of wide, French doors.

After Wystan opened one of the French doors, he and Simon walked out onto a stone balcony that overlooked the back garden,

and then Simon could see the table where he and Morag had sat to have lunch.

Wystan took off his sunglasses, polished them with a handkerchief, then after putting them back on, he smirked when he saw Simon frowning while looking at his sunglasses before blushing slightly and saying: "Um, sorry for staring."

"I suppose you're wondering why I've been wearing these sunglasses most of the time. It's because I have a problem with my eyes. I can see just fine for the time being, however, my physician is treating me for what I hope isn't glaucoma. That's an annoying sight disorder."

"I'm so sorry to hear that."

"Thank you. My vision is sometimes blurred and that's when I worry about too much glare hastening blindness, so, by wearing these sunglasses, I hope to delay the inevitable."

"That's terrible. I'm so sorry, Wystan. I didn't know."

"Oh, let's not dwell on that. I love everything colorful during the day, and enjoying walks by the gardens to look at the flowers so that I'll never forget all the many colors of...Oops! Mustn't get maudlin. Speaking of many colors, I have several closets stuffed with grand old clothes from many years ago, and I love dressing up in them. Morag does, too, so we often dine in costume, and have great fun pretending we're attending a stately ball with grand gentlemen and their lovely ladies. Let's have some fun, shall we? We'll dress in some old outfits, then stroll around the house and gardens like members of the king's court."

Wystan opened a large armoire, and as he began sorting through it, Simon saw that it was filled with very old and beautiful clothes, then Wystan said: "This outfit is much too small, and hmmm, let's see. No, neither of these will do. Maybe...No, hmmm. Ah, here we are. I'll wear this red silk outfit and....Hmmm, ah, yes, this fine, old gold outfit would look splendid on you. I'll show you how to wear the tie. Oh, and there are wigs from this particular era, too. Would you indulge me in this fun masquerade?"

"Sure, it sounds like great fun," replied Simon, grinning.

Wystan laughed as he piled clothing in Simon's arms, then he led him to an adjoining room where he could change.

Simon undressed, then as he began putting on the antique clothing, he would occasionally glance into the tall mirror, and then grin. He had worn similar clothing when he'd been in school plays, so, he was familiar with how the clothes should be worn.

The wig that Wystan had given to him was dark brown like his own hair, but the hair of the wig was longer and styled in the fashion that had been popular among wealthy gentlemen three hundred years ago.

He put on the antique shoes, adjusted the ruffles on the cuffs of the shirt that protruded from the sleeves of his embroidered gold jacket, then Simon smiled as he left the guest room, and then knocked on the door of Wystan's bedroom.

He grinned when he saw Wystan dressed in his red silk costume, and holding a large, lace handkerchief to the side of his nose, then Wystan said: "Ah, there you are, my good man. I heard your carriage arriving. Is Lady Cunnilingus with you?"

"No, I'm afraid not," replied Simon. "She's taking tea with their majesties."

"Awww, how terribly unfortunate for them. Please allow me to show you the gardens," said Wystan as they began walking down the grand staircase. "We've imported several elephants and giraffes to trample down the roses because we were having a dreadful problem with a large insect infestation. I'm having all the flowers replaced with carved and painted, wooden ones. So much less troublesome, wouldn't you agree?"

"Most certainly, sire. A wise decision, indeed. Upon my arrival, I took notice of the flowers in the east gardens. They seem to be doing well, and the topiary is magnificent, as I would have expected," said Simon.

"I greatly appreciate your compliments. Our gardens are magical at times. Woodland creatures abound at odd hours, and water nymphs frequently frolic in the pond and amidst the flowers in the morning dew. Just the other day, during an afternoon garden party, we were surprised to see a young satyr suddenly appear out of the trees. Rather randy fellows, aren't they? There he was, prancing about with an enormous erection. The rather saucy fellow called himself Simon Sunlight, and Morag found him quite entertaining," said Wystan, smiling.

"I certainly hope he had the decency to cover his erection."

"Yes, he did, but not until after he'd reached orgasm, and then zounds! His white fountain shot out with such force, and almost every spurt reached great heights to the delight of the ladies and, dare I say, a few of the light-footed gentlemen. Everyone applauded madly at the end of his erotic performance. He then stuffed his quite impressive appendage into his pouch made of oleander blossoms and little sea shells, and then he chased after sequined mermaids in the largest pond."

"You make me blush by reminding me that I was often...Well, sexually aroused while I was with Morag at the pool."

"Are you referring to the spurting white fountain?"

"You know what I mean," replied Simon, grinning.

"Oh, you mean because you lost the invitation to the party, and your dear wife missed the satyr's entertainment, but not to worry because it's a daily occurrence," Wystan said, smiling.

"I'm sure she'll be relieved to know that. Well, the bottoms of these elegant jackets hang halfway down our thighs, so, I guess we needn't worry if something arose in our pants."

"True, however, Lady Oralsex would be quite disappointed if she knew that one of us were hiding an erection from her."

"Oh, I see. She's the very short lady talking to that man over there, isn't she?" asked Simon.

"Yes, but Lady Oralsex is not as short as she appears at the moment. She's sitting in a chair, and she's not actually talking to that man standing close in front of her while grinning like a

Cheshire cat," said Wystan as they entered the kitchen, then walked over to the refrigerator, and then he said: "Ah, here we are at the cooling box. Inside it, there's a marvelous concoction we've named, 'lemonade.' Please allow me to pour you a glass, but I must warn you, it has a rather odd effect. Just as it begins cooling their throats, people begin laughing hysterically until a tiny part of their brain goes...Pop!"

"I'll risk it. Please," said Simon, smiling.

"Only if you're willing to accept the consequences. There we are. One glass of lemonade for you, and one for me. Cheers."

"Mmmmm, very nice. It tastes like...Oh-oh! It's cooling my throat just like you said! Uh! Yes! Now...Oh, no! I'm starting to feel like laughing! And my brain feels weird!" Simon exclaimed.

"Good grief! It's starting! And there isn't an antidote! Oh, well, you'll only be terribly deranged for five or ten years, then you'll be back to normal."

"Whew! Thank God for that. Oh, isn't that the Duke and Duchess of Whoredom walking in the garden?"

"Yes, it is," replied Wystan. "I love her sense of style, and as you can see, she's always setting a new fashion trend because today, she has no front to her dress above the waist. When she first arrived, I kissed her hand, then each breast, and although I tried to control myself, I felt compelled to first lick her rose nipples, and then I began sucking on her breasts. Thank goodness the servants pulled me away in time because I'd lifted her dress, pulled out my

erection, and then I was just about to...Well, I'm sure you can imagine my intentions. Yes, I rather like her dress."

"So *that* explains it. I'd been wondering why her dress was so wrinkled and why her lacy underwear had fallen to her ankles. Now I don't feel so bad about having my erection noticed because many people saw *your* erection while you were greeting the Duchess of Whoredom," said Simon, smiling.

"How true. I told you it happens all the time. I wonder where the elephants and giraffes toddled off to? Oh, I suppose they went to chat with Blaze. I understand they like equine accents."

"Blaze speaks Oaten most of the time," Simon told him.

They strolled around the gardens until Simon realized it was time to go home, then they went back into the house. After changing their clothes, Simon wrote down his address for Wystan before they walked to the stream where the horse was tethered to a tree branch.

"I had a great time," said Simon as he smiled.

"So did I. I'll be leaving this evening, and..."

"*You're* leaving, too?" Simon interjected.

"Yes, I'm going to Southampton to visit my aunt and uncle, but while I'm away, you're welcome to come here to swim, and perhaps you wouldn't mind watering the gardens."

"Sure, I'd like that," said Simon.

"Thanks. Oh, by the way, I thought you might like these."

He handed Simon two small portraits that Morag had painted; one of herself and one of Wystan. They depicted their heads and a bit of their bare shoulders, and Simon felt very pleased because Morag had painted the portraits.

"Thanks, Wystan. These are really quite good. I think she's very talented. Her eyes are almost exactly that color in the portrait. I wish she hadn't had to leave."

"But not for too long, and when she returns, perhaps you can talk her into wearing a dress like the one that the Duchess of Whoredom had on today," said Wystan, then he laughed.

"I'm sure she'd never wear one like that."

"I rather thought she might because that light dress she wore today became almost transparent when it was soaking wet. But then, I suppose you didn't notice that," said Wystan, smiling.

"I, um...Well, it...uh, yeah, her wet dress didn't hide, um..."

"Aha! Caught you! How could you *not* notice? Morag didn't realize how exposed she was in that wet dress, and I didn't want to embarrass her by bringing it to her attention. You were the perfect gentleman because any other man would've taken advantage of the situation by blatantly staring at her breasts."

"But it was sure hard not to look at them."

"It was sure *hard* when you *did* look," said Wystan, laughing.

"Oh, it sure was!" Simon agreed as he laughed.

"Well, goodbye. Oh, and if you happen to see any stray elephants, would you mind slapping their flanks and telling them to trot on back here?"

"I will. I'll take care of your gardens while you're away, too. Bye, Wystan. Thanks again for the very nice time."

"Bye. I had a very nice time, too, and I look forward to seeing you again," said Wystan, smiling.

Simon led his horse along the side of the stream to the bridge, then up onto the road. He mounted Blaze, and began riding home while thinking of the very enjoyable time he'd spent with Morag and Wystan.

ᴥ

CHAPTER NINE

Upon arriving home, Simon poured a soft drink, sat down at the kitchen table, and then looked at the portraits that Wystan had given to him.

Miranda was humming as she walked into the kitchen, and her smile broadened when she saw Simon.

"Oh, you're back home. Did you have a good time?"

"Yeah, I sure did. Mom? Look at these great watercolor portraits. They're of Morag and Wystan, and she painted them."

Miranda sat down beside him, then as she looked at the watercolor portrait of Morag, she smiled while saying: "She's a very lovely young woman, and obviously quite talented. The gardens in the background are beautifully detailed. Oh, my goodness, Wystan is an extremely handsome young man. Hmmm, he looks to be about the same age as you."

"He's really almost twenty years old, and he's taller than me, and Morag's a bit shorter than me."

"He's taller than you? You're six feet tall."

"I guess he's about...Hmmm, about four or five inches taller than me. Really good-looking, aren't they?" asked Simon.

"Yes, there are, indeed."

"They're even better-looking in real life. His eyes are an amazing color of green, and Morag's eyes are a really nice color of blue. They're a lot like the color of those flowers you planted

around the edges of that garden at the end of the porch. I think you told me that they're called twinkles or Wee Willie Winkies, or something like that," said Simon.

"Periwinkles. They're a very pretty blue."

"Yeah, they are. Her eyes sometimes get a purple shade to them, too. They sure are nice to look at."

"Oh, yes, they must be. I went to school with a girl who had blue eyes like that, and they'd become a lovely shade of violet in lower light," said Miranda.

"That's what I meant, and her cheeks always look like she put rouge on them, but it's her real color. That very different and very amazing color of green eyes that Wystan has, makes them sort of almost hypnotizing. He wears sunglasses most of the time when he's outside because his eyes are very weak, and the doctor said he has an eye problem. Glok something."

"Glaucoma. That's so sad, because that affliction usually leads to...Well, it's very sad."

"You mean that he's going to go blind soon?"

"He may do, honey, but there are wonderful eye doctors these days, so, there's a good chance they can save his sight, and he probably wears the sunglasses because bright light causes his eyes to sting and blur," Miranda explained.

"Well, I hope the doctors can stop him from going blind," said Simon. "Morag had to leave for her home that's near Hathersage, but she'll be coming back again soon. Wystan's going away, too, and he asked me if I'd water their flowers and the grass. Oh, and

he showed me through the house. It's really huge, and it used to be an old castle, and parts of it are ruined, but lots of the rooms are still all right. Then he had all these fancy old clothes in some of the closets, and they're about three hundred years old, and we put them on. I wore an old gold suit and a shirt with lots of ruffles on the cuffs, and I even had very old shoes on. After I was dressed in those old clothes, I put on this big, black wig just like the men back then used to wear, and Wystan was dressed in the same type of old clothes, and he had on a wig, too, and then we pretended we were really living back in the olden days. It was so funny. We pretended there were some guests visiting him, like dukes and duchesses and fancy people like that, and we bowed and talked to them while we walked around the lawn."

"That sounds like such fun. I'm so glad you had a very nice time there, and even a make-believe costume ball, too."

"When Morag comes back, which I hope'll be real soon, I'll ask her if she wants to do that, too. I'll bet she'll look beautiful in one of those big, fancy dresses. Just like a princess. She's also really nice, and she has a wonderful personality. Oh, and mom, she really liked those cookies. Uh, I forgot to tell her that you gave them to me to give to her."

"They *were* from you. I just chose the gift for you because I knew you'd want to give her one."

"Yeah, I did. Thanks, mom. You should've seen the expression on her face when she saw all the chocolate-covered cookies. She was so pleased and excited, and she looked so beautiful, then. She

always does, though. Hmmm."

Miranda could see that he was quite attracted to Morag, and then she smiled while saying: "I meant to tell you that if she invites you to stay for dinner, you should accept."

"Really? That'd be super! I'd make sure to take a torch with me if I left for home when it was dark, and I'll make sure there's fresh batteries in it, too."

"And if there's either a thunderstorm or a thick fog, and they invited you stay the night, I'd want you to do that, then I wouldn't be worried about you."

"Aw, mom, you're the tops. It'd be fun staying overnight in an old castle. There's lots of antique furniture and all kinds of old paintings. Oh, and there's a big one of Morag. She's wearing a dress in it that's the same color of her eyes, and there's an almost transparent, pink shawl around her shoulders, and she's holding a small bouquet of those little pink flowers you like to pick from the garden and put in that crystal vase on the dining room table."

"Miniature roses?" asked Miranda.

"Yeah, that's them. She looks so beautiful in that painting. I wonder if they're related to royalty? She's *like* a princess."

"Many people are related in some way or other to royalty, so, *she* could be, too."

"She must be. And Wystan looks like a handsome prince. Oh, I forgot to ask him if there were ghosts in the place because lots of old castles are haunted," said Simon, smiling.

"Listen for the jingle of chains next time you're there, then you

may see a man wearing a suit of armor and carrying his head under his arm."

"If I saw a ghost like that, then I'd make sure to look at the head in his arm while we're saying hello to each other. Maybe I'll hear loud, spooky laughter, too. What's for dinner?"

"We'll be having roasted chicken with that wild rice and mushroom stuffing you like."

"Brilliant! I love all the spices and other things you make it with, and it smells so wonderful while it's cooking in the oven. Hmmm, you know, sometimes I feel rather guilty about having such a delicious meal when so many people are going hungry these days," said Simon.

"I do, too, sweetheart, and you know that we're trying our best to help people survive these awfully trying times."

"I know that, mom, and I'm so proud of you and dad. We're really lucky we don't have to worry about money."

"Yes, we *are* lucky that we don't have to worry, and that's partly because your first father gave me a nice, large divorce settlement, and of course, Noel had a quite substantial sum saved before this economic disaster struck the world with a jolt."

"You're always helping people around here, and I know that lots of other rich people wouldn't do it."

"Well, I know what it's like to work for next to nothing, and to receive no thanks for it. All our neighbors work so hard for every penny they can get, and most of the time, all they receive *are* pennies for a long day's work, and many men are leaving home to

look for work anywhere they can find it. Quite a few women have told me that their husband or their son had left home to look for work and they haven't heard from them in months, and they're awfully worried because they don't know if they've been hurt in a factory somewhere, or fallen off a freight train they'd climbed onto. They're all hoping that in some city or town, they'll find work so that they can send money back to their families. The Kerrigan boys took off last month and their parents haven't heard a word from them, and as you know, Mrs. Warrington's son, Larry, ran away over a year ago with his girlfriend. They might've married and have a child by now, and they're struggling to get by in who knows where. It's a terrible time. So many families are being separated and those that remain behind are barely eking out enough to put food on the table."

"When do you think things'll change? You know, get better?"

"It can't last forever, honey," replied Miranda. "Now there's talk of an impending war. I'd hoped we'd seen the last of it when the Kaiser was in power, but now it seems that the Germans want another war. I don't like the way people in Germany have been talking about Jews for the past five or ten years, and if things get any worse, I'll seek out some organization that can arrange help for them because they'll need our financial support."

"I don't know any Jews, yet, and I don't know why people'd say something bad about them."

"Neither do I, but unfortunately there are many misguided people who blame Jews for all their woes, and now in Germany

there's much anti-Semitism."

"That's terrible. The lads at school are always talking about Adolf Hitler. He's a real big shot in Germany," said Simon.

"Oh, there's lots of big shots and troublemakers everywhere in the world, but let's hope the ones in Germany remember the last war and stop thinking about having another one."

"Yeah, I hope so, too, because I'd hate to see bombs falling and families getting killed here in this country and other countries that Germany wants to control."

"Try not to dwell on those dark thoughts, Simon, because I'm sure that world leaders won't allow another big war to happen. Why don't you go see Colin before dinner?"

"What time are we eating?" asked Simon.

"In about two hours, so that'll give you and Colin plenty of time to get into trouble," replied Miranda, smiling.

"Us? We're practically angels, mom."

"Of course you are, dear."

"Bye! I'll be back in about an hour an a half!" shouted Simon as he ran to the door.

"Bye!" Miranda called to him as she smiled, then her smile faded when she began thinking about the economic woes throughout much of the world, and she hoped that those woes wouldn't lead to another terrible war.

CHAPTER TEN

After breakfast the next morning, Simon returned to the enormous, partly ruined castle to water the flowers and lawns, and swim in the pool, then after returning home on the sixth day, he felt elated when his mother gave him the telegram that Morag had sent to let him know that she'd be returning the following day.

Just before noon on Tuesday afternoon, his heart was beating faster as he tethered his horse to a branch by the stream before walking up the small incline and through the broken wall to the garden. His smile broadened when he saw Morag coming out of the house, carrying a tray of cold drinks.

"Hi!" Simon shouted as he ran toward her.

"You're right on time," said Morag, smiling.

"Here, let me carry that tray."

"Thanks."

"So, if you're not going to your parents' cottage for a few weeks, then will you be staying here for the summer?"

"Yes, I will."

"Brilliant!" exclaimed Simon, feeling elated.

As they walked to the patio, Simon looked at her hair glistening in the sunlight, her lovely smile framing her perfect, white teeth, and he almost forgot that he had a tray in his hands, or that they'd reached the patio, until Morag suggested that he set the tray down on the table.

"Mmmmm? Oh, right. The tray," said Simon, setting it down.

"Did you bring your bathing suit?"

"Oh! I forgot!"

"That's all right. You can swim in your knickers."

"Naw, I'll just watch *you* swim," said Simon.

"Why? What's wrong with my suggestion?"

"Well, I guess they're almost like a bathing suit."

"Of course they are. Thank you for tending the gardens."

"You're welcome. I did some weeding, too."

"Yes, I noticed, and you mowed the lawn, too. That must've taken you a long time," said Morag, smiling.

"I liked doing it."

"I feel sorry for your horse down by the stream, all alone. Why don't you bring him up here?"

"Well, Blaze'd really like that, but he'd have a problem getting over all the fallen pieces of stone from the wall."

"I'll help you clear some of them away. Let's do that."

"Are you sure?" asked Simon.

"Absolutely," she replied.

Twenty minutes later, they'd cleared enough stones to lead the horse up into the garden, and then Blaze whinnied happily while walking slowly around the enormous lawn.

"He won't step on the flowers," said Simon.

"I didn't think he would. You're his owner, so, I knew he'd be a gentleman just like you. There's a pail over there. You can fill it

with water for him, and while you're doing that, I'll run back to the house and get an apple for him."

"Thanks, Morag. He'll like that treat."

"After filling the pail, get undressed and get into the pool."

"All right," he said smiling while watching her hurrying away, then he filled the pail with cool water, and put it in a shaded area of the garden, and then Simon undressed and dove into the pool.

Morag had been wearing a dress similar in length to the one she'd swum in during his first visit with her, and he wondered if she'd wear that dress to swim in this time, too.

Recalling how the material had become transparent, Simon suddenly thought about his undershorts which were white and made of a thin cotton. He was about to climb back out of the pool to see just how transparent his undershorts had become, when Morag ran back onto the patio, placed two apples on the table, then dove into the pool wearing her thigh-length dress.

While they laughed and talked in the pool, Simon often thought about when he'd have to get out of the water wearing his wet undershorts, which he felt sure would be mostly transparent.

Fifteen minutes later, Morag suggested that they get out of the pool to finish their drinks before they got warm from the sun. Simon told her that the umbrella shading the patio table would keep their drinks cool, however, she swam to the edge of the pool where the steps were, and climbed out of the water.

Simon's thoughts whirled when he saw how her sopping wet, pale blue dress clung to her body, and he could almost see through it, then Morag spread out a large towel as she smiled at him and told him to hurry.

He waded over to the steps of the pool, and as his body rose above the water, he looked down and blushed when he saw that the wet undershorts clung to him and exposed his genitals.

He tried to look nonchalant as he held his hands in front of himself while hurrying over to lie on his stomach on the towel.

"That water's so refreshing," said Morag. "Mmmmm, it's such a beautiful day, isn't it?"

"Yeah, sure is. Like you," replied Simon, then he coughed.

"Just a moment," she said while getting up off the towel, then Morag walked over to the table and picked up a folded towel.

Simon hadn't noticed the folded bath towels on the patio table because his attention had been centered on her.

"I'm stepping behind the hedges to remove this wet dress, and then wrap this towel around me. I brought one for you, too."

"Oh, thanks," said Simon.

He waited until she'd walked around behind the hedge, then he took off his wet undershorts, laid them over the back of a chair, and wrapped the big, thick towel around his waist, and then seconds later, Morag walked out from behind the hedges, and smiled as she sat down beside him and said: "Now, doesn't that feel much better than having on cold, wet clothing?"

"Yes, it does."

"Our clothes won't take long to dry. Did you know there are beaches where people swim and sunbathe in the nude?"

"Yeah, I heard about that," said Simon.

"I think that's rather sophisticated. Wystan swims nude here at the pool."

"He does?"

"Yes, I've seen him from an upstairs window, and I've swam nude in the pool, too, and it felt wonderful. Have you ever swum in the nude?"

"Sure, lots of times when I was alone with my friends at a part of the beach," Simon told her.

"How could you be alone if you were with your friends?"

"Hah! You know what I mean. We always swim nude when there aren't any girls or women around."

"There's just us here, so, we could get nude," said Morag.

"Huh? No."

"Why not?"

"Because we're different."

"So what? People in other countries don't seem to be bothered by those differences, and I'm sure there are many people in *this* country who don't mind being nude at a beach."

"Yeah, I'm sure they don't mind, but this isn't a nude beach."

"I'm well aware of that," she said, smiling. "But we could pretend we're at a nude beach. I dare you to swim nude."

"I only do that when you're not here."

"Oh, you do? Hmmm, I see. Well, it wouldn't bother me to swim nude right now, with you here."

"You can't do that. What if someone came out of the house and saw you?"

"But we're alone, so, I'm going to do it. You don't have to look if you don't want to," she said, then she laughed.

Before Simon could protest, Morag jumped up, and as she ran to the pool, she dropped her towel and dove into the water. She resurfaced and laughed, then exclaimed: "This feels so wonderful! Well? Now it's your turn!"

"Naw! I don't think so!" shouted Simon, smiling.

"What a coward! I'll turn around 'til you're in the water! All right? Simon? Come on!"

"No!" He shouted, laughing.

"Oh, stop being so shy! Come on in!"

She turned her back to him, and then after thinking about it for a few moments, Simon stood up, walked over to the pool, took off his towel, and dove in.

"You did it! Good for you! Won't my parents be surprised when they come out onto the patio in a few minutes?"

"Morag! You told me there wasn't anyone else here!"

"I did? Oh, what I should've said is that there wasn't anyone else here at the pool, but there's quite a few guests in the house. That's okay, though, because I'm sure they'll understand when I tell them that you insisted that we swim nude."

"I'm going to put my clothes on right now," said Simon.

"Wait! Don't go. What would happen if just as you're getting out of the pool, they come out of the house? They might not be as sophisticated as us, so, you'd better stay in the water."

"We can't stay in here all day!"

"Oh, calm down. I was just joking. I love teasing you because you look awfully cute with that shocked expression on your face. Mmmmmm, doesn't it feel wonderful swimming nude?"

"Yeah, it does," he replied.

"I'm going to do this more often from now on. Hmmm, cold water makes my nipples stiffen. Does it do that to yours?"

"Um, yes."

"The first time you came here, I noticed that the water didn't only make your *nipples* stiff," said Morag, grinning.

"Uh...um, I...well, I..." stammered Simon as he blushed.

"Yes, your wet hair was stiff and standing up and out at various angles, and it looked so funny," she said before laughing.

"Oh, *that*! Um, yeah, I suppose it did."

"My hair's too long to do that. I love the way your hair is much longer at the front so strands of it curve down onto your forehead. You know, you should let your hair grow longer because I think it'd look rather nice that way."

"I've been planning to get it cut even shorter," said Simon.

"Oh, please don't do that because it's so beautiful as it is. I love the waves in it, and it'd be even wavier if it was longer."

"Naw, I don't like it much longer than this. Sorry."

"Oh, well. C'est la vie," said Morag. "Bet I win the next race around the pool."

"Hah! Bet you won't! Okay, one — two — three — go!" shouted Simon, laughing.

He began trying to catch up with her as they swam around the pool, and Simon was getting more excited each time he saw quite a bit more of her nude body rise above the surface of the water.

After playing in the water for over half an hour, Simon turned his back to her, and Morag got out of the pool, wrapped a towel around herself, then she held up his towel and giggled as she told him to get out of the pool and take the towel from her.

"Uh-uh. Turn around," said Simon, smiling.

"But I wanted to see the difference between a boy and a girl."

"Then go to the library. There's lots of art books with pictures of nude statues and paintings of nude people there."

"How shocking! I'll go get a library card, immediately."

She turned around until he'd wrapped the towel around his waist, then they laid on the patio.

"Wystan told me that he gave you a partial tour of the house, and about the two of you wearing antique costumes."

"Yeah, it was fun,"said Simon.

"We often dress in costume, and when Wystan returns, it'd be fun if we had dinner while wearing the costumes. Would you come to dinner sometime?"

"Sure, I'd love to."

"Fine. When Wystan returns, the three of us will have dinner while dressed in some of the old costumes. Well, I shouldn't say costumes, but rather, *old clothing*. In a hundred years, what we wear now, people will call old fashioned," said Morag.

"That's true, but the clothes we wear today aren't as grand as those that were in fashion many years ago. The old shirts alone must've taken many hours to make."

"All the clothes were made so beautifully. Some of the wigs are so big that I don't know how women could wear them every day, especially if their own hair was about as long as the hair in the wigs they wore."

"I never thought about that," said Simon. "But I guess all that hair *would* weigh a lot. I bet women are really glad that hair styles have changed. I forgot to ask Wystan, so, I'll ask you. Most of the house used to be a castle, right? Many castles are said to have ghosts in them, so I was wondering if..."

"Ghosts? Why, of course, we have ghosts because they wander around in *every* castle. We had twenty at last count. Some are just heads floating through the air, and some are missing the bottom half of their bodies, and other ghosts carry an extra head with them in case they misplace their own. It gets quite hectic whenever they invite their ghost friends to a party because some of those guests are twenty feet tall, and some can sit in the palm of your hand."

"Yeah, I thought they came in different sizes," said Simon. "I know you have to be careful not to clap your hands when you have

a tiny ghost sitting in the palm of one of your hands."

"Yes, we lose so many little ghosts that way. Tragic."

"But ghosts can't die," said Simon, grinning.

"Oh, but they do! Didn't you know? After you've clapped your hands and killed a tiny ghost who was sitting in one of them, he becomes a live ghost again, a little later. That's why it's so awfully tragic. Poor wee things. You see, they're so tiny, that besides getting applauded to death, they also get stepped on, and then they're temporarily a dead ghost."

"Aw, no," said Simon, feigning a pout.

"Yes, and it just keeps happening to them, over and over. Whether they're dead ghosts or alive ones, those tiny ghosts live in fear of some gigantic hand or foot slamming down on them."

"That sure is very tragic."

"Then be careful where you step."

"Oh, I will," he said with a crooked smile.

"By the way, there's been over a dozen tiny ghosts blowing their hot breaths on me while we were talking, so, I'm going back into the pool to cool off. Coming?"

"Yes. I'll turn around 'til you're in the pool," said Simon.

"Oh-oh. Blaze is looking over here at me."

"It's all right. He can't see this far without his glasses."

"Well, thank goodness for that, because I was so worried. Meet me in the water, handsome," said Morag, then she laughed.

They laughed, swam, and talked for the rest of the afternoon, and then Simon rode home, feeling sexually aroused when he

recalled how often he'd seen Morag's towel loosen enough to almost expose her breasts, and one time, her towel had almost fallen completely open until she'd quickly adjusted it again.

He'd felt elated when Morag had invited him to lunch the following day, and she'd also asked him to visit every day from then on.

The next day, they swam nude before and after lunch, and Simon was enjoying every moment with her, then Morag told him that she had to go away for two days to visit relatives.

When she returned, Simon was ebullient after kissing her cheek before he left for home, then soon he was kissing her cheek every time he arrived, as well as when he left for home.

Each time he kissed her cheek, his lips moved closer to hers, and he decided that on his next visit, he'd see how she reacted when he kissed her directly on the lips. His plans were dashed, however, when he arrived at the house the following day, and he felt disappointed when Morag told him that she was leaving to visit relatives who lived in the next town.

"Um, well, I hope you enjoy your visit," said Simon.

"Thank you. I'll be back tomorrow before noon."

"Tomorrow? I see, so, you'll be staying overnight with your relatives, then."

"I always spend the night when I visit them, because after dinner, we play one or two of the many board games for hours, and it's so much fun. Oh, and Wystan is arriving in a few days, so, why

don't we plan to have dinner soon? We'll dress up in some of the old-fashioned clothes and act like very important people from many years ago."

"Sure, I'd like that. So, when are you leaving to go visit your relatives?" asked Simon.

"I was supposed to leave an hour ago, but I waited until you got here so that I could say goodbye. I'm terribly sorry to have to rush away, but the car's waiting for me."

"Bye," he said, leaning over to kiss her cheek.

"Your kisses are exciting. Thank you. I'll see you on the morrow. Tra-la!" Morag cried out as she hurried away.

"Bye! See you soon!"

Simon felt both elated and pleased that she'd said his kisses were exciting, then he grinned as he walked to the patio and pool area. Now that Wystan would be returning, Simon knew he'd have to wear his bathing suit, but if Wystan was only staying for the day, and then Morag returned, then...Then he became very excited when he thought about being alone at the pool again with Morag.

When he rounded the hedges and walked onto the patio, he saw a big, white cloth draped over something on the patio table, and there was a note pinned to the cloth.

Simon smiled as he read Morag's note, telling him that she'd prepared a lunch for him, then he removed the white cloth and saw the plates of fruit, croissants, and sugarcoated biscuits.

She had also written in the note that there was a spare key to the house, where to find that key, and that in the refrigerator there

was a plate of assorted cheeses for him, as well as soft drinks. Simon draped the cloth back over the plates before he undressed, then ran nude to the pool, and dove in.

CHAPTER ELEVEN

The following day, Simon rode off to visit Morag, and before leaving home, he'd picked a large bouquet from the garden, tied the flowers with ribbons, and wrapped them in pretty, colored paper that his mother had given to him.

He had told Miranda that there was the possibility that he'd be invited for dinner, and she'd smiled while saying she hoped he would have a very nice time, and she had advised him to take a flashlight in case he left for home after dark.

He hurried through the broken area of the huge wall, then as he began leading his horse toward the patio, Simon saw Wystan walking along the lawn toward the house.

"Wystan! Hi!"

"Oh, Simon! It's so nice seeing you again!" He then grinned as he walked over to Simon and shook his hand.

"I thought...Well, Morag told me that she expected you back in a few days, but here you are, already," said Simon.

"Morag always seems to get things mixed up. I told her that my aunt and uncle were having guests for a few days, and that I'd planned to spend only one day with them."

"Oh, I see. Did you enjoy your visit?"

"Yes, thanks," replied Wystan. "I'll bet that after your long ride here, you'd love to cool off. Morag's on the patio doing just that."

"She is? I'll go say hello to her."

"Would you please stay for dinner?"

"Sure, I'd really like that. Thanks," replied Simon, smiling.

"I won't be joining you on the patio because I have to drive into the village to do a bit of shopping. I won't be back 'til oh, probably an hour before dinner, which we'll be having at seven. You two enjoy yourselves, and I'll come out to the patio to let you know when dinner is almost ready."

"All right," said Simon. "So, you do the cooking, huh?"

"Surprising as it may seem, I'm considered quite the cook for my age."

"I'm not. All I can make is breakfast and sandwiches."

"Well, that's a start," said Wystan, grinning.

"I guess your eyes must feel a lot better today, huh?"

"I beg your pardon?"

"You're not wearing sunglasses, and you told me that the bright sunlight bothered your eyes," said Simon.

"Oh? Oh, yes, of course. I was suffering from eyestrain, which I imagine was caused by excessive reading in low light one

evening last week. But that problem was resolved after I used an eyewash that I bought at the pharmacy in town."

"I'm so glad to hear that because I thought it you had a serious problem with your vision."

"No, not at all, but thanks for your concern...Hmmm, it *is* Morag I'm talking to, isn't it?" asked Wystan with a slight smile.

"Hah! Yeah, sure, it is. Can't you tell by my tits? Oops! I mean, *breasts*? And this favorite dress of mine I'm wearing?"

"Oh, then it *is* you, Morag. I didn't recognize you at first because your voice is rather deep today."

"That's because I've started growing hair on my chin, and I'm starting to grow a pair of testicles."

"Aha! I knew there was some odd chemical in the drinking water. Thank God I only drink wine and other booze because the water seems to have begun making you rather masculine, Morag, so, Simon's going to be disappointed by the changes in you."

"Yes, he sure will be, so, I'd better go see him right away before my mustache and beard grow any longer," Simon said while suppressing a grin.

"Bye, Morag. Hmmm, that's rather sad. Tsk-tsk, and she used to be so pretty and petite."

Simon hurried to the patio, and after walking around the hedges, he grinned when he saw Morag standing near the pool. She had on another short dress, and again it was a different color. This one was a bright yellow with a pattern of tiny green flowers,

and Simon thought she looked more beautiful than he'd ever seen her. Of course, he thought that every time he saw her.

"These are for you," he said, handing her the flowers.

"Oh, thank you, Simon. You've wrapped them so beautifully, too. You always go to so much trouble to please someone with a gift. Hmmm, I don't want to tear the paper too much because it's so pretty."

Morag untied the ribbons, then she carefully pulled back the wrapping paper.

"Oh, they're lovely!" she exclaimed.

"Not as lovely as you."

"You're so sweet, and so very handsome. I'll put these in a vase while you get undressed."

"Wystan's gone shopping, so, um, he said he won't be back for about three hours, so, I guess we...I mean, if you want to...Um, we could, uh..."

"You sound nervous," said Morag.

"Well, we swim in the nude when he's not here, and now that he *is* here...I mean, he's not right now, so..."

"Oh, I know what you're trying to say. We've often been swimming nude for the past while, and you're wondering if we should or shouldn't now that Wystan's here. He wouldn't care if we swam nude."

"He wouldn't?" asked Simon, raising his eyebrows.

"Of course not. Why would he? It's not like you and I are stepping beyond social limitations, and he often swims nude, too,

so, don't be so shy. Get undressed and I'll be right back."

"Uh, sure, okay," he replied as he blushed.

He undressed and dove into the pool while excitedly looking forward to swimming nude with Morag. She returned, and when she started to remove her dress, Simon turned his back to her, then hearing her dive in, he turned around and swam to her.

"Thanks for the very nice lunch you made for me yesterday."

"You're most welcome," she replied with a smile.

"Wystan invited me to dinner."

"I do hope you accepted."

"I did," said Simon, smiling.

"Good, because we're dressing up in such elegant old clothes. I love wearing long, beautiful gowns and a tall wig with them, and there are so many to choose from. Wystan and I dress up like that every chance we get."

"I noticed that the clothes aren't dusty at all."

"That's because they're professionally cleaned all the time, except for the wigs. They're kept in tightly sealed, large boxes because there's not too many shops that clean wigs, anymore. At least, not wigs like those," said Morag.

"No, I guess not. You know, I've often wondered if men who wear wigs, wash them at home, or if they have to take them to a shop to have them professionally cleaned."

"The next time you see a man wearing a wig, ask him."

"No, I'd never do that," said Simon, smiling.

"Oh? Then *I'll* ask the next bald man I see in town if he's wearing a wig. Oh, but he wouldn't be bald if he had on a wig. Well, I suppose I'll just have to ask every man I meet if he's wearing a wig because he's bald."

"You can't do that. You'd embarrass them."

"Hmmm, I see. Oh, I forgot to ask. Are *you* wearing a wig?"

"No!" exclaimed Simon, laughing.

"Now were you embarrassed when I asked you that?"

"No, I wasn't."

"You see? If it didn't bother *you*, then I'll ask other men if they're wearing wigs."

"There's going to be quite a few men blushing around here."

"You may blush *now* if you don't turn around because I'm getting out of the pool and diving back in," said Morag.

"I'd rather see you're...Never mind. There, I'm not looking."

They took turns getting out of the pool to wrap a towel around their bodies while the other person had their back to them, then they laid together on the extra large towel.

"After dinner, we always play games, or sometimes Wystan plays beautiful music on the piano. He's so talented."

"Do *you* play the piano?" asked Simon.

"Yes, but not as well as Wystan. Mmmmm, he's so handsome. When I was much younger, I was quite infatuated with him, and I used to dream of the day we'd be married."

"To your own brother?"

"My brother? Oh, I never bothered to tell you. Wystan is my cousin. Third cousin, really, but our family is rather close."

"Oh, I see. I thought he *was* your brother. Do you still feel the same way about him?"

"At times. After all, he's not only exceedingly charming, but he's also very handsome. You are, too, of course, and I love being with you because you have many fine qualities, and we have so much fun together. I'm certain that I'm the envy of every young woman in the country because I have the friendship of both Wystan *and* you."

"Oh? I'm glad you think that because you'll always have my friendship. So, um, about Wystan. Do you ever think about the time when you wanted to marry him?"

"No, not anymore," she replied while smiling. "I've stopped thinking of him as my future husband, and I suppose that's because I'm maturing, and because I met you."

"Uh, I see. So, um, did Wystan know you felt that way about him when you were younger?"

"Hmmm, well, if he did, he never let on. I'm not the only one who felt very attracted to him because, after all, there are few men in this, or any other country, who are blessed with such very handsome features like Wystan's, and that includes his marvelous physique. Wouldn't you agree?" she asked.

"Yes, he's really quite handsome. He's also very nice."

"There, you see? I'll bet if you'd been a young woman, you

would've been infatuated with him, too."

"And I'll bet there's not a young man anywhere who wouldn't be infatuated or in love with you because you're the most beautiful girl I've ever seen."

"Oh, really? What about your mother? I imagine if your father saw me, he'd think *she* was much more beautiful."

"I'm sure he thinks that because they're very much in love. He has a really super personality, just like my mother."

"Love is wonderful. Oh, I never asked you. How many girls have you been in love with?"

"None," he replied. "Oh, sure, I liked many girls quite a lot, but I never felt that I was in love with any of them."

"Well, I've been infatuated with many young men. It's a very nice feeling, and it makes one so happy."

"I know it does," said Simon, wanting to kiss her.

"It's time to cool off again. You go in first, and I'll get us fresh drinks and some apples and grapes."

"All right. Hurry back."

Simon had felt so pleased when Morag had told him that she was probably the envy of every girl in the country because she was his friend, and that he had so many fine qualities.

He swam slowly around the pool while thinking about her, and he felt certain that because she'd told him how she felt about him, they'd soon be kissing more intimately.

He then thought about Wystan, and he hoped that Morag's infatuation with him was indeed a thing of the past because he

knew that if Wystan wanted her, he'd only have to smile and hold out his hand to her. Simon sighed when he realized that Wystan was also taller, and with a better physique.

His thoughts were interrupted when he saw Morag appear on the patio, smiling and holding a tray of cold drinks and fruit. They laughed as he turned around before she dove nude into the pool, and Simon envisioned her beautiful body gliding in the water as if she were flying nude through the air and smiling at him as she flew down into his arms.

They'd swam and played several times in the pool whenever they hadn't been basking in the sun and now that Simon was again lying on the blanket with her, he felt so excited. He had an erection as he gazed at her lying on her back, with a towel covering her nude body from just above her breasts to halfway down her thighs, and he recalled the number of times he'd caught a glimpse of her breasts above the water.

"Cocktails!" exclaimed Wystan.

"Cock tales?" asked Simon when his erotic thoughts were abruptly interrupted, and then he blushed when he realized that he'd misinterpreted the word, '*cocktails*.'

"I made cocktails," said Wystan, smiling.

"Oh, hi. I didn't know you were back, already."

"It's been over three hours since I left you and Morag."

"The time passed so quickly because Simon and I were having

so much fun. Have you time for a swim?"

"No," replied Wystan. "I'd love to, but I'm preparing dinner for us. I'll have a few sips of my cocktail with you, though."

"I hope they're not too strong because I wouldn't want Simon walking into walls or falling into the pool."

"Then it'd be your chance to play lifeguard, and save me, right? Mmmm, this tastes great," said Simon. "Thanks, Wystan. I haven't had anything alcoholic to drink since Christmas."

"Well, there's not much alcohol in these cocktails, so, you won't get the least bit tipsy. I see that you're both in towels. Swimming nude, were you?" asked Wystan, grinning.

"Yes, we were. I didn't want to, but Simon tore off my dress, then pushed me into the pool."

"What? Morag! Don't believe her, Wystan. She pulled off *my* clothes and I was so shocked," said Simon, laughing.

"I wouldn't doubt it because Morag can be rather impetuous at times. She loves playing the wanton water nymph, however, she only runs around nude in the garden when we have many guests. She's such an exhibitionist."

"Why, that's not true! I had to plead so often with Simon to stop making me swim nude with him. *He*'s the exhibitionist. He heard you coming, so, he wrapped a towel around himself, but he's been nude all afternoon," said Morag, then she giggled.

"Oh, really? I see, so then I presume you'll want to dine nude, as well, Simon."

"No thanks," he said as he laughed.

"You're quite sure?" asked Wystan. "If you like being nude most of the time, we could all dine nude. Yes, marvelous idea."

"I'd rather dress up in the lovely old clothes, but you men can be nude during dinner," said Morag.

"So, what's it to be, Simon? Fancy old clothes or nudity?"

"Hmmm, well, I *do* like dressing up in the wigs and old, fancy clothes, so, this time, we'll wear clothes," he replied.

"Fine," said Wystan. "Dinner will be ready in a little less than an hour, so, we can start getting into costume. I'll select an outfit for you, Simon, and you can change in the guest room next door to my bedroom. All right? Hmmm, now let me see. Yes, you were dressed in gold, last time. There's a copper velvet outfit, or the emerald green one, or..."

"Excuse me for butting in," said Morag. "But whereas you're still undecided about what to wear, I've decided on *my* costume. I'm dressing in white and I'll pretend I'm Marie Antoinette or a lady of the court, or perhaps a famous countess."

"Hmmm, I have it!" exclaimed Wystan. "Why not add a dash of adventure? Morag, you can pretend to be a lady-in-waiting to the Queen of Spain, but you're also a princess from some country, somewhere on an old map. You're on a grand galleon sailing to Spain with a huge treasure of jewels and such, and Simon and I are pirates. We take command of the ship, hold you as our prisoner, and ransom you for the treasure. What say you?"

"I think it's a marvelous idea!" cried Morag.

"Do we put her in chains?" asked Simon, grinning.

"Many of them, and we'll gag her, too," replied Wystan.

"Oh, no you won't," she said. "I'm a fine lady, therefore, your lives would be forfeit when the king learns of your dastardly deed of dressing me in many chains, then gagging me, too."

"Oh, very well, then," said Wystan. "But what guarantee do we have that you won't dive overboard?"

"I'd never do that. Too many sharks," replied Morag.

"Hmmm, can we trust her, Simon?"

"Certainly. She'd never want to be devoured by sharks."

"Perhaps. We'll chance it. Off to your boudoir, my lady! Enjoy your freedom for only a little longer," said Wystan.

"Hah! My guards will cut you down if you try to board the ship! I shall take my leave whilst you rogues weigh your folly."

"Simon the Terrible and I shall abduct you before any of your guards are able to raise a sword to us."

"Such foolhardy arrogance!" huffed Morag as she hurried away to the house.

"Are you the pirate captain, or am I?" asked Wystan.

"We'll both be captains. Partners in crime," replied Simon.

"Agreed! Let the performance begin! Come-come!"

Wystan and Simon went into the house, then upstairs, and while walking by Morag's closed bedroom door, they shouted that their ship was already gaining on hers.

Simon followed him into his bedroom and he grinned as he

watched Wystan sorting through several closets and tossing clothes and accessories onto the bed.

"Ah, here we are," said Wystan. "Silk sashes, jeweled scabbards. Boots. Daggers. Oh, and pistols. You do realize that because our pirate crew all died of scurvy, that we'll have to take her ship by ourselves."

"So? That shouldn't be a problem because there's only forty of the king's best swordsmen guarding her," said Simon.

"Yes, you're right. Absolutely no problem, at all. Here's a waistcoat for you. An ivory shirt, and...Hmmmm, and these tan trousers. I'll dress completely in white, with a bright red cape. You wear these black boots, and I'll wear the brown ones. Now, hurry to your quarters and change. Time is of the essence."

"Aye-aye, Captain Wystan. I shall be ready to take action in ten minutes or less."

"Good man," said Wystan as he began undressing.

Simon rushed to the guest room, undressed quickly, then he noticed how damp his underwear was because they'd been laying too close to the pool, and water had splashed on them.

He knew that if he wore his damp underwear, it would appear that he'd accidentally urinated in the pants of the costume, so, he decided to take off his underwear.

Simon put on the cream colored shirt, fastened the buttons on the cuffs of the long, wide, puffy sleeves, and because there

weren't any buttons at the front of the shirt, he understood that it was meant to be tied at the waist.

He picked up the tan trousers, and it wasn't until he'd unfolded them, that he noticed they were similar to long stockings made of very thin material. Simon realized that they were tights, so, he struggled into them, sat down on the bed, and smiled as he put on the black, knee-high boots.

He stood up and fastened the scabbard to the wide, brown leather belt that hung low on the left side of his hips, then he put on the three large, jeweled rings that Wystan had given to him.

He whirled around to face the full-length mirror, then he bared his teeth as he drew his sword and slashed the air with it. Simon grinned as he looked over his costume, and then blushed when he noticed that because he wasn't wearing underwear, and the color of the tights were a slight shade lighter than his tanned skin, he looked almost nude from the waist down.

He left his guest room, knocked on Wystan's bedroom door before entering, then he saw that Wystan was dressed in the same style of clothing, but they were all white, and his white tights were also rather revealing.

"So, I, uh, I'm ready," said Simon.

"Ah, yes, you look rather splendid, indeed."

"Um, when we dressed up before, we didn't wear tights, and, uh, these are sort of really tight-fitting."

"That's why they're called tights," said Wystan.

"I know that, but these are almost the same color as my skin, so, it looks...Well, it looks like I..."

"Oh, yes, you're right. They're *almost* similar in color."

"Well, um, my underwear got wet when we were at the pool, so, I had to leave them off, and I didn't know 'til I put these tights on that you can see everything I got, and, uh, because they're this color, I look sort of nude," said Simon.

"Hmmm, yes, well, it simply looks natural to me. I never wear underwear when I wear tights because that was the fashion back then. It's not as obvious as a codpiece, and in some paintings I've seen, the men wearing codpieces look like they have erections."

"I've seen those, too. Codpieces, I mean. But these tights are sort of just as daring because they're like...Well, you know, like silk stockings."

"That's because they're made of silk," said Wystan.

"Yeah, but very *thin* silk. It's just that...Um, I think it makes my dick noticeable."

"And your point is?" asked Wystan as he put on his vest.

"My point is that it's not small. My dick, I mean. When I've been in the change room at school, I've only seen two other guys who've got dicks as big as mine, and...Well, with these tights on, it really shows off my dick."

"If you were living back in the time when tights were fashionable, I'm sure you wouldn't feel in the least self-conscious. Besides, one tends to look at the entire outfit, instead of staring at the crotch."

"Even if it's really big?" asked Simon. "I mean, yours is twice the size of mine, and thicker, too, so, it's hard not to look at it, and I can see your big juicers, too."

"Juicers?"

"You know, your knockers, or nuts, testicles or whatever. The material's so thin, I can see everything you've got."

"And *I* can see everything *you*'ve got, and your *juicers*, as you call them, too, but I really don't know why that should bother you. You should be proud of your genital endowment because few men are as gifted. Besides, Morag'll be wearing a dress with so much cleavage that her breasts'll barely be covered, and that was also the fashion back then, therefore, if she's baring most of her breasts, I'm certain that'll make you feel more at ease. We often dress in costume with our guests, and several of the men have had stubby little penises that stick straight out, which I'm sure you'll agree is much more obvious. But Morag's never given it a second thought whenever she's seen a penis like that. Our penises may be larger than average, but at least they hang at a polite angle down our thighs, so, stop all this nonsense about dick display. All right?"

"Yeah, all right," replied Simon, then he laughed.

"Good man. Yes, you look quite fine as a pirate. Oh, I almost forgot. Here, wear this big, gold hoop earring. It'll make you look even more authentic."

Simon clipped on the earring, then Wystan put one on, winked at him, and then grinned and said: "Ready?"

"Yes, but I...Well, I still feel like I'm nude from the waist

down, but you look the same way in those white tights, and you said that Morag's used to seeing you and other men dressed like this, so, I guess I'll get used to wearing these tights after I've had them on for a while," said Simon, smiling.

"Of course you will."

"You look very good in your outfit, and I like your gold waistcoat. Lots of jewels on it."

"And every one of them stolen from various kings. You know, Captain Simon, I remember when you looted the Emperor of China's lead ship and stole those magnificent, large pearls you have sewn on your fine waistcoat. The pearls were originally from Fiji, if I recall correctly."

"Yes, they were. My favorite tailor spent six months sewing them all into the material," said Simon as he smiled.

"Fine craftsmanship, and excellent taste, too. Morag will take much longer getting ready because after putting on a gown, she'll try on various wigs. Come-come. Let's go downstairs and have drinks. Oops! I mean, *grog*," said Wystan, grinning.

Wystan prepared two glasses of dry, white sherry and ginger ale before going to the kitchen, then Simon sat at the dining room table, drinking the cocktail while admiring the two tall, silver candelabra and the expensive place settings.

Five minutes later, Wystan began making trips back and forth from the kitchen, carrying covered serving dishes, and when he'd

finished setting the table, he freshened their drinks, then he sat down, and slid two pieces of paper and a pencil across the table to him. Simon noticed that one piece of paper was blank, and the other had numbers written on it, then he smiled and asked: "Is this the amount of ransom we're asking for her?"

"Nope. For the past two years, I've been waiting to have a telephone, and yesterday, I was told that a serviceman will be arriving sometime this month to install the thing. That'll be my phone number, and I was hoping that you'd write down yours."

"Sure, now we'll be able to call each other," said Simon, smiling as he wrote down his phone number, and slid the piece of paper back across the table to Wystan.

"Just about everyone I know have had their phones disconnected until they'll be able to afford the monthly payments again, so, my parents had an extra phone installed for our neighbors to use," said Simon, feeling proud as he smiled. "My father had a phone booth built at one end of the porch, and it looks like a tiny cottage with curtains on the windows, and there's even a little upholstered bench in it, too."

"Your family's generosity is quite admirable," said Wystan.

"You'd be surprised at the extent of their generosity. It's so wonderful what my parents do for our neighbors and friends."

"Well, I had an inkling they were, because you're very generous and kind yourself."

"Thanks, and I think you are, too. I'm glad to hear you'll be getting a phone, and I know it takes quite awhile to get one, so,

I'm not at all surprised that you've waited so long," said Simon.

"After it's installed, I'll be able to contact you immediately if I'm ever called away for some family emergency, such as one of my relatives tripping over his or her shadow, then falling on it, and wrinkling it badly, or even tearing part of it."

"My shadow hasn't been torn or wrinkled yet, but I know how dangerous shadows can be because I've slipped and fallen on mine many times," said Simon.

"That's why I always stomp instead of step. Hmmm, our prisoner is keeping us waiting. I hope she hasn't leapt overboard because sharks can be rather voracious at this hour."

"Aw, she's a fast swimmer," Simon said as he smiled.

"And speak of the devil, our lady arrives."

Simon looked over at the staircase and saw Morag dressed in a huge, silver gown and wearing a very high white wig as she descended the stairs.

He gaped at her bodice because the neckline was so low, and it was designed to lift her breasts so high, that it looked as if they could pop out with the slightest movement. She seemed to drift over to the table, with her chin held high, and then she sat down with a flourish.

"Drink and dine heartily, you swine. This shall be your final repast because the king will send fifty ships to cut you down and rescue me," said Morag, haughtily.

"Ah, but he'll never find us because we've changed our direction and we now sail for the West Indies," Wystan told her.

"Fools! He'll search the ends of the earth for me! Well, if I am to be temporarily at your mercy, I shall partake of your food and drink, and I do hope it's of high quality."

"Only the best for such a beauty. Captain Simon, would you please fill Lady Morag's goblet?" asked Wystan.

"I'd be honored to."

"And no servants? Hah! I expected as much," said Morag.

"I'll serve. Is trout to your liking, ma'am?" asked Wystan.

"Mere trout? I suppose it'll suffice, although I'm used to sautéed hummingbird tongues."

They played their roles as they dined and laughed. Simon had never drank much alcohol before, so, after a few glasses of wine, he felt both tipsy and quite relaxed.

Morag reached for a salt shaker, and Simon's heart leapt when one of her breasts lifted out of the low-cut bodice of her dress, but she didn't notice that as she continued eating and chatting. He was in a quandary because if he told her that her breast was exposed, Morag would feel embarrassed, and if he didn't tell her, she'd be embarrassed because it hadn't been brought to her attention.

Simon looked at Wystan whom simply winked at him and smiled, then he slowly shook his head and held the index finger of his right hand to his lips. Wystan stood up, walked over to her, cupped her breast, then as he blocked Simon's view, he placed her breast back inside her dress.

"Thanks, Wystan. This dress shows off so much cleavage that...Well, this sort of thing often happens."

"You're still such a child because I still have to tie your bows and such," Wystan told her as he smiled.

"Have you thought of an after dinner game?" she asked him.

"Several, but I lean toward Gods and Goddesses."

"Yes, let's play that, Wystan! I love that game!"

"How is it played?" asked Simon.

"You choose your favorite Roman or Greek god and pretend you're him – or her, in my case," replied Morag. "Wystan of course is very convincing as Adonis or Apollo, although, when given enough compliments, he plays Narcissus quite well, too. But then you could play Narcissus, too, Simon, because you're every bit as handsome as Wystan."

"And whom will *you* play this time?" Wystan asked her.

"Hmmm, either Venus or Aphrodite. I'll surprise you."

"I'll play Hercules, and Simon can play Apollo."

"Perfect! With your height and very big muscles, you'll be so convincing as Hercules, and Simon'll make a splendid Apollo. Mmmm, this wine is delicious. Gentlemen, my glass is empty."

"Please forgive me, milady, for not noticing. Here, you have wine and Simon and I'll have cognac. Did you enjoy the meal?"

"It was so delicious. Wonderful," replied Simon, grinning.

"A splendid repast, as usual, Wystan," said Morag.

"Thank you, dear guests."

Wystan served coffee and glasses of cognac for Simon and himself, then Morag suggested they sit in the largest living room.

Simon felt so comfortable as he sat on the big, soft couch, looking from Morag to Wystan to the flickering flames in the fireplace. Wystan lit a cigarette, inhaled deeply, then passed it to Simon whom smiled as he took the cigarette.

He had previously smoked three cigarettes with Colin and a few other friends, so, Simon wasn't worried about choking and coughing while smoking a cigarette with Wystan.

He and Wystan talked as they passed the cigarette back and forth to each other, then slightly over five minutes later, Simon felt a little dizzy. He wasn't aware that Wystan had lit a cigarette made of marijuana, so, Simon felt even more relaxed as his gaze often lingered on Morag's almost exposed breasts.

"I'm going upstairs to prepare for the game," she said.

"Fine. *Our* costumes are in the solarium, so, Simon and I'll change there. The stage is still decorated from our last game of Gods and Goddesses."

"Oh, good. I'll be back downstairs in about twenty minutes, gentlemen. Tra-la!"

"Let's change our clothes, Simon."

"Hmmm, all right. You're a wonderful cook. The dinner was superb, and I'm having a great time."

"We must do this again, and soon, too. Perhaps tomorrow night if you'd like."

"Sure, I'd really like that," said Simon, smiling.

"So would Morag and I."

PART THREE

CHAPTER TWELVE

Reality Or Fantasy?

Simon felt pleasantly high as he accompanied Wystan through the house, passing open doors of many grand rooms, then a few minutes later, Wystan stopped at two, very tall and wide, ornately carved and gilded doors. He opened one of them, and then smiled while saying: "This is the solarium."

Simon followed him into the enormous room that had many floor-to-ceiling windows, with about a dozen domes of various sizes forming the ceiling, and a massive chandelier hung from the huge, central dome.

When he'd entered the solarium, Simon had been quite surprised because most of the plants and tropical trees had been removed, and now it looked like a large room in an ancient Greek or Roman palace.

The solarium had never looked like this at any time in his past, therefore, Simon tried concentrating to recall the solarium as it should be, but he couldn't change what he was seeing.

He then presumed that he had lost temporary control of his game again, and now he was only dreaming this situation, so, he

decided to accept everything his confused imagination was creating until he could eventually concentrate completely again on true memories of his past.

He relaxed, then smiled while looking around at what he knew were imaginary changes in the solarium. At one end of it, there was a big platform about eight inches high, with six, white marble pillars standing at three sides of the platform, then Wystan explained that it was the stage for performances they often participated in with their guests.

In the center of the stage, there was a six-foot-wide by eight-foot-long couch, with low arms at each end of it, and the couch was draped with long, white, diaphanous material.

All six pillars had similar white material wound loosely around them, and besides the dozen life-sized statues of nude men and women around the perimeter of the solarium, there were also hanging baskets of flowers, potted ferns and palms, and many flowering plants in large, ornate urns.

Wystan led him to the opposite end of it to a small, upholstered bench that had folded, white material on it.

"These are our costumes, so, off with your clothes."

"All of them?" asked Simon.

"Yes, because then the costumes will fit much better."

"Oh, okay."

After undressing, Simon stood looking around the solarium at the statues, which he found to be rather erotic. While he'd been looking at the statues, Wystan had put on his costume.

"Simon? Come put on your costume."

"Mmmm? Oh, right. Wow! You look...Um, uh, convincing."

He gaped at Wystan's costume, which was simply a long, narrow, almost completely transparent white cloth draped over one shoulder, then it swooped down just below his genitals, and then up over his opposite forearm.

He looked down at Wystan's sandals that had thin, gold ribbons tied in crisscross fashion up to his calves, then Simon grinned and said: "Jeez, Wystan! You look like a god. Like a statue with golden skin. You really are....Oh, I just noticed that your legs are still hairy, but all the hair on your chest and stomach is gone. I guess you shaved it off, huh?"

"Yes, I thought that shaving it off would be quicker and less painful than spending hours plucking out one hair at a time with a pair of tweezers," replied Wystan with a crooked smile.

"Smartass!"

"It itches like hell when the hair starts growing back in, and thankfully, that only takes about two weeks."

"The way you've rubbed a little bit of oil all over your arms and torso makes your skin look like shiny marble."

"That's the effect I wanted to give the suggestion that I'm a statue of a god whom has just come alive for the evening."

"Yeah, a *nude* statue who came alive because that cloth you've draped around you doesn't hide anything."

"Yes, *I* thought it made me look rather authentic, too."

"So, what sort of pants or whatever are you going to put on

with that?" asked Simon.

"None."

"What? But that cloth doesn't hide anything."

"That's because I haven't finished adjusting this material, and after I do, then the folds in it will hide my fun parts."

"Yeah, maybe the folds'll do that for now, but you better watch how you move around, or else your dick'll show."

"Sometimes it will, sometimes it won't, but we'll be too busy playing our roles that neither you nor Morag will notice. Incidentally, how do you know this isn't the sort of thing the gods sometimes wore whenever they strutted around bare-assed? Now *you* get into *your* costume," said Wystan, chuckling.

Simon gawked at him when Wystan handed him a similar, long length of almost completely transparent material.

"It's the same as yours."

"Of course it is," said Wystan. "What did you expect to wear as a god? A suit of armor?"

"No, but I'd thought we'd be wearing at least a cloth fig leaf with some strings to tie it on somehow. You know, like a fig leaf made out of gold cloth, or maybe silver cloth."

"I'm sure that even if there *were* strings on either a gold or sliver cloth fig leaf, they would eventually loosen or break, then the fig leaf would fall off."

"Hmmm, yeah, I guess you're right," said Simon.

Wystan helped him drape the cloth in the same manner as his own costume. Simon then walked over to the long, narrow mirror

propped up against a wall, and then while looking at his almost nude reflection, he wondered how revealing Morag's costume would be, if his and Wystan's costumes were so transparent.

"Hmmm, I don't know about this. I mean, I can see right through this cloth, and...Well, I don't know."

"There you go again, Simon. You went on about the tights being too revealing, and now you say *that* costume is, too. But I refuse to waste any more of my time trying to convince you that there's nothing wrong with partial nudity, so, for fuck's sake, stop you're whining," said Wystan, then he laughed.

"Yeah, yeah, I know, I should be thankful my dick's a fair size. You should be even *more* thankful."

"Thanks. I didn't think you'd noticed."

"But what'll Morag think if the folds in this material smooth out at times, and she can see our dicks and our pubic hair, too?"

"She'll think we've reached puberty," replied Wystan.

"Hmmm, I don't know about this. I mean, it looks like we're not wearing anything, so, Morag will see our...Are you sure she's seen other male guests dressed like this?"

"Awww, stop being such a prude. Now we look like statues of mythical gods."

"Yeah, totally naked statues."

"Simon, Simon, Simon. Whine, whine, whine. But regardless of your not-too-convincing protests, you look stupendous. Yes, you make quite a fine Apollo to my Hercules. When Morag comes back downstairs, she'll go directly to the small room behind the

stage, and then after I turn off all the lights, she'll prance out onto the stage, then the performance begins. She knows her way around in the dark, so...Hmmm, now *there*'s an understatement if there ever was one. As I was saying, she'll start the performance, so, you sit down, and I'll turn off the lights, and when Morag appears, I'll turn on two lights that'll light the stage. They're low lights, so, they'll give the illusion that we're really gods and the white material will glow brightly in the dark. Don't fall asleep."

"I don't think falling asleep is possible because I'm feeling very excited in a way," said Simon, smiling.

"All right, lights out."

Wystan turned off the lights, and then Simon sat in the dark, sliding his hands slowly over his thighs, chest and stomach while wondering if when the lights were turned back on, the solarium would suddenly appear the way it should be, and he'd be fully dressed again.

About ten seconds after Wystan had turned off the lights, low, rather pleasant music began playing at the same time the stage began slowly lighting up.

Simon's heartbeat quickened when he saw Morag reclining on the couch while she plucked the strings of a small harp, and a pastel blue, semitransparent cloth was draped over her nude body.

Her wrists were tied together with gold twine, then after Simon's gaze moved slowly down over her beautiful body, he saw that her ankles were bound together, as well.

She stopped humming and plucking the strings of the harp when Wystan appeared, then stepped up onto the stage, grabbed her, and then easily lifted her high over his head, with one hand.

"Oh, Apollo! Rescue me from Hercules!" cried Morag.

"The only way he can do that is to insert one finger into my navel, then turn it three times!" exclaimed Wystan.

Simon laughed as he stood up and walked over to them, then he pushed the tip of his index finger into Wystan's navel, then after turning it three times, Wystan groaned as he lowered Morag down onto the couch, and then he fell onto his back beside her while pretending to be unconscious.

"Oh, quick! Untie me before he awakens!" Morag pleaded.

"Yes, sweet goddess. Immediately," said Simon, grinning.

He tried to untie her hands, but the thin, silk twine was too intricately bound, and as he fumbled with the knots, Wystan began moaning, then he sat up and glared at them as he shouted: "Aha! I shall fight you to the death, Apollo!"

"Damn! I mean, by Jove! Or Jupiter! Or whatever appropriate god to swear by! Hercules has awakened and he's now going to harm us! Use your magical strength, Apollo!"

Wystan grabbed him, and they started to wrestle as Morag slipped off the couch and sat on the floor, watching them. Wystan was much larger and stronger, so, Simon was having a difficult time trying to fend him off, then he looked at Morag and saw that she had somehow managed to loosen her wrist bonds.

A moment later, she'd untied the ropes binding her ankles together, then she leapt onto Wystan's back, wrapping her legs and arms around him as she tried to pull him away from Simon.

Morag worked her way around to the front of Wystan's body until she and Simon were both lying on their backs, and then Simon started becoming highly aroused because of Morag's nude body squirming against his while she pretended to help him fight off the supposed Hercules.

The almost transparent material that had been draped on their bodies had pulled off them while they'd been wrestling and squirming all over one another.

Simon was concentrating as hard as he could not to get an erection while feeling certain that if this god and goddess game continued, he'd soon have an orgasm.

Morag squirmed out from under Wystan, then knelt close beside him, and began pounding his shoulder as Wystan laughed and playfully slapped her hands away. Simon's heart then leapt when Wystan began sucking on one of Morag's breasts while she moaned in pleasure.

Wystan was still sucking on her breast when he pulled her down closer to Simon, then Morag's other breast pressed against his mouth, so, Simon began kissing, licking, and sucking on it.

Moments later, they were caressing one another's bodies while playfully wrestling, and Simon was about to ask them if Gods and Goddesses was usually played like this, but when he opened his

mouth to ask them that, Morag slid her tongue into it, then Simon began murmuring: "Mmmm, oh, my God. Ohhh, yeah, mmmm."

"Woman! Help me subdue your rescuer, or you die!"

"Yes, I obey, oh, mighty Hercules!" she cried out.

Simon's thoughts swirled faster when she chose to subdue him by fellating him, and he began humping his hips to meet every plunge of her mouth.

Wystan spread her legs, then began fucking her as Morag fellated Simon. The Gods and Goddesses game had turned highly sexual so quickly, then Simon threw away his inhibitions, and joined in on their torrid lovemaking.

At one point during the wildly uninhibited sexual acts with Morag and Wystan, Simon stopped participating after looking over at a very dark area of the room, where he saw a nude man lit by what appeared to be a spotlight in the ceiling.

The man was screaming and struggling while being forced into an odd-looking steel framework by hands reaching out of the dark, and Simon was surprised that neither Wystan nor Morag seemed to hear the man's screams while they made passionate love.

He watched the steel framework lifting the screaming man off the floor at the same time slowly turning him upside-down. The man continued screaming as syringes were quickly inserted into the sides of his neck, his arms, and inner thighs.

A few moments after blood began flowing down through long,

narrow, rubber tubes attached to the syringes, the man stopped struggling and shouting in terror.

Simon thought that the man was being initiated into some sort of bizarre religious sect, then suddenly, that bloodletting scene was cast into total darkness when the spotlight shut off.

He then immediately forgot that bloodletting scene when he began groaning loudly in ecstasy as Morag fellated him while Wystan knelt behind her, gripping her hips as he fucked her.

Although none of these erotic scenes or that man being hoisted in a strange, steel cage in the dark had been part of his past, Simon didn't care because he'd never felt so sexually excited before in his life, and their very passionate lovemaking continued for what seemed hours before he fell asleep from exhaustion.

He wasn't sure how much time had passed before he slowly opened his eyes, then Simon smiled and began falling asleep again as Morag sucked on his nipples. Just as he was drifting into an erotic dream, Wystan picked him up, and carried him upstairs.

CHAPTER THIRTEEN

Simon sat up in bed, then feeling light stinging sensations on most of his body, he stumbled out of bed, turned on the light, and stood in front of the full-length mirror.

He was then surprised to see that he had small scratches on his arms and legs, and on several other areas of his body. It took him a few moments before he could recall how he had received the scratches, and then he blushed while thinking about the many sexual variations he'd eagerly engaged in earlier that night.

Simon felt sure that he would never consider having any sexual contact with a male, yet because he'd felt astoundingly sexually excited, he had willingly participated in a lusty threesome with Morag and Wystan.

He could hear the faint sound of a piano, so, he picked up the dressing robe that had been spread out on his bed, then put it on, opened the door, and walked along the hall to the bathroom.

After he flushed the toilet, Simon went over to the staircase where he could hear the piano clearer. He hesitated before walking slowly downstairs, and along the hall to the room he saw light and heard music coming from.

He felt dizzy as he swayed closer to the entrance of the enormous room, then looking inside, he saw Morag playing the piano. She had on a long-sleeved, purple dress, and Wystan was

dressed casually in ivory-colored trousers, and a burnt orange polo shirt as he sat in a wing chair near Morag.

"Simon!" exclaimed Wystan when he noticed him.

Morag stopped playing the piano, and then she and Wystan hurried over to him.

"Oh, Simon, I was so worried about you!" she exclaimed.

"I was quite worried about you, too," said Wystan. "I'm so sorry about what happened. That wasn't ordinary tobacco in that cigarette we smoked. It was marijuana, and I had no idea that you'd react so badly to the effects of it."

"Marijuana?" asked Simon.

"Yes," replied Wystan. "I thought you'd smoked some before with your friends, so...Well, I was mistaken. I'm sorry."

"You shouldn't have let him smoke so much of it. Oh, Simon. How do you feel? Wystan, help me lead him to a chair."

They helped him over to an armchair, and then after he was seated, Simon looked up at them, and said: "Thanks. I feel sort of half asleep, or in a dream, but I remember that we'd been in that big solarium, then things got quite wild."

"Just after we entered it, you must've panicked for some reason when I turned off the lights, and it was then that I heard crashing sounds," said Wystan. "When I turned the lights back on, I realized that you'd run out the side door, and into the garden. I'm so sorry, Simon. By the time I got to you, you'd run through the rose garden and you were trying to climb a tree, so, I called to you, but you didn't seem to know who I was."

"It all happened so fast, too," said Morag. "I came downstairs and went to the solarium, and that's when I heard shouting and laughing. I rushed outside and saw you just as you fell from the tree. Wystan tried to hold you from running, but you broke free of him and ran through the open part of the wall and down to the stream. I thought you'd cut your feet badly when you ran over all the broken stones, but I was so relieved to find that you didn't."

"I did that?" asked Simon, as his thoughts slowly swirled.

"You must still be confused from that marijuana. I had no idea that it had such a devastating effect on some people, otherwise, I would've warned Wystan not to let you have even a tiny puff of it. Oh, Simon, I keep picturing you racing through the gardens and then over all those broken pieces of the old wall, then all the way to the stream! Thank goodness Wystan got to you before you ran any farther. When you fell from that tree not far from the solarium, the rose bushes and a few other bushes scratched your body, but I noticed that your clothes weren't torn. Oh, this has turned out to be such a disastrous evening. Damn you, Wystan."

"Yes, I *should* be damned. After you fainted, Simon, I carried you back into the house, and then upstairs. Can you ever forgive me for letting you smoke some of that marijuana cigarette?"

"But I thought we...Uh, on the stage. We...We did things, and I...Ohhh, mmmmm," said Simon, feeling slightly disoriented.

"I'd laid out some masks and togas for us to wear, and then Morag was supposed to walk in dressed as a half-deer, half-nymph with big antlers, and then we were to pretend we shot her with

magic bows and arrows, then...Well, unfortunately, we didn't have a chance to begin playing Gods and Goddesses because of the marijuana's effect on you, and it's all my fault. Oh, this is so embarrassing. I'm so sorry the marijuana had such an odd effect on you. You must've thought that Morag was in the solarium with us at the time because you started calling out to her that you were Apollo and that you were going to free her from slavery. I've never seen marijuana have that effect before."

"You mean we weren't...Nobody was nude?" asked Simon.

"Nude? Of course not," replied Wystan. "Hmmm, why would you...Oh, I think the reason you thought that was because we'd talked about the tights you had on, and you felt they were...Well, slightly revealing, so, I suppose *that*, combined with the effects of the marijuana, most likely led you to imagine that you were actually nude. That'd explain why you ran over to the stage where there was a pile of material, which you threw around yourself before you ran out into the gardens."

"When I first saw you with reams of white material wrapped around you, I thought you were a ghost running through the gardens," said Morag, frowning. "I was so worried that the material would fall over your face while you were running, and then because you wouldn't be able to see anything, you'd run into a tree. After you climbed that tree just outside the solarium, then fell out of it, then ran down to the stream, you stopped, and then you looked around and asked where all the gods and goddesses had run off to, then you started turning around until you became

dizzy. Wystan got to you just before you fainted, and then he carried you upstairs and applied lotion to your scratches. I was so certain that you'd sleep until morning, but here you are out of bed only half an hour after that frightful experience."

"Half an hour? That's all?" asked Simon.

"Yes, all that frightening commotion happened so fast, and I was so surprised that you came back downstairs just minutes after Wystan had carried you upstairs. You must've been devastated by all that happened, and so quickly, too, because it's now just a few minutes after eight o'clock."

"It is? It's that early?" Simon asked her.

He looked at his wristwatch and he was astonished to see that it was indeed only a few minutes after eight. He recalled that when Morag had told them that she was going upstairs to put on her costume, he had glanced at his watch and seen that it was almost seventy-thirty, so, he'd only imagined that they'd all been nude and participating in highly sexual acts for what seemed like four or five hours.

"But it all seemed so...I thought we'd started playing Gods and Goddesses, and then it...We, uh...And then the three of us had...Hmmm, I'm a bit confused," said Simon.

"I don't doubt you're feeling a bit confused because this has been quite an astonishing evening, and I hold you responsible for all that's happened, Wystan," Morag said while scowling at him.

"Whew! The reaction I had to the marijuana made me have hallucinations, and it all happened so fast, too."

"How do you feel now?" Wystan asked him.

"A bit dizzy, but I'm sure for just a minute or so longer."

"You have no idea how relieved I am to hear that. Please stay seated, and I'll fetch you a cup of strong tea. Morag, please get him a stool for his feet."

Wystan rushed away as Morag brought an upholstered stool over to Simon, then after placing his feet on it, she said: "Oh, Simon, I wasn't aware that Wystan let you smoke that marijuana cigarette with him. I thought it was tobacco. Now I suppose you're terribly angry with me, and definitely with Wystan."

"No. No, I'm not angry with either of you. Honestly."

"Oh, thank goodness," she said. "He calls *me* immature, but sometimes, like tonight for instance, Wystan can be much more immature. So irresponsible."

"I had some wild hallucinations."

"It certainly looked like you'd seen something wild. It must've been such an awful experience. You might've had even more of those dreadful hallucinations if you'd seen me in my deer costume because the headpiece looks so real, and the antlers are so frightening. You might've thought you'd seen a deranged deer that had somehow found it's way into the solarium, and it was about to charge you after you'd startled it, then that surely would've caused you to leap over the garden walls."

"I thought you were going to dress like a goddess."

"I was supposed to be a goddess who had been changed into half-deer and half-forest nymph, then after you and Wystan shot

me with magic, invisible arrows, I'd rush behind the curtain, pull off that costume, and dance back onto the stage, wearing a lovely white gown and a crown that sparkles like diamonds. Are you sure you're all right? All those scratches must sting and hurt so."

"No, not anymore. Whew! Marijuana sure makes you think very, very differently," said Simon.

"I've never seen it have that effect when Wystan smokes it. He told me that when he smokes marijuana before he goes to bed, it sometimes makes him have erotic dreams. He said *very* erotic. Well, it certainly didn't have that effect on *you*."

"Oh, there sure was...Uh, well, there was a moment when I thought about something a bit erotic. At least, I think I did. Hmmm, I feel rather confused."

"And so you should. The next time he offers you that stuff, promise me you'll smoke very little of it, and the moment you start feeling out of the ordinary, like you did earlier, stop smoking it. All right? Wystan should've told you that you're supposed to smoke it gradually. A few puffs a day 'til your system can adjust to it. Damn him. Sometimes he never thinks. He said he'd thought you'd smoked it before. You haven't, have you?"

"No, I haven't," replied Simon. "I really liked the effects, initially, though. Well, I'll know better next time. A few puffs, and that's all."

Wystan returned, carrying a mug of strong, hot tea for Simon, then as he handed it to him, he said: "This tea will help freshen you. I suppose you hate me now."

"No, because, after all, you didn't know I hadn't smoked marijuana before. I should've told you," said Simon, smiling.

"I'm so relieved that you're feeling better. Your eyes were wild for a few moments after you smoked some marijuana."

"And you're to blame," said Morag, glaring at Wystan.

"Oh, I know that for sure, and now I almost feel like a murderer. What a frightfully terrible evening this has turned out to be. Now what should we do for the rest of the evening?"

"I wanted to serve dessert at nine, but now I don't think I'll be able to do that because Simon'll probably want to go home after what he's experienced," said Morag as she pouted.

"No, I feel fine, now," Simon told her.

"You really do?" she asked while frowning.

"Yes, I really do," he replied, smiling.

"Oh, I'm so glad. When Wystan carried you upstairs, I fed Blaze. He was quite startled when he saw you shouting and running around, then he reared up when you suddenly ran toward him. But not to worry, I spoke softly to soothe him as I patted him. I brought him up to the garden and I talked to him before I came back in to play the piano just before you came downstairs."

"Thanks for taking such good care of my horse. Hmmm, it's only been half an hour, and I thought hours had gone by. That was quite a wild hallucination I had."

Simon's thoughts whirled while he recalled the intense sexual acts that he'd only imagined had happened.

"Perhaps a game of cards might be calming," said Wystan.

"What say you, Simon?" asked Morag, frowning.

"Yeah, sure, I'd like that, but let me rest for a minute first because I'm still trying to collect my thoughts. I feel embarrassed about what happened."

"Nonsense! It was entirely my fault," said Wystan.

"Yes, it certainly was, and you should punch him, Simon. He deserves it," Morag said, sticking her tongue out at Wystan.

"No! Please! Spare me, Simon!" cried Wystan, grinning and cowering away from him.

"Behave yourself. Oh, I just remembered that there's a concert on the wireless at nine, so, we can listen to that while we're playing cards," Morag told them.

"Oh, we listen to that program every Tuesday night at nine at home, too, and I really like it because they often play a bit of jazz and blues," said Simon.

"Then it's settled. Cards and music it is, but only if you're sure you feel up to it. Do you?" asked Morag.

"Yes, I do. Honestly," he replied, smiling at her. "I'll run upstairs and get dressed, and be back in no longer than ten minutes," said Simon while hurrying away.

They sat in a smaller room, which impressed Simon because it was exquisitely furnished, and as they played poker, his heart beat faster when he recalled the erotic hallucination about making love with both Morag and Wystan.

He felt that by having dreamed of being so intimate with them, it would make them closer friends, but he dared not tell Wystan that he'd imagined the three of them involved in so many sexual acts together.

The tremendous sexual excitement he'd experienced from the effects of the marijuana had lessened considerably, however, Simon's cheeks flushed when he suddenly recalled the highly erotic things he'd done to bring Wystan to several orgasms during his marijuana-induced hallucination.

He began wondering if other males had had erotic thoughts about a male, then he felt sure that his erotic thoughts had only been unusual, sexual suggestions that had been subconsciously sparked by the effects of the marijuana.

Simon realized that any close friendship between two men had to have a love of some kind to make that bond, however, the marijuana had distorted his perception of that bonding.

His thoughts were interrupted when Morag lightly tapped his hand and told him it was his turn to play a card, then Simon apologized as he smiled and placed one of his cards on the table.

Later in the evening, Morag suggested that they stop playing cards until she prepared dessert and tea. Simon suddenly realized that it was almost eleven o'clock and he'd listened to most of the music program on the radio.

When Morag served tea and cake with an ice-cold, fresh fruit

sauce, Wystan asked to be excused, then fifteen minutes after he'd hurried away, he returned, smiling while telling Simon that he'd taken Blaze around to the stable at the side of the house, and settled him in for the night.

"Oh, thanks, Wystan," said Simon, smiling.

"It's late, so, obviously you'll be spending the night with us, and I wanted to ensure that your horse was comfortable."

"That was so considerate of you. And this is wonderful cake. The fruit sauce on it is very delicious, too," Simon remarked.

"Thank you. Oh, Wystan, why not pour us all a glass of that delicious, mixed-fruit liqueur?" asked Morag.

"Certainly. Good choice. No marijuana for you this time, Simon, but you can get a tad giddy on a little alcohol, then drift upstairs to sleep and have contented dreams."

"I'm sure I will. The marijuana had a soothing effect at first, but until I'm more used to it, I'll only take a few puffs each day."

"I told him to do that, Wystan, but you shouldn't have let him smoke so much of it. Oh, well, you've been chastised enough, I suppose. Big, bad boy," said Morag, smiling.

"Ah, good, you're smiling. I'm greatly relieved that you're not going to nag me all night," said Wystan, smirking. "Here, Simon. Ambrosia of the berry gardens."

He handed Simon a small snifter half-filled with the liqueur, then he smiled and said: "Now, by the time you finish drinking that, I'm sure you'll feel nicely drowsy and be thinking much better thoughts than you had during that frightful ordeal."

"Thanks, but I'm sure I'll sleep very well tonight. Mmmm, very nice. So smooth," said Simon, savoring the liqueur.

"And light. You don't need anything stronger," said Morag.

"Now let's get on with the card game, shall we? Hmmm, who won last time?" asked Wystan.

"I did, of course," replied Morag, then she giggled.

"Sheer luck. Simon'll soon have the giggles, too, because the marijuana's effect will take until tomorrow morning at least to wear off, but nothing like before. Just very erotic thoughts. I feel a similar effect now, and visions of pretty women are dancing through my head. Nude ones at that," said Wystan, smiling.

"Oh, I know. You always have those naughty types of thoughts whenever you smoke that stuff, so, please concentrate on the cards, instead of those erotic thoughts. Hmmm, are you having erotic thoughts, too, Simon?" she asked, then she giggled.

"Well, a few, but only about every two seconds," he replied.

They all laughed, and then Wystan exclaimed: "Hip, hip, hooray to the raunchy effects of marijuana!"

Simon often chuckled, then Morag told them that she was well aware of what they were thinking, which made Simon and Wystan burst out laughing.

He had stronger erotic thoughts as the time passed, and Simon wondered if Wystan's thoughts were similar to his, and that made him start laughing again.

Morag decided to go to bed, and she advised them to do the same, then she kissed each of them on the cheek, said goodnight, and went upstairs.

"Now we can snicker and giggle whenever we want because of our marijuana high," said Wystan, grinning. "Morag chastised me for having erotic thoughts when I smoke marijuana, but she didn't know that I've been getting erections for the past hour."

"So have I," Simon told him as he smiled.

"And your eyes are slowly closing, so, I can well imagine the dreams you'll have tonight."

"Hmmm, yes, I'm feeling very tired. It's been a stressful evening. Oh, not because of you or Morag, but because of that hallucination I had earlier this evening," said Simon.

"Yes, I imagine that *would* make you feel exhausted, so, you'd better get to bed. I've prepared one of the guest rooms for you."

"Thanks, Wystan. Ahhhhhh-hmmm, mmmmmmmm."

"That was an enormous yawn."

They walked slowly upstairs, then Wystan said goodnight to him before closing the guest room door.

CHAPTER FOURTEEN

Simon undressed, climbed into bed, and fell asleep. He began to dream about the sexual acts he'd had with Morag and Wystan, and he smiled as he squirmed around on the bed while slowly sliding his hands over his chest and stomach.

He dreamed that Morag entered his room, let her nightgown drop to the floor, and then completely nude, she slipped into his bed, and they began making love. He felt the right side of the mattress tilt down, then looking to his right, his heart leapt when he saw Wystan smiling at him as he crawled closer to them, and instantly added more sexual excitement to their lovemaking.

Hours passed slowly by, coating their bodies with sweat, and Simon felt so sexually aroused, that he didn't care what he did to or with Morag and Wystan to satisfy his almost crazed lust.

He bent back his head and cried out in ecstasy when he had another intense orgasm, and when he slowly bent his head back down, Simon was startled to find that he was alone in bed.

He sat up and looked around, feeling confused because the sex acts had seemed so realistic, but Morag and Wystan weren't on his bed, hence, he had to conclude that he'd been dreaming.

He fell back onto the bed, then Simon became aware that his chest and stomach were streaked with drying semen, then he realized he must have ejaculated while having a very erotic dream, so, he decided to take a bath.

He got out of bed, picked up his dressing robe, and then he hoped he wouldn't be seen nude and streaked with semen as he hurried down the hall to the immense bathroom.

Simon leaned over the bathtub to plug the drain, and then after turning on the taps, he leaned back up, and hung his robe on a hook on the wall near the bathroom door.

He was just about to lean over the tub to test the temperature of the bath water as it filled the tub, when he heard somebody knocking on the bathroom door, so, he quickly wrapped a towel around his waist just as the door opened, and then he saw Wystan.

"Oh, Simon. I thought you'd be sound asleep by now."

"Uh, hi, Wystan. I was just running a bath."

"So I see. I thought you'd fall asleep the moment your head hit the pillow, but here you are, wide awake, and less than five minutes after I left your room," said Wystan, smiling.

"Then you *were* in there. I thought I was just dreaming."

"You almost *were* dreaming on the way upstairs."

Suddenly, Morag appeared at the bathroom door and stood slightly behind Wystan as she smiled and said: "I saw you two coming upstairs just now. Don't tell me you're going to stay up all night, giggling and talking nonsense. Wystan, let him get to bed. Honestly, you can be such a pest at times."

"You're dressed," said Simon, staring wide-eyed at her.

"Of course I am. I waited near the top of the stairs 'til I was sure you men would be coming up to bed before I went into my bedroom. What are you two up to in here?"

"I...I was...Uh, just going to have a bath," replied Simon.

"Oh, really? Well, then I do hope that you intend to undress before getting into the tub," said Morag, giggling.

Simon looked down at himself, and his jaw dropped when he saw that he was fully dressed in the same clothes he'd had on when he had played cards with them downstairs.

"I...I thought...I was sure I'd undressed."

"Marijuana certainly has a very odd effect on you."

"And on *me*," said Wystan, then he laughed.

"But I was sure that...I mean, that we...I thought...Whew! That was so wonderf...Uh, yes, marijuana really does have a very odd effect. Uh-huh, *very* odd," said Simon, feeling confused.

"Simon, while you're in your bedroom getting undressed for your bath, I'll use the bathroom, all right? Oh, and I'll shut the water off when the tub is filled. And you go to bed, Morag."

"You get to bed, too. Goodnight, you naughty youngsters."

"Goodnight, little bossy mother," Wystan said as he chuckled.

"Goodnight again, Morag," said Simon.

He and Wystan gave her a quick peck on the cheek before she walked away to her bedroom.

"Hmmm, well, I'm about to piss my pants," said Wystan.

"Oh, sorry! I'll go back to my room and undress for my bath."

"Thanks. Goodnight."

"Yeah, um, goodnight, Wystan."

Simon walked slowly back to his room, astonished by the effects of the marijuana. As he began undressing, he trembled as

he thought about the realistic hallucination he'd had about a very erotic threesome with Morag and Wystan.

Simon put on the robe, returned to the bathroom, and then heaved a big sigh as he lowered himself into the tub. The warm, soapy water had a very soothing effect on him, and he soon felt quite drowsy, so, he stepped out of the tub, dried off with a big, soft and thick towel, put his robe back on, and returned to the guest room.

He frowned when he noticed that the bed was still made, then he assumed he'd made it before he had gone to take a bath. He then got back into bed, and fell asleep less than five seconds after he laid his head on the pillow.

A few minutes after Simon fell asleep, he opened his eyes and saw that he was walking along the rooftop of what seemed to be a high office or apartment building somewhere in the midst of a very big city.

A full moon and many lit windows in tall skyscrapers, and other big buildings cast enough light on the roof that he could see where he was walking, so, he didn't have to worry about falling off the edge of the roof.

He could see black structures of various sizes protruding up from the roof he was on, then his heart leapt when he noticed one of the structures move.

He relaxed when he saw that it had been Wystan turning his

body slightly to look back at him, smile, and then raise his hand to beckon him. Simon hurried over to him, and saw that Wystan was sitting at the edge of the roof, with his lower legs dangling off the edge, so, he sat down beside him.

"It's about time you arrived," said Wystan, smiling. "I was wondering what was taking you so long to get here."

"Sorry. What are you doing here?"

"I'm looking at that lit window directly across from us. There's some sort of meeting in progress."

There was an alley separating the building they were on from the one with the lit window that Winston was looking into.

"That building's taller than this one," said Simon. "If more windows were lit up, then someone could see us sitting here."

"No, that's an office building, and all the people with offices on this side of the building, have gone home, or to wherever they go at night to do whatever they do before going home."

"Oh. So, what's so interesting about those men?"

"They're gangsters?"

"Gangsters?" exclaimed Simon while quickly standing up.

"Yes. You see that white-haired man at the end of the table? He controls most of the illegal drug trade in this city, and he also runs a prostitution ring, and of course, most of the prostitutes are drug addicts because of him. The men who work for him have killed many people, so, I feel it's about time that *they* were killed."

"But you can't do that! They've probably got guns!"

"Probably."

"Have *you* got a gun?" asked Simon.

"No, of course not. Why would I need one?"

"To protect yourself if you try to confront them!"

"I definitely won't need a gun to do that."

"Oh, I get it now," said Simon. "You plan to throw or shove something very heavy off the roof, then it'll fall on them."

"Don't be silly. Ah, now they're getting up from the table, so, it shouldn't be much longer before they walk out onto the alley below us."

"Please don't try to take them on by yourself!"

"All right, then we'll *both* confront them."

"They'll probably shoot us to death before we can even get close to them!" Simon whispered loudly.

"Impossible."

"But they've got guns!"

"Shhhhh! We want to take them by surprise."

"We won't be able to do that because they'll...Oh, maybe I'm dreaming all this. Yeah, I must be, because I don't remember how I got up here on this roof."

"Stop muttering to yourself, and sit back down," said Wystan.

Simon sat beside him again while watching the gangster boss close the door after his employees left, then he walked back to the table, and began talking on the phone as he lit a cigar.

A few minutes later, the door to the alley opened, and Simon felt both excited and slightly scared as he watched the five gangsters walking out into the alley.

Simon's heart leapt and he felt terrified when Wystan suddenly grabbed his left arm before leaping off the roof, then they were both plummeting feet-first to the alley below.

He had started shouting in terror, then he gasped in surprise when they alit lightly on the ground, then Simon just stood gaping in astonishment while only being able to comprehend a blur of whirling bodies, and then suddenly, he and Wystan were standing in front of a closed door in a very dark hall inside the building.

Simon was still too stunned to speak as he watched the door burst off it's hinges, and then as Wystan began quickly picking up and tossing the unconscious gangsters into the office, their boss cowered back against a wall.

He was then only vaguely aware of the gangster boss and his employees sprawled out on the office floor and slowly dying while Simon was thinking that the effects of the marijuana he'd smoked had caused him to have another rather strange hallucination.

His thoughts began spinning again as his eyesight blurred, then after his vision cleared, he saw that he was standing beside Wystan as they chatted and drank wine from glass tumblers while looking out the office window at the city landscape.

After they finished drinking over a dozen glasses of what Simon deemed to be a rather delicious wine, Wystan walked away from the window and over to the now doorless entrance to the office, then he stopped, turned around, and looked at Simon whom

became alarmed when he saw small splotches of blood on the front of Wystan's white shirt. He was about to rush over to him to see whether Wystan had been shot, but the moment he took a step forward, a closed door suddenly appeared in front of him.

Simon opened the door, walked through it, and when the door quickly slammed shut behind him, he saw that he was standing on the moonlit road outside Wystan's ancient summer house.

He walked off the road, past the high bushes and trees, then he saw a light in one of the large windows. Simon made his way over to the window, and when he looked in and saw Morag playing the piano, he wondered if she knew that Wystan was sitting on a roof somewhere in the midst of a huge city.

He watched Morag playing the piano, then after Simon turned away from the window, he gasped when he saw Wystan a short distance away from him, leaning back against a tree, and the small splotches of blood were still on the front of his white shirt.

He felt certain that Wystan had been repeatedly shot by the gangsters, so, he rushed toward him to ask if he could help tend the wounds, but when he opened his mouth, he found that he was unable to speak.

Simon suddenly thought about Morag, and he hoped that she could use her voice, so, he ran back to the window and started knocking on it while he watched her smiling and playing the piano louder and louder.

He kept knocking hard on the window, trying to get her attention, and then his heart leapt at the same time he almost

jumped into the air when he felt Wystan's hot breath in his ear as he whispered: "Boo!"

Simon whirled around to face him, and he watched Wystan fading back into the darkness until he'd completely disappeared. Simon looked back at the window when he heard it open, and he saw Morag smiling as she leaned out, and looked around.

"Morag! Wystan's been murdered!"

"Hmmm, too late. Simon and Wystan have already left."

"No, I'm here. No, not over there. Morag, look. I'm standing right in front of you. Morag? Morag! Look at me!"

"I thought they were still upstairs getting ready to go out, but obviously while I was playing the piano, I didn't see them walking by me on their way out of the house, and damn it, I wanted to go with them."

"No, I was already outside of the house, and then I saw Wystan while I was on top of a roof in a really big city, and then he was killed, but he came back here, and now he's gone."

"But you're *not* gone, Simon. Why would you tell me that? You can't fool me because you're lying right there on the bed."

"Oh, you can see me now. I thought you couldn't before."

"Hi, Wystan," said Morag.

"He's not here. He's dead," Simon told her.

"Oh, you! You just love to tease me. Wystan looks perfectly fine to me, and without a drop of blood anywhere on him."

"But he was shot at least five times. He had blood on the front of his shirt before he disappeared into the shadows."

"Simon, what are you going on about?"

"He's just babbling," said Wystan. "You know how marijuana sometimes causes him to do that."

"Wystan! I thought you were dead!" exclaimed Simon.

"It may look dead at the moment, but once Morag sucks on it for a few seconds, my dick'll be as hard as steel again."

"Huh?" Simon uttered, while looking down at Wystan lying nude on the bed.

"Simon, do me a favor?" asked Morag. "I'm going to kneel over him, so, would you please kneel behind me, and fuck me while I suck on his dick to get it hard again?"

"But I don't understand! I mean, not about you sucking on Wystan's dick, but about the way I was just standing outside the house, and now suddenly, I'm upstairs here in the bedroom."

"Well, Simon? Are you going to fuck me or not?"

"Morag! I can't believe you asked me that!"

"Hmmm, then I'll take that as a no," she said, pouting.

"Wait! Morag! Where are you going?" asked Simon.

"If I'm not getting fucked, then I'll come back in a month."

"A *month*?"

"Was that Simon I heard talking to you? Oh, it was. Hi, Simon. I see you're awake again. Hmmm, good," said Wystan.

Simon's thoughts swirled when he saw that he was suddenly nude, and lying close beside Wystan on the bed, and Morag had left the room before he could persuade her to stay.

He began turning his head to ask Wystan if he knew where she

was going, when he heard a horse whinnying, so, Simon looked back over at the closed door, and his eyes widened when he saw a huge, golden horse with a long, black mane and tail.

"Wow! Look, Wystan! Isn't he an absolute beauty? Wystan? Where did you go?" Simon saw that he was alone in bed, so, he got up, walked over to the horse, but just before he could pat it, the horse leapt from the floor and began slowly galloping up through the air toward the ceiling that started opening in the center like a pair of enormous doors.

Simon watched the horse disappear into the night sky, then the room started slowly revolving as he rose toward the ceiling, and then he heaved a big sigh when he was far above the roof, and gliding over the night landscape.

His heart began beating faster when he saw the golden horse laying on its side and slowly swirling as it drifted toward him. Moments later, Simon gripped onto the horse's mane, swung himself up and around until he was seated astride the golden horse, and riding bareback across long wisps of moonlit clouds while he looked up at a spectacular display of shooting stars.

Simon felt exciting sensations throughout his body as he rode through the night sky, then turning his head, he saw that he was now racing by a gigantic mirror, and his jaw dropped when he saw that the golden horse he'd been riding had turned into a centaur.

He looked down at his hands when he felt the long, black mane he was clutching suddenly turn silky, and then he watched it rapidly lessening in length while forming a thick mass of black

curls on the centaur's head. He then looked back into the colossal mirror, and he gasped at the same time he sprung an erection when he saw that the golden centaur was Wystan.

He could see the roof of the house off in the distance, and as they raced toward it, he noticed that the horse part of Wystan's body was changing back into human form, then after the change was complete, Simon started shouting in ecstasy as he clung to Wystan's back, and rode him with deeper and faster strokes.

He was nearing orgasm when they reached the opening in the roof, then as they were slowly spiraling down to the bed, Simon threw back his head and roared as he tried to thrust his erection even deeper while experiencing an exquisitely pleasurable orgasm.

He slowly lifted himself up off Wystan, when Morag suddenly leapt at him from the other end of the bed, and Simon toppled sideways after she'd thrown her arms and legs around him, then they began making wildly passionate love.

Over an hour later, Simon began feeling quite drowsy while watching Morag start fellating Wystan again, then just before he fell asleep, he wondered how many more times Wystan and Morag would want to make love before they fell asleep, too.

CHAPTER FIFTEEN

Sunlight flowing into the room awakened him, and Simon stretched his arms and legs as he grinned while recalling parts of the highly erotic dreams he'd had.

He put on his robe, hurried to the bathroom to relieve himself, then he ran a bath, and laid back in the tub, smiling. He decided that he'd definitely smoke more marijuana if Wystan offered it to him because he'd experienced such a realistic sexual fantasy, and Wystan had told him that those types of fantasies were often caused by the effects of marijuana.

It wasn't until he felt the bath water cooling, that he suddenly realized that either Wystan or Morag could be waiting to use the bathroom, so, he pulled the plug, and as the bath water was draining, he rinsed his body with fresh, warm water.

He returned to the bedroom, and hummed as he sorted out his wardrobe for the day, then he dressed and whistled as he went downstairs and saw Morag and Wystan sitting at the dining room table, drinking tea and chatting.

"Good morrrr-ninnnnng!" chimed Simon.

"Good morning, sleepyhead," said Morag.

"Morning, Simon."

"I feel sohhhhhh great this morning," said Simon.

"I was sure you'd feel much better after having a good night's sleep, and now it's almost noon," she told him.

"It is?" asked Simon. "Mmmm, I hadn't realized I'd slept so long. I hope I haven't overstayed my welcome."

"Not at all," said Morag, smiling. "It's a lovely, sunny day, and Blaze is enjoying it by strolling around the gardens."

"Yes, Blaze is enjoying the sunshine," said Wystan. "I heard you getting up, so, I prepared breakfast for you. Scrambled eggs, bacon, ham, toast, muffins, and recalling your American heritage, I made coffee for you."

"You did? Breakfast, and all?" Simon asked, smiling.

"Yes, breakfast, and all. We had kippers with our eggs and slim sausage. Sit down and I'll get your breakfast. More tea, Morag?"

"Yes, please. Thank you. You look so refreshed, Simon. I must apologize again for all the scratches you got last evening after dinner because I'd hoped you'd love to play Gods and Goddesses with us, but you had to suffer that terrible incident. This was the first time someone's been hurt after smoking that stuff. Wystan should've warned you about the marijuana's effects," she said while shaking her finger at Wystan.

"Aw, stop scolding him, Morag," said Simon, then after he laughed, he said: "I really enjoyed the effects, later, because I had some very nice dreams."

"From what Wystan has told me on several occasions, many of the dreams are of an erotic nature," said Morag, smiling.

"Oh, yeah, that's right because I dreamed about riding a horse, with a partially nude young woman in my arms," lied Simon.

"Ah, that explains the smile on your face," she said.

"I had somewhat similar dreams, and awoke feeling blissfully content," said Wystan, then he winked at them and grinned.

"Hmmm, I've never felt more content in my life because I slept so well. It's a very comfortable bed," said Simon. "So, um, what are your plans for the day?"

"I'd like to go riding on your horse, if I may," replied Morag.

"Sure. Blaze is quite gentle," said Simon.

"I wanted to ride into the next village to pick up a few groceries, so, I'd be gone for several hours. You can swim in the pool 'til I get back, then I'll join you. All right?"

"Sure, I'd like that. Oh, I just thought! I should start heading home soon. Naw, it's all right. They know where I am. Mmmm, this breakfast looks delicious. Thanks, Wystan."

"You're welcome. Try the coffee. I hope it's all right."

"Mmmm, it's perfect," said Simon after tasting the coffee.

"I ground the coffee beans, then poured hot water over the grounds in the same manner I make tea," Wystan told him.

"It's wonderful. Really. Mmmmm, and so are the eggs. Nice and fluffy and so tasty. You're quite the chef," he said, grinning.

"Thank you. It's another very nice day. Much sunlight, so, I'm going to loll by the pool."

"Now that you've given me permission to ride your horse, I'll leave for the village after you finish breakfast," said Morag.

"What time will you be back?" Wystan asked her.

"I've planned to stop in for a cup of tea with Mrs. Saunders, so, that means I won't be back here for at least three hours."

"Please give her my regards. It's a great day for a swim, so, I'm going upstairs to change, then I'll sit by the pool and read the paper. I'll see you there shortly, Simon."

"Sure. Bye for now," said Simon, smiling.

Wystan left the room as Simon ate his breakfast and Morag sipped on her tea, then she smiled while saying: "Blaze is such a beautiful horse. I knew right away that he was gentle the first time I patted and spoke to him."

"Yeah, I think he's beautiful, too, and you're right. He does have a very gentle nature."

"That he does, and you've got a very good appetite," said Morag, as she giggled.

"I certainly do this morning. Wystan is a marvelous cook."

"I agree. I fare well with salads," she said.

"I thought so because I'll bet you'd fare well with anything you'd set your hand to."

"Well, I'm watching Wystan, very carefully, as he prepares food, and I hope I'm just as good as him in a year, or perhaps two. Oh, would you like another cup of coffee?"

"Please. Thank you. He made a full pot. Do *you* like coffee?"

"Yes, but I have it usually after dinner," replied Morag.

"Mmmmmm, that was a delicious breakfast."

"Now that you've eaten, I'll be on my way. Oh, and you don't have to worry about suntanning nude because I won't be back until later this afternoon," said Morag, smiling.

"And don't *you* worry about handling Blaze."

"Oh, I won't. I'll get much attention riding him because he's so beautiful. You keep him so well-groomed," she said before getting up from the table, then she leaned over and kissed his cheek.

"Oh, um, thanks."

"Have a nice time," said Morag.

"Thanks, I will. You, too."

"I enjoy Mrs. Saunders company. Tra-la."

"Bye," said Simon, smiling.

He carried his breakfast dishes and cutlery into the kitchen, rinsed them off, and set them on the counter beside the sink, then he walked to the door leading to the garden, and smiled up at the sky. Simon stepped outside, took a deep breath of fresh air, and then began walking to the pool.

He rounded the high hedges and saw Wystan wearing a bright yellow terry cloth robe as he reclined on a chaise longue, reading his newspaper, and sipping on a cold drink.

"Hi."

"Oh, hello, Simon. There's two extra robes here, and they're both the same size as the one I've got on. I was just in for a dip. Nothing like swimming in the nude, is there?"

"Yeah, it feels great," Simon replied as he began undressing.

"Hang your clothes beside my bathing suit on that board with the line of hooks near the end of the patio," Wystan told him.

"Okay. I see you brought a big pile of towels here."

"Yes, some of them are very big to spread out on the patio, and you can use two or three as one big pillow."

"Great idea," said Simon.

He stripped nude, picked up a towel, ran to the pool, and dropped the towel before he whooped and dove into the water. Simon had initially felt a sudden shock from the cold water, but within seconds he became used to the water temperature, then ten minutes later, he climbed back out, and sat on the edge of the pool as he towel-dried his hair.

He draped his damp towel over the back of a deck chair, and after spreading out a much larger towel on the patio, he sat down and brushed his hair back from his forehead with his fingers.

Simon began applying suntan lotion as he looked over at Wystan reading the newspaper, and then he asked: "Anything shocking in the paper?"

"Hmmm, more talk of war. Rather disturbing."

"Yes, it is," said Simon.

"Well, enough bad news for today. I'll concentrate on the funny pages. Here, I'll pour you a glass of lemonade."

"No, don't bother, I can get it. May I refill your glass?"

"Please."

Simon picked up a smaller towel, wiped the excess suntan lotion off his hands, then he walked over to Wystan, took his empty glass, refilled it, and smiled as he handed it back to him.

"Ahhhh, good man. Thanks," said Wystan.

"You're most welcome."

He poured a glass of lemonade for himself, then Simon walked back to the towel, sat down, and said: "It looks like it's going to be a great summer."

"I'm sure it will be, and that means we'll have very good tans soon. Speaking of which, it's time for me to roast a bit more."

Wystan stood up, removed his robe, and after sitting back down on the chaise longue, he began applying suntan lotion to his body.

"Do you mind if I ask you where you buy the marijuana?"

"Not at all. I buy it when I'm in London," replied Wystan.

"Oh, of course, I should've thought of that. London's so big, so I guess you can get almost anything you want there. Do you go there often?"

"Yes, I make it habit of going there about ten days a week, and then the other eight or so days of the week, I spend lounging here by the pool."

"You've got a lot of days to your weeks," said Simon, smiling.

"That's because I've got a lot of things to do every week both here and in London. I love going to all the clubs, and enjoying everything that big city nightlife has to offer. Dancing, partying, kicking ass, and all that carry on."

"I love visiting London, too, because not very much happens around here, but in London, there's so much more to do."

"Higher crime rate in London, so, country boys beware."

"That's true of every big city, though," said Simon.

"Yes, it is, but murders also happen in towns."

"Well, not anywhere close to here, though."

"No? Haven't you heard of all the mysterious disappearances in villages near here? People just vanishing into thin air?"

"Sure, but that's because lots of unemployed men are hopping freight trains to travel across the country, looking for work."

"Ah, but what of those who've been found dead?"

"Oh? I've never heard about that. Are you sure?" asked Simon.

"Certainly. Every now and then a body wearing fogged-up glasses turns up kneeling in a field, or a dead man is found sitting on a toilet with a tortured look on his face, and sometimes a body is found upside-down in a rocking chair on a porch, and rocking back and forth very fast, or...Well, they've found bodies in all sorts of odd places and in awkward positions. There's a local legend about a teenaged killer who never grows old, and from what I've been told by several of my more elderly neighbors, who in turn were told of the legend by their parents, the teenager had himself been a murder victim, and his aunt and uncle, too."

"Oh, yeah? How long ago was that?" asked Simon.

"Some say hundreds of years ago, and he still wanders very close to this area. Shhhh! Quiet! Did you hear that?"

"What?"

"The rustle of bushes. Wait! I swear I just saw the teen killer crouch down behind those bushes over there! Quick! Run!"

"Hah! Doesn't scare me," said Simon, smiling. "But seriously, was there a murder somewhere around here?"

"Oh, yes, and countless dozens of them for approximately three hundred years, and I'm sure they're all well-recorded in the local

libraries. From what I've been told of the spooky legend, it started after the teenager was murdered while he'd been visiting his aunt and uncle who lived just outside one of the small villages that you see scattered throughout this area of the country. The aunt and uncle had invited a farmer and his wife, and their two teenaged children to dinner and to spend the evening playing cards or charades, or riding drunk cows from room to room, or whatever. During that evening, some men crept toward the house, then inside it, then they murdered everyone in it. It was quite a shock for the local police to see six, battered and bloody bodies in that house."

"No, *seven* bodies, right? Four adults and three teenagers."

"Ah, but the nephew's body was never found. Creepy, huh?"

"Maybe the nephew killed them all," said Simon.

"No, because there was evidence to prove that he didn't, and they found blood splatters in the upstairs guest room he always occupied while staying at his aunt and uncle's home, and the police could tell there'd been quite a struggle in that guest room."

"Oh, really. Hmmm, and they were sure it was the nephew who was killed upstairs in that room?" asked Simon.

"Absolutely."

"But how could they determine that if there wasn't a body?"

"There was quite a bit of blood all over the phone in the nephew's room, and the police found his fingerprints on that phone, therefore, they knew that he'd tried to call for help."

"Oh, I see."

Simon never thought about asking him how it'd been possible

for the nephew to have called the police if there hadn't been any telephones three hundred years ago.

"I just thought of something," said Simon. "It's not likely that they'd have just one telephone, and that it'd be in the nephew's guest room. Right? There must've been another phone downstairs, so, somebody else would've called for help, besides him."

"Hmmm, yes, I see your point," said Wystan. "I suppose that's because his aunt, or his uncle, or one of the other murder victims didn't have time to get to a phone downstairs before they were attacked, and the police determined that the nephew most probably ran upstairs to call for help, but then he must have dialed the wrong number because he'd been feeling a bit nervous."

"Hell, I'd've been more than a bit nervous. I would've been scared out of my wits, especially if I heard the killers coming up the stairs while I was dialing a wrong number," said Simon.

"Hmmm, my theory is that he really *did* call someone for help, and that person rushed over to the house, but arrived too late to save him, so, he carried the nephew's body out of the house, and that's why the police never found him."

"But then why wouldn't he have told the police he had the nephew's body?"

"My guess is that the person who carried away the nephew thought that the police might very well accuse *him* of the murders, so, he never told anyone. Anyway, that's the explanation *I* like, and it sounds perfectly reasonable to me."

"Hmmm, you could be right," said Simon. "I mean, I can see

that happening, sort of. So, the murderers got away, did they?"

"It seemed that way at first, however, about two or so weeks later, the police found the bodies of the two men who'd murdered the family and their guests. Legend has it that the nephew avenged the deaths of his aunt and uncle and the others, and then after that, he refused to stay dead."

"You mean, he became a ghost?"

"Well, not a ghost as we know it. You see, according to the legend, he became one of the undead, but not really a zombie. I think they call people like him, 'playful spirits,' which would make him a good-hearted ghost, and for about three hundred years or so, he's wandered around the moors and nearby towns at night, killing people, but only murderers, of course. Saves the police a lot of bother because all they have to do is sweep up or mop up after every murder," Wystan told him as he suppressed a smile.

"Aw, you don't really believe that, do you?"

"Bloody right, I do. I've always believed in benevolent ghosts, and obviously other people throughout this country believe in them, too. The old folks who I heard the story from, told me that he's called The Moors Bull," said Wystan.

"The Moors Bull? Then he must be really big and strong."

Wystan tried not to laugh as he began telling Simon more of the fake legend, starting with: "No, he supposedly got that name for three reasons, and the first one was because whenever he killed another murderer, people would say, 'Bully for him,' and the second reason he got that name was that his first few victims were

found on the moors. But I'm not sure what the third reason was, unless of course, it had something to do with his sexual stamina, but combining the first two reasons was enough reason to name him The Moors Bull."

"Oh, I see," said Simon. "Hmmm."

"You sound skeptical."

"No, I'm not. Really."

"After all, everyone who has ever heard of the legend, believe it, and so they should because The Moors Bull still exists, which is why there's always a few unsolved murders every year. Of course, each new generation of police officers refuse to believe The Moor Bull's spooky legend until they see the evidence for themselves."

"They've found evidence that The Moors Bull exists?"

"Certainly. Why else would they keep it such a big secret by not telling anyone about that evidence?"

"Oh, yeah, I see your point. Hmmm, and it all started with the nephew avenging the deaths of his aunt and uncle and the other people who were in the house at the time," said Simon.

"That's right, and it gives me the jitters sometimes. But I was shocked and quite dismayed when I first heard all about that spooky legend because apparently that aunt and uncle were so well-loved by the entire community, so, their deaths were mourned by many people for many years."

"That sure is a sad story. I've heard of some awful murders that were committed by people who everyone used to think were very nice, mild-mannered people."

"I have, too, and that's why I'd never close my eyes while I'm lying here basking in the sun because *you* could be that spooky Moors Bull. You might suddenly rush at me at any moment and stab me fifty or sixty times, then run off with my head simply because you wanted all the lemonade for yourself."

"Damn, and here I was hoping you wouldn't realize that, so, now I'll have to share it with you," said Simon as he laughed.

"Awww, too bad for you. Well, before I have another glass of lemonade, I'm going to cool off in the pool," Wystan said as he grinned while sitting up.

"You've been lying out in the sun for a while, so, the cold water'll give you quite a shock."

"Yes, and my dick'll be so shocked that it'll shrink back in fright from the cold water."

"Hah! But in your case, it probably just shrinks back to the national average," said Simon, then he started laughing.

"True, but I've never been average in any respect," Wystan said, grinning, and then he ran to the pool, dove in, resurfaced, and shook the water from his mass of curly hair before he swam around for a few minutes, and climbed back out of the water.

"So what do you think? National average, now?"

"Well, it only shrunk a bit," replied Simon, laughing.

Wystan then fell forward onto his hands, and after doing two dozen pushups, he did about twenty quick sit-ups, then several other exercises, which included slow cartwheels before he ended up in a handstand.

"How do I look from your upside-down point of view?"

"Hmmm, sort of upside-down," replied Wystan.

"Are you getting dizzy yet?" asked Simon as he smiled.

"Nope. I think I'll walk around on my hands for the rest of the day. However, if *you* want to get a bit dizzy, you could smoke some marijuana with me."

"Sure, I'd like that."

"Good, then I'll roll one right now."

Simon grinned as he watched him walking across the patio on his hands, then reaching the table, Wystan lowered his legs, and when his feet touched the ground, he crouched down, and then sprung high in the air, twirled around once, alit again, and took a bow as Simon applauded him.

"You're so athletic, and you've got an amazing build."

"So true. Don't forget handsome, clever, and charming, too."

"But of course," said Simon, grinning. "And I'll even say your smile's fantastic, all right?"

"All right," Wystan said, and then he laughed.

"I'm going to do some exercises, too."

"Good man. Exercise is just as refreshing as a shower."

Simon began with knee-bends, and a few other exercises before doing forty quick sit-ups, then two dozen pushups, and then he tried standing on his hands for as long as Wystan had managed to do, but he finally gave up.

"Well, I won't be walking around on my hands for the rest of the day like you because I can't balance myself for very long."

"You did better than most people," said Wystan.

"Nowhere near as good as you, though. Oh, well."

"Morag told me you play quite a few sports, and it's more than obvious you've been lifting weights for some time, too."

"Yes, I have," said Simon. "You've got such a great build, so, I guess you've spent quite a long time lifting weights."

"One or two hours every other day for just over six years."

"It sure paid off for you, and you haven't built yourself up to extremes like those men you see doing publicity stunts. You know, the ones who lift horses or pull big, heavy trucks by a rope clenched in their teeth. Instead of that, you've got what they call perfect symmetry like those ancient Greek or Roman statues. But you always wear big loose-fitting shirts, so, nobody'd know you have a great physique unless they saw you with your shirt off."

"Thanks for your compliments. If you keep to your current regimen, it won't take you long to have a build equal to mine. But you have a far better than average build, now," said Wystan. "Diet's very important, as well as proper exercise, and that usually leads to a healthy body and mind."

"I agree," said Simon, smiling. "The meals you prepare are very healthy and delicious, so that's why I've enjoyed every one of them, and especially the dinner you served last night."

"Oh, and speaking of that, I apologize again for that marijuana fiasco last evening after dinner."

"Aw, forget it. It wasn't your fault because you didn't know I'd react like that," said Simon.

"Well, I'll make sure that we share just this one marijuana cigarette until you're more used to the effects. I rather enjoy the effects because they often evoke wonderful, erotic thoughts."

"Yeah, they sure do," said Simon. "I didn't dare tell Morag just how erotic *my* thoughts were."

"I'm glad you found them so enjoyable. Not everyone feels the same when they smoke marijuana, but I see that we do."

"I'm sure that's why I slept so well," said Simon.

"I'll light this one up now because I love swimming when I'm feeling the effects of marijuana. The water seems much more refreshing, and rather like I'm floating through cool, moist clouds instead of water."

"I know what you mean. The water in the bathtub felt almost like warm satin. Mmmmm, this lemonade tastes so delicious."

"I added a dash of...Hmmm, what is that juice? I can't recall just now, but it's Chinese, and similar to Mandarin orange."

"Whatever it is, I really like it. You cook well, too, and you make very nice drinks. You're quite talented."

"Aw, more compliments. Now I'll start blushing."

"I do so much of that, lately," said Simon, then he laughed.

"That'll stop when you grow older and more jaded."

"Um, I wanted to ask you something when Morag wasn't around. It's, well, when you smoke marijuana, how real are *your* fantasies?" asked Simon.

"Sometimes while I'm asleep, I have very erotic dreams that seem quite real."

"Oh. Hmmm, well, I couldn't tell the difference. My fantasies are so real that it's difficult for me to tell if I'm having a fantasy while I'm asleep or while I'm awake."

"If the person or *persons* you had such wonderful sex with in your fantasies seemed so real, then you'd know they hadn't been real after you awoke. Right?"

"Of course, but when I have those fantasies, I can feel their bodies, hear their voices clearly, and everything, so, that's what I meant about not being able to tell the difference between fantasy and reality," said Simon.

"Then perhaps you shouldn't smoke marijuana again."

"No! I really, really love the fantasies, but because they're so realistic, I...Well, it feels so fantastic that I love having them, so, I'd love to smoke more of it with you whenever you offer to share it with me."

"You're sure?" Wystan asked as he grinned.

"Absolutely," replied Simon, laughing.

"Does that mean you'll just enjoy your fantasies and not be bothered if they seem too real?"

"Not at all, because they feel so wonderful."

"All right, then we'll share this marijuana cigarette."

Wystan lit the joint, inhaled deeply, handed it to Simon, and then said: "Here, take a puff. Now inhale it slowly, hold your breath for a few seconds, then exhale. All right?"

"All right." Simon inhaled some smoke and held his breath.

"Perfect," said Wystan as Simon slowly exhaled the smoke while passing the cigarette back to him.

They talked as they passed the marijuana cigarette back and forth, then Simon started to feel a very pleasant, tingling sensation flowing through his mind and body. When he'd finished smoking, Simon laid back down on his stomach on the towel and looked at the sunlight sparkling much brighter than usual on the surface of the water in the pool.

He felt so relaxed as he laid on the towel and watched the sparkling ripples whenever a hot breeze blew gently across the surface of the pool. Simon was still gazing at the sunlight on the water when he glimpsed a movement beyond the pool, and then propping himself up on one of his elbows, he cupped his hand over his eyes to see what was moving far back amongst the bushes near the rear of the property.

He looked over at Wystan to ask him if he'd heard or seen something moving in the bushes, but he'd left the patio, so, Simon looked back at the area where he'd felt sure he'd seen something or someone moving.

A moment later, he sat up when he saw Wystan almost at the far end of the property, walking through the bushes, and Simon presumed that Wystan had also become aware of an intruder, and he'd gone to investigate.

He decided to help Wystan search for the intruder or some sort of animal that must have climbed over one of the high walls, so, Simon walked to the far end of the patio, and began making his

way around trees and high bushes while looking ahead to see where Wystan was now searching.

"Wystan? Did you see who or what that was?"

He didn't receive an answer, so, Simon began walking around more bushes toward the area he'd last seen Wystan, and then after looking in all directions, and still not seeing him, Simon realized that Wystan must have walked closer to the wall where it was very dark because of shadows cast by big trees near the wall.

He continued onward, then Simon thought that Wystan might not have noticed an intruder, but instead, he'd only come back this way to urinate, and the thought of Wystan doing that, caused Simon to feel that he had to relieve himself, too, so, he stood closer to a bush to urinate.

He finished pissing, then thought of how carefree he felt being nude, and he began getting an erection, so, he continued making his way toward the high wall at the back of the property while hoping he'd lose his erection before Wystan noticed it.

Simon kept looking down at the ground to make sure he didn't step on anything sharp as he walked, then he stopped walking when he caught sight of something moving ahead of him. He wondered if it was the intruder he thought he'd seen earlier, then a moment later, he caught a glimpse of Wystan's head and shoulders beyond some high bushes.

Simon looked down at the ground when he stepped on a branch that had broken off a bush, and when he looked back up, he didn't

see Wystan, then he spent the next few minutes trying to determine which way Wystan had gone.

Simon climbed a tree, but because of all the other trees and big, high bushes he wasn't be able to see Wystan anywhere at the rear of the property.

He jumped down from the tree, and began moving among the bushes again while wishing more sunlight was penetrating the tops of the trees. While nearing one of the high walls that bordered the property, he saw the structure that he'd once thought had been a guard house until Wystan had explained that it was a sealed entrance to a tunnel that led all the way back into part of the basement of the old mansion.

After walking closer to the entrance to the tunnel, Simon was surprised to see that the stone door was slightly open, then he pulled it open wider and looked inside, and saw a narrow stone staircase. He pushed the heavy, stone door closed, and when he turned away from it, he noticed someone's bare footprints in the soft soil, leading away from the door.

Simon leaned over to have a closer look at the footprints, and he determined that they'd been made by a male with a wider and slightly shorter foot than his own, then recalling Wystan's big feet, he knew they definitely couldn't be his footprints, either.

He made his way around bushes and through tall weeds, looking for both the stranger and Wystan, but he still hadn't caught sight of either of them.

A few moments later, he saw what appeared to be a nude man walk very slowly behind some bushes, and by the weight and height of whoever it had been, Simon knew that it couldn't have been Wystan.

There were too many bushes growing tightly together, so, Simon couldn't walk directly toward the area where he'd just seen the nude stranger, so, he had to circle around many other big bushes and trees to find out where that man was headed.

He had managed to get nearer to the area where he'd seen the man disappear, then he smiled when he saw Wystan crouching down, and he seemed to be looking at something on the ground, but because of bushes blocking most of Simon's view of him, he couldn't see what Wystan had found.

"Hi!" Simon called out to him. "I didn't know you'd come this way, too. Good thing none of the branches are sharp on any of these bushes, or else I could've got scratches all over stomach and legs. But it feels so great being nude out here, doesn't it? So, what are you looking at on the ground?"

He presumed that Wystan hadn't answered because he'd found something very interesting.

"Wystan? What is it? Is it a small animal?"

"No, of course not."

"Oh, I thought it might've been. So, what *did* you find?"

Wystan didn't answer him, so, Simon pushed his way through the waist-high bushes, then he gasped when he saw Wystan kneeling beside a nude man whom was obviously dead.

"Oh, no! What happened to him?"

"He died," Wystan replied with a wink and a smile.

"But how?"

"Well, my guess is that his heart stopped beating."

"Wystan! Be serious! This isn't funny, at all. He was alive about five minutes ago because I saw him walking around over here. Or I *think* it was him. If it wasn't him, then there has to be somebody else around here."

"No, I'm sure there isn't."

"He must've climbed over the wall at the back of the property, and then he took off all his clothes, and then he had a heart attack while he was heading over to the patio to talk to us."

"No, I'm certain that he wasn't going to do that."

"Then what do you think he was up to?"

"Hmmm, well, the top of his head came up to my chin, so, I'd say he was about as tall as you," replied Wystan, then he laughed.

"I didn't mean his height! Awww, you know exactly what I mean, and I don't know how you can laugh about this man who just died of a heart attack!"

"What man?" asked Wystan.

Simon looked back down and was astonished when he saw that the dead man had vanished, and then he looked back at Wystan and asked: "What happened to him?"

"Who?"

"Ohhhh, no, not again! I've just had another bizarre reaction to the marijuana. I swear I saw a naked dead man on the ground and

you were crouched over him, and...Wystan? Where'd you go? Whew! I just imagined *you*, too! Jeeeez!"

Simon's thoughts began whirling slower, then he rubbed his eyes, and when he opened them again, he found that he was on the patio, lying on his stomach, and looking at Wystan walking back from the pool.

He knew that if he'd imagined the corpse, then obviously the man hadn't appeared from the tunnel to the house, then Simon recalled the expression of terror on the face of the dead man whom he'd only imagined seeing.

He looked at Wystan hanging his damp towel over the back of a deck chair, then as he watched him walking nude back over to the chaise longue, Simon pictured himself again, looking down at Wystan crouching beside the dead man, and he was astonished by how real it had seemed.

He stood up, and looked over at the bushes and trees beyond the pool, and when he didn't see anyone walking or standing anywhere, he slowly shook his head as he thought about how strange his recent hallucination had been.

"Seeing that man on the ground like that was really strange."

"*What* was strange?" asked Wystan, sitting back down.

"Oh, um, just a sudden feeling I got running through me."

"Happens sometimes. I call it a rush," said Wystan, smiling.

"Yeah, that's what it did. Rush through me. So, uh, I'm going to lie out and get some sun."

"Put more suntan lotion on before you do."

"I will. Thanks for reminding me," said Simon, smiling.

He applied more suntan lotion to his body before he laid on his back, closed his eyes, and thought about the dead man he'd only imagined, but his thoughts soon turned to sex, and he smiled as his penis began hardening.

He loved the warmth of the sunlight, and he almost drifted off to sleep, but the sound of water splashing when Wystan dove into the pool, caused him to open his eyes.

He laid on his stomach with his chin resting on one of his crossed forearms while he watched Wystan swimming in the pool, then Simon rolled over onto his side, facing away from him, and closed his eyes again.

Ten minutes later, Wystan climbed out of the pool, then knelt at the edge of it, dipped his cupped hands into the pool to fill them with water, and then after standing back up, he ran over to Simon, and threw the water on him.

"Aaaaa! That's cold!" cried Simon, sitting up quickly.

"But refreshing, isn't it?" Wystan said as he grinned.

"Yeah, a few seconds after it hit my hot skin."

"You looked a bit drowsy, and I'm sure that's because of the effects of the marijuana."

"Mmmmm, yeah, I feel a bit lightheaded and rather nice."

"So do I," said Wystan, walking back to the chaise longue.

"The sun feels great," said Simon. "I hope it stays sunny for the rest of the afternoon."

"I'm sure it will because according to the latest weather

forecast, there won't be any rain for at least another week."

"Great."

Simon loved feeling the effects of the marijuana, basking in the sun, and feeling the occasional breeze wisp over his nude body. He recalled the very erotic fantasy he'd had about having sex with Morag and Wystan, and then he yawned closed his eyes, and within seconds he fell asleep.

‑✸‑

CHAPTER SIXTEEN

Voices awoke him, then Simon sat up and yawned while wondering how long he'd been asleep. He then saw Wystan and Morag walking through high grass while heading toward a large group of trees.

Simon hurried to catch up with them, and it wasn't until after he'd walked past the patio that he remembered he was nude, so, he rushed back to put on his bathing suit.

He looked in the direction he'd seen them walking, then his heart leapt when he saw Morag brushing something off her bare breasts as she talked to Wystan.

He felt sure that she'd be embarrassed if she knew that he could see her, but because she'd had a close relationship with Wystan since childhood, Simon assumed that was why she felt comfortable about baring her breasts in front of him.

He started walking toward them while intending to make his presence known to her when he was still far enough away to give her plenty of time to cover her bare breasts.

He saw them turn and begin walking toward a few people, and Simon noticed that the recently arrived guests seemed to have lost their direction because they were frowning while looking around at the trees.

Morag hadn't covered her breasts, so, Simon presumed that the guests must be close family members who were used to seeing her

that way in the summer. Wystan smiled and waved to him, and when Simon saw Wystan beckoning him, he began walking toward them while vowing to himself to try his best to be as sophisticated as the others by not gawking at Morag's bare breasts.

He came across a very tall, broad bush, and by the time he'd walked around it, Morag, Wystan and their guests had walked out of sight behind another large group of bushes, so, Simon hurried to catch up with them.

He stopped walking when he heard a long, loud moan, and then moving closer to the source of the sound, Simon heard someone else utter a loud moan.

Simon pushed his way through bushes near the area where he'd heard the loud moans, then he saw Morag and Wystan holding big, crystal glasses of wine as they sat in front of three middle-aged people who were seated on the ground, and looking around in confusion at the overgrown garden.

"Oh, hi, Simon," said Morag, smiling up at him.

"Hi. Hi, Wystan."

"I wondered when you'd arrive," said Wystan.

"Sorry, but I dozed off, and when I woke up, I saw you back here with your guests," Simon said, smiling at the guests.

"Yes, I suppose they *are* guests, in a way," said Wystan.

"This area here hasn't as much brush and tall weeds, but I didn't notice that 'til I got past those high bushes back there. This is like a very nice, small garden here," said Simon, smiling.

"A rather tasteful setting while we taste the delights of this

vintage they've supplied. Mmmmm, yes, our guests, as you called them, do have good taste," Morag said, then she giggled.

He tried not to look at Morag's breasts while she talked to him and Wystan, then Simon wondered why he hadn't been introduced to their guests, and why they hadn't been offered wine.

Simon initially thought it was a little odd that Morag and Wystan's guests mumbled and stared at them in confusion, but then he presumed that they'd been smoking much marijuana, or they'd previously drank too much wine.

He felt sure that they were hospital patients on a brief outing from being treated for some sort of kidney or liver problem because of the strange apparatuses attached to them. The woman and one of the men had several very long, narrow, rubber tubes wound around their chests to somewhere behind their backs, and all those tubes were attached to another tube around their necks.

Each of the tubes around their necks was attached to a syringe that was imbedded in their necks, and all the tubes were filled with blood, which Simon presumed was being transferred from veins in their necks to veins in other parts of their bodies.

The other male guest had a similar, long, narrow, rubber tube tied around the upper part of his right arm, and another one around his left wrist, and both tubes were attached to syringes that were obviously withdrawing blood and distributing it to other parts of that man's body.

While Simon had been looking at all the tubes attached to syringes imbedded in the three guests, Morag and Wystan had

been refilling their glasses with wine. A moment later, Wystan nudged him, and Simon turned his head to look at him, and then he smiled when Wystan winked, grinned and said: "Here, I poured you a glass."

"Thanks," said Simon, taking the big glass of wine. "Your guests aren't drinking?"

"I offered, but they refused," said Morag.

"Oh, right. I guess they can't drink wine or anything else alcoholic while being treated for...Uh, well, whatever they're being treated for. Mmmmmm, this sure is a delicious wine. So sort of...Well, *full-bodied*," said Simon, smiling.

"I enjoy a good pun. Don't you, Wystan?"

"Good or bad, I don't particularly like puns. You drank that wine so quickly, Simon."

"Uh, yeah, I did. I hope I didn't appear rude, but it tasted so delicious that I just gulped it all down."

"It wasn't rude of you, at all. It's quite a compliment to see how much someone enjoys the wine I serve them. Oh, and Simon? Would you mind running over to that huge, dead tree, and getting Morag's blouse?" Wystan asked him.

"Oh, yeah, sure. Be right back," he replied.

He handed the empty glass to Wystan, then Simon began hurrying around bushes, and he'd only gone a short distance when he realized that he should have asked Wystan which huge, dead tree he'd meant because there were at least six of them spread out through that area of the property.

He turned around to go back and ask for directions to Morag's blouse, when he saw her effortlessly dragging one of the guests by the hand along the ground toward the cement structure that was the entrance to the tunnel leading back to the basement of the house.

Simon then saw Wystan come into view from behind bushes, clutching a guest in each hand while dragging them like they were merely paper dolls as he headed in the same direction as Morag.

"Oh, my God! What happened?" exclaimed Simon.

"Dead," replied Wystan.

"Dead? What do you mean, *dead*?"

"As in no breath."

"What? All three of them?"

"Uh-huh."

"But how?" asked Simon, wide-eyed.

"I just told you, remember? They stopped breathing."

"No, that's not what I meant! Wystan! Stop laughing! This is terrible! They were alive about three minutes ago, and now they're dead, and you and Morag are taking them to...Where *are* you taking them, anyway?"

"Not *any* way, Simon, but *this* way because I want to take them over *that* way."

"Wystan!" Simon exclaimed.

"I don't know why *you're* so shocked. After all, you're the one whose nude, *and* with an erection."

"What do you mean? Oh, no!"

Simon looked down and saw that Wystan was right, so, he

quickly covered his erection with his hands at the same time he hurried behind a bush to hide his body from the waist down.

It was then that he saw that the bush he'd rushed behind had branches that hadn't grown dense enough to hide what he'd wanted to hide.

Simon turned around and stood with his back to Wystan, then he exclaimed: "My bathing suit couldn't've just fallen off! Even if it had, then I would've felt it falling down my legs! Did Morag see me like this? Wystan? I sure hope she didn't! Did she?...Wystan! God damn it! Would you please just answer me? Did she, or did she *not* see me like this? Well? Answer me! This isn't funny, you know! Awww, fuck ya!"

Simon turned his head to look back at him, and saw that Wystan was gone. He couldn't see Morag, either, then suddenly, someone behind him grabbed his waist, and when he spun around, he saw Wystan and Morag standing close in front of him.

Simon was about to ask them what had happened to their guests, but before he could speak, Wystan pulled him down to the ground, and then Morag kissed him. He moaned happily as he started making love with Morag and Wystan, and his lust quickly reached fever pitch.

🌿

CHAPTER SEVENTEEN

He squinted from the bright sunlight when he opened his eyes, then saw that Morag was gone and Wystan was still lying on the chaise longue.

Simon then realized that when he had fallen asleep for about five minutes, he'd had another highly erotic sexual fantasy, and although he could recall the sexual acts that he'd participated in during that fantasy, he had forgotten about the three dead people.

"Wystan?"

"Yes?"

"I, uh, when I dozed off for a few minutes, I thought that I was in another sex fantasy that felt so real."

"Oh?"

"Yeah, and, uh, well, as I told you before, I find it hard to tell if I'm in a sex fantasy because it's so real when it's happening. But even though I'm horny right now, I know I'm not in a sex fantasy because if I were, then I'd be having sex."

"Hmmm, I see," said Wystan. "Sounds a tad perplexing. If you sometimes can't distinguish between reality and fantasy, then you might only be imagining that we're having this conversation."

"Oh, I can tell I'm *not* imaging it, because nothing sexual is happening. I can never tell when I'm starting to have a sex fantasy, then they're always so real. But I love having dreams about having

lots of sex. I'll shut up now, and try to have a nap for fifteen minutes or so, and if I start snoring, then just wake me up. Okay?"

"Okay."

"Thanks, Wystan."

"You're *very* welcome, Simon."

They laughed, then Simon closed his eyes, and because Wystan had *his* eyes closed, too, Simon began slowly masturbating. He tried to stifle his loud moans of pleasure as he quickened his strokes, and he was aware of how reckless he was being because Wystan could sit up at any moment and see what he was doing.

He stopped masturbating when he heard someone groaning loudly in pleasure. He sat up, and then Simon's eyebrows shot up, and his jaw almost fell to his chest when he saw Morag nude and straddling Wystan's hips as she rode his erection.

Wystan grinned and winked at him when he noticed Simon observing them, then he said to Morag: "We have an audience."

"I guess he's stopped wanking," she said before giggling.

"Oh, my God, Morag! What are you doing?" asked Simon.

"Can't you tell? I thought it was rather obvious."

"I don't believe this!" exclaimed Simon, wide-eyed.

"I sure as hell do," said Wystan, smirking. "And it feels so great with half my dick, and sometimes more, stuffed up inside her. Mmmmmm, awwww, yeah."

"Oh, yes, this is what I call being fulfilled by being fully filled because your hardon's stretched my cunt to the limit."

"My God, Morag! The way you talk!" cried Simon, aghast.

"I'm much more interested in the way Wystan fucks."

"But I thought you were a virgin!"

"How can she be a virgin if she's in this lascivious fantasy of yours? And in your other fantasies, too?" asked Wystan.

"Huh? Oh, so this *is* another sex fantasy," said Simon.

"Apparently. Are all your sex fantasies this realistic?"

"I'm so confused! Is it really a fantasy?"

"I *feel* real, and I'm sure Wystan feels real, too."

"Then it *isn't* a fantasy. Right, Wystan?" asked Simon.

"While you're wondering if this is or isn't another sex fantasy, I'll keep fucking Morag. Awww, yeah, this feels great."

"Man, I can't believe what's happening, and all this time I thought you were a virgin, Morag."

"You've never fucked me like I was a virgin."

"My God! You even swear!" exclaimed Simon.

"I do? Oh, I suppose I should've said you've never treated me like a virgin anytime you'd had sexual intercourse with me, and neither have all the other men. Ohhhhh, I love pretending I'm not a virgin with Wystan," said Morag while panting and smiling.

"Whew! Mmmmm, that looks so sexy," said Simon.

Ten minutes later, he was startled when Morag began screaming, growling and groaning, then moments later, she was panting heavily while she and Wystan reached out for him as Simon's thoughts whirled, then he began making love with them.

Hours later, Simon closed his eyes while lolling in the lingering effects of the very intense orgasms he'd had, and the effects of the marijuana.

He began drifting off to sleep, then Wystan picked him up, carried him into the house, and then after lowering him down onto the bed, Morag kissed him as Simon slowly fell asleep.

Simon awoke smiling, and as he licked his lips and slid his hands over his body, he recalled how wonderful it had felt having carefree, highly exciting, and quite satisfying sex with Morag and Wystan on the patio by the pool.

He got out of bed, walked over to the full-length mirror, and smiled at his reflection as he flexed his biceps while imagining that Morag and Wystan were nude and standing close beside him, and whispering erotic suggestions to him.

He decided to bathe before going back out onto the patio to join Morag and Wystan in their lovemaking. Simon took a long bath, dressed, and then started humming as he went downstairs.

While walking along the downstairs hallway, he wondered if Morag and Wystan were still making love near the pool, and then he looked into the dining room and saw them dressed and sitting at the dining room table.

"Good morning!" exclaimed Wystan, grinning.

"Good morning, sleepyhead," said Morag, as she smiled.

"*Morning*? What time is it?" asked Simon.

"A few minutes after ten," Morag told him.

"Ten in the morning?"

"If it were ten at night, then it'd be dark out. Right?"

"Oh, right," said Simon, feeling confused. "I'm not quite all awake yet. Anyway, now I know it was just a dream. Oh, and I hope I haven't overstayed my welcome."

"Not at all," said Morag, smiling. "It's a lovely, sunny day, and Blaze is enjoying it by strolling around the gardens."

"Yes, Blaze is enjoying the sunshine," said Wystan. "I heard you getting up, so, I prepared breakfast for you. Scrambled eggs, bacon, ham, toast, muffins, and recalling your American heritage, I made coffee for you."

"You did? Breakfast, and all?" Simon asked, smiling.

"Yes, breakfast, and all. We had kippers with our eggs and slim sausages. Please sit down, Simon, and I'll get your breakfast. More tea, Morag?"

"Yes, please. Thank you. You look so refreshed, Simon."

"Uh, yeah, I feel refreshed."

He had felt certain that he'd fallen asleep after very passionate sex at the pool with them, and that it had lasted well into the late afternoon, but it was still only morning.

"So, um, is Blaze all right?" asked Simon.

"Oh, don't you worry about him because as I said, he's enjoying a stroll around the gardens. He's so clever because he's being careful not to step on any of the flowers," said Morag.

"Yes, Blaze *is* quite clever. Mmmm, I slept so well because it's

a very comfortable bed," said Simon while feeling slightly ashamed of himself for thinking that someone as sweet and innocent as Morag would ever consent to having such wild sex with him.

His face flushed when he thought about the sexual things he'd done in his dream with Wystan whom would be just as shocked as Morag if he knew that he'd been in another male's very explicit, sexual fantasy.

Wystan returned with Simon's breakfast, and a plate of fresh, hot muffins, then he sat back down at the table.

"So great. Thanks, Wystan," said Simon, smiling.

"You're welcome," he replied, pouring coffee for him.

"I love your freshly baked muffins," Morag said as she took one out of the wicker basket.

"I know, and that's why I made more of them."

"Everything you cook is super great," Simon told him.

"Thanks guys," said Wystan, smiling at them.

"I should be getting home soon," said Simon. "So, what are your plans for the day?"

"Wystan and I are going to the village to do some shopping."

"That sounds very nice, and it looks like a great day to do that. Lots of sunshine," said Simon. "Mmmmm, this breakfast looks delicious. Thanks again, Wystan."

"You're welcome again. Try the coffee. I hope it's all right."

"Mmmm, it's perfect," Simon said, tasting the coffee.

"I ground the coffee beans, then poured hot water over the

grounds in the same manner I make tea," Wystan told him.

"It's wonderful. Mmmm, and so are the eggs. Nice and fluffy and so tasty. You're quite the chef," said Simon, grinning.

"Thanks," said Wystan. "It's another great day, with much sunlight, so, I'm sure you'll enjoy your ride home this morning."

"Thank you for a wonderful dinner and evening."

"Next time, I'll be careful to make sure you don't smoke too much marijuana with me."

"And I'll make certain he *is* careful, Simon," said Morag.

"She certainly means that, too, because she's always watching me. Sometimes when I think she's not watching me, I suddenly hear something rolling along the floor, and then I look down, and see Morag's eyeballs coming to a stop at my feet, and then staring up at me."

"Hah! If I'd been watching you closer, then I would've been able to stop you from letting Simon share some of that marijuana with you," she said while smiling.

"Ah, but you wouldn't have seen us because we would've been hidden amid huge clouds of smoke. Well, now that I've had breakfast, I'll go out to the solarium to read the paper. I look forward to seeing you again, and very soon, Simon. Perhaps tomorrow if you're free."

"Sure, I'd like that."

"And every time you have dinner with us, and hopefully stay long into the evening, you can spend the night here in any of the guest rooms. Morag and I would love to have you stay with us as

often as you'd like. It'd be even better if you could stay here with us for several days, or longer if you enjoy our company as much as we do yours."

"Thanks, Wystan. I enjoy our time together, too."

"Good. Now enjoy your breakfast, and I hope you'll be returning very soon."

"I'd sure like to," Simon said, smiling up at him.

Wystan strolled out of the room, and Simon smiled as he looked at Morag and said: "He's a real nice guy."

"Yes, I've always thought that, too."

"Mmmmm, this breakfast is so delicious."

"I must say, you've got a very good appetite," said Morag as she giggled.

"I certainly do this morning. Wystan's a marvelous cook."

"I agree. I fare well with salads."

"I wouldn't doubt that because I'll bet you'd fare well with anything you'd set your hand to."

"Well, I'm watching Wystan very carefully as he prepares food. I hope I'm just as good as him in a year or perhaps two. Oh, would you like coffee? You're almost finished that cup."

"Please. Thank you. He made a full pot. Do *you* like coffee?"

"Yes, but I have it usually after dinner," replied Morag.

"Mmmmmmm, that was a delicious breakfast."

"I'm so glad you enjoyed it. Well, now that you've eaten, I suppose you'll want to be on your way."

"Yes. Sorry for having to rush, but I've got to get home. I've

had a great time here, and you've both been wonderful hosts."

When Simon had come downstairs for breakfast, he'd been surprised because he'd had the same conversation with Wystan and Morag before. He then felt sure that the prankster responsible for that duplicate scene was nearby, grinning and watching him to see if Simon had been aware that his game had been manipulated.

"Will you be coming by, tomorrow? I really hope you will."

"Sure, I'd love to," said Simon, smiling. "I was worried about overstaying my welcome."

"Oh, nonsense. I'll accompany you to the stream."

"It's such a nice, sunny day," said Simon.

"Yes, isn't it, though?"

She kissed his cheek before he began leading Blaze away, then he grinned as he said goodbye to her again, and then he started making his way along the stream.

Simon then grinned while thinking that if his jubilee game had been amusingly manipulated to duplicate a breakfast scene, then it was quite likely that other fun things had happened during other phases of his game, and that included all the decadent sexual activity that he hadn't experienced at this time in his past.

He felt sure that although he often became confused and had bizarre dreams and sometimes what seemed to be hallucinations, that he'd be able to control the end of his game. Simon then laughed after deciding that when he ended his jubilee game, he'd pretend that he was still playing it.

He began concentrating on the next phase of his game while

wondering how often it would be playfully manipulated, and then each time it was, Simon knew that he'd have difficulty sorting out which were his real memories, and which ones were being staged to make him think that they were part of his past.

PART FOUR

CHAPTER EIGHTEEN

Nearing the end of the game

Simon arrived home, then went into the bathroom to shower, and he'd just finished dressing when he heard his stepfather's car drive up to the house, and then he heard his mother's laughter as they came into the house.

He hurried downstairs to greet them, then Miranda stepped back out of Noel's embrace while smiling and saying: "Hi, Simon. How was your dinner and evening with your new friends?"

"It was wonderful, thanks."

"It must've been, because you look so happy," said Noel.

"They're super people. The dinner was so delicious and we had trout with small, roasted potatoes, asparagus, and a few other fresh vegetables. Oh, and we wore those old fashioned clothes I told you about, and Morag wore a very tall, white wig like Marie Antoinette. Her really big dress was all silver, and she looked so beautiful. We listened to the concert on the wireless while we played cards 'til it was time to go to bed, and I stayed in a really nice, big guest room, and the bed was so comfortable. Their bathroom is huge, too, and I had a nice, long bath in it."

"That sounds quite delightful," said Miranda. "If they invite

you to stay the night again, then you must remember to take your toothbrush with you."

"I'll do that. Oh, and they told me I could stay overnight as often as I liked because we all had such a good time together. We have the whole place to ourselves, and Wystan's a very good cook, too. He's sort of in charge of Morag while they're there, but then sometimes, she bosses him around, but it's only in fun. She's like a really refined lady. Very proper, but she's much fun, too. She's what you'd call elegant. Very nice manners."

"You're very well-mannered, too, Simon, and I'm sure they could see that, immediately. I'm sure even the king would be impressed by you," said Miranda, smiling.

"I do, too, and because of that, I think Simon would be a good catch for Morag. He's just like a handsome prince, and she's the beautiful princess," Noel said, winking at Miranda.

"Aw, you know what I mean. She'd never swear or even say anything bad about anyone. It's not proper manners," said Simon.

"No, it's not. She's as refined as you are," Miranda told him.

"Yeah? Thanks, mom. So, anyway, I'm going up to my room for awhile."

"I'll call you when lunch is ready," said Miranda.

"Okay. See you later, mom. See ya, dad."

"Bye for now," said Noel, smiling.

"Do you want a cup of coffee?" Miranda asked him.

"No thanks," replied Noel. "I've got to get on my way. I should be back in a couple of hours, and perhaps by that time,

Simon might've talked your ear off about Morag."

"I don't doubt that because he's quite enamored with her, for sure. All right, then. Bye, dear."

"Bye, gorgeous," said Noel, kissing her.

Simon tried to concentrate on the book he'd started reading, but he was getting very sexually aroused because he kept looking across his bedroom at the portraits Morag had painted of Wystan and herself.

He unfastened his pants and pulled out his hardening penis while envisioning Morag and Wystan as they'd been in his erotic fantasies; nude and participating in many rather raunchy sexual acts with him.

He went over to his bedroom door, opened it, and when he didn't hear his mother and stepfather talking, Simon assumed that they'd gone for a walk, so, he began quickly undressing as he walked back to his bed to masturbate.

Simon panted, groaned loudly, and often shouted in ecstasy while recalling how quite realistic his sexual fantasies had been after every time he'd smoked marijuana with Wystan.

His mind reeled while he was thrilling to a very intense orgasm, then as those sensations began slowly subsiding, Simon panted heavily as he felt that he had to masturbate again to satisfy his sexual excitement.

He resumed masturbating, but much slower while wondering

what his mother and Noel would've thought if they'd been home when he'd made so many loud sounds of pleasure while masturbating to the first orgasm as the headboard of his bed had constantly banged against the wall.

After thrilling to another, just as intense orgasm, Simon was sweating and panting heavily as he got up off his bed. He went to the bathroom to shower again, then he dressed, went downstairs and through to the kitchen, and then Simon was very surprised to see his mother.

Miranda was sitting at the kitchen table, drinking coffee while reading a magazine, then she looked up and smiled at him when Simon said: "Oh, uh, hi. So, um, when did you get back from your walk with dad?"

"We didn't go for a walk. Just after you went upstairs, Noel went over to see Bill Grayson, so, I decided to make some coffee, and read this magazine I bought yesterday."

"Oh? Um, I see," said Simon.

He felt so embarrassed as he wondered if she'd heard the headboard repeatedly banging against the wall, and his loud groans and shouts while he'd masturbated twice.

"So, uh, what time is dinner?"

"In about an hour and a half," replied Miranda while looking at the magazine.

"I'm going to run over to Colin's and see what he's up to."

"Don't bother. I invited him and his parents for dinner."

"Yeah? Thanks, mom. His dad's really having a hard time finding a job, but don't worry, because I didn't tell Colin where all the money and food are coming from. So, what time are they coming over?"

"Who? Oh, yes, Betty and James and Colin. They should be here soon."

"I'm going out to watch for them. Maybe Colin and I can have a game of handball or horseshoes before dinner."

"All right, dear. Have a nice time. Oh, and please make sure that if you two are going to play horseshoes, that you use the ones that aren't on the horses. All right? Those poor horses get so dizzy after you've tossed them back and forth a few times," she said while suppressing a smile.

Simon laughed as he stood at the open door and said: "Gee, mom, we only toss *one* of the horses. Bye."

"Just one horse, now. Promise," said Miranda.

When Colin arrived with his parents, he played horseshoes with Simon, and then after dinner they went riding for an hour, but Simon still hadn't told him about Morag.

He'd decided that after he'd known Wystan and Morag for a few weeks, he'd tell Colin, Jennifer, as well as his other friends about them.

They talked and laughed while riding slowly back to the house, then Simon rode his horse closer to Colin, slapped him on the

back, and laughed as he raced away with Colin in pursuit. They slowed their horses while nearing Simon's home, and then they dismounted and laughed as they led the horses into the stable.

"I heard my parents asking yours to come to dinner again on Saturday, and after they were asked for the tenth time, your parents finally accepted the invitation. You're coming, too, aren't you?"

"Yes, of course," replied Colin, smiling.

"Then I'll ask Jennifer to come, too, and then we'll plan something for after dinner. All right?"

"Sure, that'll be great. How about getting together tomorrow, or sometime during the week?"

"I'm not sure yet, because my dad has some plans."

"Let me know, when you're sure, okay?" asked Colin. "By the way, I was meaning to ask you what you've been doing lately because I haven't seen much of you."

"Oh, well, I've just been working with my dad, and going over to Brian's, or Nigel's, or Maggie's place for a while, and well, all kinds of things," lied Simon. "Sorry I haven't gotten together with you lately."

"I see. When you became scarce, I thought you were seeing a lot of some girl. Maybe Evelyn?" asked Colin.

"No, I like her, sure, but I just saw her for a while one day during the week. So, um, how about you?"

"I'm keeping busy, too, as usual. Still dating as many girls as I can 'til I find one who'll put out."

"There's always Hilary Janson," said Simon.

"Yeah, for sure there's always her, but she's such a tart that I'm sure she wouldn't even know I was doing it to her."

"Yeah, she *does* get a lot of attention."

"Never from me," said Colin. "It doesn't matter to me if the girl I marry isn't a virgin, but I'd want one who hasn't got a dick in her all day long, and always a different one, too. I like sex, but I don't want to get some tart pregnant because then she'd want me to marry her, and then I'd have a wife who had dozens of lovers, and then I'd never know which kids were really mine."

"Good point. Just have Hilary suck you off."

"Oh, yeah? Has she done that to you?" asked Colin.

"If she had, I'd've told you right away, right?"

"Yeah, you would've. Well, I wouldn't have to worry about getting any girls pregnant if I have them suck me off, instead of shagging them," said Colin.

"They'll probably do that, too, because just about every girl in school thinks you're very good-looking, and you know that."

"Yeah, but I'd get a hell of a lot more girls if I had *your* looks."

"Thanks, but if we're so good-looking, then why are we just wanking ten times a day while dreaming about shagging them all ten times a day?" asked Simon, grinning.

"I must wank even more than that, and if we keep talking about sex, I'll get so randy that I just might bend you over that fence, and shag you silly," said Colin, smirking.

"Oh, yeah? I'm a hell of a lot stronger than you, so, I'd bend *you* over the fence, and shag you 'til I shot off a few times."

"Hah! Not bloody likely, because you haven't seen me in a fight, because if you had, then you'd know I'm a hell of a lot stronger than I look, so, I'd have you bent over a fence before you had time to think."

"Nope. Two seconds after you raised your hands to grab me, I'd have your arm twisted behind your back, and then your arse'd be mine."

"Bollocks!" exclaimed Colin, laughing.

"I bet Hilary could wrestle you to the ground in less than a minute, then tear off your pants."

"I'd help her do it," Colin said as he grinned.

They laughed and talked while throwing stones at an old tin laundry basin hanging on the outside wall of the stable.

"Too late to sniff out a randy girl because by this time, they're either having dinner or getting ready to go out on a date."

"Too bad Hilary wasn't here because we could shag her."

"Then we'd be arguing over who shags her first."

"Maybe not," said Simon. "We could get her to suck on one dick while she's being shagged by another, right?"

"Oh, yeah, and I'm right randy now from thinking about that, and if I keep thinking about it, I'll go bloody bonkers."

"I just thought of a great way to keep your mind off sex."

"Then you'd be a genius," said Colin.

"I already am. How about coming up to my room and playing poker for a while? And if you let me shag your arse sometime next week, I'll let you win," Simon said, laughing.

"If I'll be winning lots of money, then I'd let you shag me *while* we're playing cards," said Colin as he laughed.

"Oh, yeah? Then how about I pay you a million pounds?"

"Brilliant. I hope I can walk back downstairs after, though."

"And if your parents ask you why you're walking a bit bent over and bowlegged, you can just tell them that you rode extra hard, and I had to apply some liniment up your arse."

"I bet you think they'd believe that," said Colin, grinning.

"Yeah, I do, because I bet they've heard that excuse from you dozens of times before."

"You really know how to take the piss, don't you?"

"Aha! See? You're laughing, so, I know you *have* used that excuse before."

"Just for that, I'll only let you shag me once."

"Awww, damn. Oh, well, I'll try to make do."

"I bet you make do a lot with those raunchy pictures you've got hidden in your bedroom," Colin told him as he laughed.

"I wish I could get more, though," said Simon, grinning.

"I was thinking the same thing because I've seen them so often, too, so, I asked around, and Kirby told me that Joel's got about twenty very sexy nudes of women with real big tits. He got them from his cousin in London, and Kirby's trying to talk him into lending them out after a while, so, let's hope we get to borrow them soon."

"I bet not for at least two months, though," said Simon.

"Yeah, probably. I don't mind getting off on photos of the same women a few more times, though," said Colin, smiling.

"Too bad they're only photos."

"Hmmm, you're hard to get hold of most of the time, lately. You haven't been getting in touch with either me or Jenny, and whenever we've called you, your mother's said you'd gone out riding for a while. *You've* told me that you've either been busy helping your dad work on things, or that you've been hanging out with some of our friends, but they've said they haven't seen you for over a week, either. So what's up? Are you seeing a girl we don't know about?"

"I...Well, I wasn't going to tell you 'til I knew them better, and then I..."

"What? You're dating twins?" asked Colin, then he laughed.

"No! It'd be nice, though, wouldn't it? No, what it is, is that I met a very nice girl and her cousin, and they..." Simon told him how he'd met Morag and Wystan, where they lived, and he described them to Colin.

"If she's *that* beautiful, I can see why you were reticent to tell me about her, and if he's one of those real handsome guys, I bet that's the reason you didn't tell Jenny about him because you thought she'd start coming by their place when she knew you were visiting them, and get to know him. Right?" asked Colin, smiling.

"No, I never thought she'd do that. Jenny has a lot more class than that, so, she'd have waited for an introduction when I felt like

I knew Morag and Wystan well enough to ask them if I could bring my best friends around to meet them."

"Okay, I'd like that. Hmmm, you said Jenny's got class, so, does that mean that you don't think *I* have, and that's why you didn't tell me about Morag because you thought I'd follow you to her place and gawk at her?"

"No! You're my best friend because you've got tons and tons of class, okay?"

"No money, though. Not as much as your family's got."

"So, what's money got to do with class? If I thought that, then I'd make sure I'd only be friends with rich guys, right? But even if there were hundreds of rich guys living around here, I wouldn't want to be friends with them unless they had at least *some* of your great qualities," said Simon.

"Thanks. I'm not being insecure, okay? It's just that I thought you might be slowly changing into a snob, and if you were, then *I* would be avoiding *you*," Colin said with a smile.

"No chance that I could ever be a snob. I'm really sorry if I've been avoiding you, and there's no excuse I can offer you that'd make up for the way I've been avoiding both you and Jenny. It's just that sometimes Morag's only at the summer place for a few days at a time, and she still isn't sure if her parents'll let her stay there longer. But when I know she'll definitely be there for a two or three-week period, then I'll..."

"Her periods are that long?" interjected Colin.

"Hah! Always the clown. But all joking aside, I'm going to introduce you and Jenny to her and her cousin, Wystan, for sure, very soon. Okay? I promise, and I know they'll love meeting you. I'm fairly certain they'll be there for at least another week, so, sometime this week, I'll take you and Jenny to meet them."

"That'd be super. Oh, and I hope you're not in love with Morag because I'm very sorry to tell you that beautiful girls find me rather irresistible, so, when I meet her, I know she'll tear off my clothes while trying to stick her tongue down my throat."

"Oh, of course. That's the only drawback in being your friend because whenever we come across girls, I get bruised by their elbows while they're poking me out of the way to get at you. You know, it's sort of disgusting how they don't care if anyone sees them ripping off their clothes and begging for your dick. Don't you ever get embarrassed about shagging in public?"

"Uh-uh. Never," replied Colin. "You see, I was born to help women get rid of their sexual frustrations, so, when they see me and lose complete control of themselves, then I feel it's my duty to shag them giddy."

"You're a good man, right now, but I know that if you keep shagging huge droves of women who've come looking for you for the absolute ultimate orgasm, day after day, week after week, then you'll be a *great* man, someday."

"So true. Thank God I'm not conceited."

"Yeah, really," said Simon.

"Hmmm, I just thought of something. You know when you said that the only drawback in being my friend was that sex-crazed women are always throwing themselves at me? Well, it got me to thinking about other drawbacks in this world. For instance, do you know what the biggest drawback in the jungle is?"

"Being bitten by tsetse flies?"

"Nope. An elephant's foreskin," replied Colin.

They laughed as they walked over to the house, and then after dinner with their parents, they went upstairs to play poker in Simon's bedroom.

They played cards for almost two hours before they went back downstairs just as Colin's parents were telling Simon's that they should be getting on their way home.

Simon told Colin that he'd see him when he came to dinner on Saturday with his parents, and then after he waved goodbye to him, Simon went into the house, took a soft drink from the fridge, and went upstairs to his bedroom.

He kept glancing at the watercolor portraits of Morag and Wystan, and wishing that he had photographs of them the way they'd looked during his sexual fantasies that he'd had about them after he had smoked marijuana.

CHAPTER NINETEEN

Simon awoke the next morning, and while showering, he recalled Wystan's invitation to stay overnight as often as he wanted to. He grinned while thinking about spending the rest of the week with Morag and Wystan, and then introduce Colin and Jennifer to them sometime during the following week.

He hoped that his mother and stepfather would agree to let him spend a few days with Wystan and Morag, then he hurried downstairs and found his mother sitting in the living room.

"Morning, mom."

"Good morning, honey," said Miranda.

"Really nice day again, huh? I'm only going to have a salad and some orange juice this morning because I'm planning on doing something," said Simon.

"Doing something sounds interesting, so, I might try doing something, too."

"Very funny," Simon said as he grinned.

"Are you going out right after you eat?" asked Miranda.

"No, I was...Well, I'll tell you in a sec."

Simon rushed to the kitchen, prepared a salad, then while eating it and drinking orange juice, he tried to think of the best way to ask his mother and stepfather if he could spend a few days with Morag and Wystan.

He walked back to the living room, and waited until his mother had turned a page of her book before he spoke to her.

"Where's dad?"

"He went riding a little over an hour ago, so, I expect he'll be back any minute now because he's going into town with Mr. Blake to get a new part for his car."

"Dad needs a new part for his car?"

"No, Mr. Blake's car broke down, and Noel's driving him into town. Noel's lending him the money for the new part."

"Oh, sure, a loan," said Simon, smiling. "I'll just bet that when Mr. Blake starts paying him back for that supposed loan, then money'll start magically appearing in Mr. Blake's mailbox."

"Well, we might not have castles around here with ghosts inside them, but we do have ghosts *outside* of castles who sneak around at night, leaving little gifts for people," said Miranda.

"Yeah, I know all about that, Mrs. Claus."

"Now what was it you wanted to discuss with us?"

"I wanted to ask you and dad if it was...Oh, here he is now."

Simon rushed through to the kitchen, and after greeting his stepfather, he asked him if he could talk to him in the living room about something very important.

Noel smiled when he noticed how excited Simon was as they walked to the living room, then he sat in an armchair across from Miranda, and suppressed a grin as he waited for Simon to begin explaining what he felt was so important.

"Okay, what I wanted to ask you is, well, it's about Morag and

Wystan staying for most of the summer at that castle...Well, it used to be a castle, but now it's just the old part of the huge house, but anyway, they really like me, and I really like them, and they asked me if I'd like to stay with them more often. Okay? So, I was wondering what you'd think if I stayed with them for a few days."

"Hmmm, what do you think, Noel?" asked Miranda, smiling.

"Well, now let me see. Three young people on their own in a big place like that, having much fun together, *and* proper meals? And Simon takes his toothbrush along with him? Yes, I think he'd behave himself," said Noel, winking at Miranda.

"Really? Aw, thanks, dad. You're swell. Oh, and I'd make sure I helped buy the groceries and...Well, whatever else. And some gifts, too. Morag loved those fancy chocolate biscuits you chose for her, so, I could buy some more for her. Oh, and some pretty wrapping paper, too. Something elegant and refined, and I could think of something nice to buy Wystan, too. But that'd be hard to do, though, because it seems like he's got everything. You know, he's got really nice clothes and all that, but I'll find some gift for him. Maybe I should get him some good magazines because he spends a lot of time reading. What do you think?"

"Yes, that's a good idea," replied Miranda. "I'm sure he'd like a few of the newest magazines, and perhaps you could give Morag watercolor paints and some paper, or brushes, or both."

"That's a brilliant idea! So, I was thinking of leaving for their place now, all right? And I'd be staying for a few days, and on my way there, I'll shop for some gifts for them, and if I'm not back for

a few days, then you'll know where I am. Right? Gee, spending every day there with Morag'll be great. Swimming in the pool, and watching her paint. Maybe she'll paint *my* portrait, too. *I* should try to do some painting, too, and that way I'd paint...Or *try* to paint *her* portrait. Blaze has such a good time there, too, and Morag loves patting and talking to him, and feeding him an apple or a carrot, and she told me that he's a very beautiful horse, too. Oh, and they've even got a nice stable for him to stay in for the night. Morag really likes Blaze. He really likes *her*, too. I think she's the prettiest girl I've ever seen, and she's also the smartest one, too. Most refined girl, too."

"I see. Take a breath," said Melinda, trying not to laugh.

"Oh, uh, yeah, right. So, what do you think if I left for their place right now?"

"Now? This very moment?" asked Miranda, smiling.

"Poof! A puff of smoke and he disappears!" exclaimed Noel.

"Aw, you know what I mean," said Simon as he laughed.

"You'll be taking a few pairs of underwear?"

"And your toothbrush?" asked Noel, grinning.

"Toothpaste too?" asked Miranda.

"And a comb?"

"Or a brush?" Miranda asked him.

"Socks, too?"

"Okay! I promise to pack all that!" cried Simon, laughing.

"Then start packing," said Noel, smiling.

"Don't forget it's for three days," Simon reminded them.

"If they can tolerate it, then we can," said Miranda.

"Brilliant! Aw, thanks so much! I'm going to look for my best clothes, and I'll make sure to put lots of socks and underwear in my bag, too, and I'll take extra food for Blaze, and if he needs more, I can pick up feed at the store down the road from them. It's only about I think, hmmm, just over two miles from their place. That's where I can buy Morag some watercolor paints. So, anyway, I'll be back downstairs in about ten minutes, all right? Yeah, I'll be back real fast. Bye," Simon said, rushing away.

They waited until they heard Simon running up the stairs before they laughed.

He's so excited," said Noel. "It's quite obvious where he'll be spending most of the summer if she's going to be around."

"Yes, I'm sure you're right. I do believe Simon is madly in love with a princess," said Miranda, smiling.

"We should tell him to put a pea under her mattress and see if she screams in agony."

"Oh, no, she's much too refined to scream, dear. Perhaps just a slight moan. Simon's so taken with her, so, I hope he doesn't become too depressed at the end of the summer when she goes back home."

"Absence makes the heart grow fonder," said Noel.

"Yes, and I'm sure they'll keep the post office quite busy. Simon's almost doing cartwheels. A first love can be so strong. I know that because you're the first man I've ever loved," she told him, meaning it with all her heart.

"You're the only woman I've ever loved, and I'm so happy because you've given me a wonderful son, too."

"Hmmm, I've been thinking about giving you a daughter."

"Oh, you have, have you? You must tell me how you'll manage to do that," Noel said, grinning.

"With Simon away visiting for a few days, I'll teach you all about it. I'm sure you'll learn quite quickly."

"I'm so pleased that he's in such a rush to visit with his friends because as soon as he's gone we can spend a few hours in bed before dinner."

"But I'm not tired," said Miranda, kissing him.

"I was hoping you weren't. Hmmm, I'd better sit down because I wouldn't want Simon noticing my trousers stretched out of shape. Mmmmm, I want to make love to you, right now."

"Oops. Here he comes, so, you'd better sit down."

Simon rushed into the room, grinning and holding a large, leather shoulder bag, then after leaning over to kiss his mother's cheek, he grinned and said: "All right, I'm going now."

"Bye, dear," said Miranda, smiling.

"Bye, dad," he said, kissing his cheek.

"Gee, a kiss. Thanks," said Noel, grinning.

"Say hello to Mr. Blake for me, and I hope they have that new car part he needs in stock at the garage. I'm just going to pack some feed bags for Blaze. Well, I'm leaving now, and I'll see you on Friday. Bye."

"Oh, you're leaving now? Oh, all right. Goodbye, dear."

"Bye, mom. Dad. I'm leaving now."

"Yes, it seems that way. Bye, son," said Noel.

"And I didn't forget to pack my toothbrush."

"Good."

"All right, then. Bye," said Simon, rushing toward the door.

"Bye," Noel and Miranda said in unison.

After Simon raced out of the house, they burst into laughter, then ten minutes later, they waved goodbye to him as he rode off on Blaze.

"Time for your lessons on how to make a baby."

"Mmmm, come here, beautiful woman," said Noel, smiling.

CHAPTER TWENTY

Simon arrived in the town that Wystan and Morag often shopped in, and then he bought a big box of fancy assorted biscuits, a pad of watercolor paper, and six tubes of paint for Morag, and four magazines for Wystan.

He felt ebullient as he rode away from town, and then a few minutes later, he began seeing hitchhikers on the road, but with so many bags strapped to Blaze, he couldn't offer a ride to one of the young people.

He saw three children playing in a field close to the road, so, he slowed his pace, reached into his pocket for coins, then after beckoning them, he gave them the coins, and they excitedly thanked him as they smiled, and then Simon felt rather pleased that he'd brightened their day.

After crossing over the bridge near Wystan's huge summer home, he dismounted, and began leading Blaze along the road, then as he led his horse partway along the path at the side of the house, Simon smiled while looking at the two, large wooden doors to the stable, then moments later, he led Blaze through the opening to the rear gardens.

He took the saddle off Blaze, then Simon knocked on the back door of the house, and when Morag opened the door, she smiled and said: "What a delightful surprise! Please come in!"

"Hi, I decided to drop by for a visit."

"I'm so glad you did," she said, smiling.

"Where's Wystan?"

"Oh, somewhere in the house. Can you stay for dinner?"

"Sure, thanks, I'd love to," replied Simon, smiling.

"And a card game, after?"

"I sure can. Oh, I brought you a gift. Just a sec."

Simon started taking her gifts out of the bag, and placing them on the table while hoping that she'd like the wrapping paper, ribbons and bow he'd put together while in the store.

"Oh, what beautiful gifts. I love how you've wrapped them. You didn't have to buy me gifts," said Morag, smiling.

"I just wanted to. So, open them. No, open *that* one first."

"All right."

She slipped off the bow, then tried not to tear too much of the wrapping paper, and then Simon was delighted to see her smile broaden when she saw the gift.

"Biscuits like the ones you brought me before. Oh, Simon, you're so sweet, and much too generous. Thanks so much."

"I hope you like the other one," he said, feeling so pleased.

"This gift is much larger. Hmmm, what's this? Oh, a big pad of watercolor paper! You must've noticed I had almost used up my last pad! Thanks ever so much. Oh, and tubes of paint! This is so extravagant. I love the colors you chose, and now I wish I had a very nice gift to give to you. If I'd known you were going to bring me these lovely gifts, then I would've gone into town to..."

"Aw, I never meant for you to do that. I just felt like getting you a few little gifts because I had a wonderful time here. Um, with you."

"I loved having you here for dinner with me, and we had such a nice time that evening. Well, except for that terrible incident caused by the marijuana," Morag said as she frowned.

"That was only for a little while, then I felt much better."

"Well, if you smoke more of that while you're here *this* time, you can just go upstairs to sleep for the night. I wish you were able to stay here as our guest for a few days or longer while I'm here because I enjoy your company so much."

"I told my mom and dad I'd been invited to do just that, so, I packed some clothes, and I brought extra feed for Blaze, too."

"Really? Oh, Simon! That's wonderful! I'm so excited! Wystan will be so pleased, as well."

"I got *him* a gift, too. I didn't know what to get him, at first, but I decided...Well, I hope he likes what I decided on."

"You're so wonderful, and I know he'll love his gift. Please sit down and I'll get you a cool drink, then I'll look for Wystan and tell him you're here. He'll be so happy because he was just saying...Oh, I'll get your drink first."

Morag returned with a glass of lemonade for him before she went looking for Wystan, then Simon felt elated now that he knew he'd be staying with them for a few days, if Wystan agreed.

Five minutes later, Wystan appeared with Morag, and he rushed over to shake hands with Simon.

"Morag told me you're staying for dinner *and* not only overnight, but for a few days. I'm delighted. We're becoming such good friends," said Wystan as he grinned.

"I sure hope we are. Oh, I got you something. Here," Simon said, handing him the gift. "I thought you might like this."

"And bearing gifts, as well. You know that wasn't necessary. Now whatever could this be. Hmmm, I like the nice wrapping paper and the ribbons, too. Oh, Simon, thank you. I love these magazines. But how did you know these were my favorites? I don't have any of them laying around the house."

"Oh, I just thought you might like those ones."

"I do. I truly do," said Wystan. "You know, this is astonishing because I was going to buy one or two of these the next time I was in town. You're surprisingly generous. Thanks so much. I'll be spending some enjoyable hours reading these magazines. Well, this calls for a celebration, so, I'm serving our best wine with dinner tonight, which I'll make sure is cooked to perfection."

"Naw, there's no need for you to go to all that trouble just for me. Even just a sandwich would be nice," said Simon.

"Nonsense! Only the best for you. I can't get over how wonderfully generous you are. Oh, while I'm finishing up a few things, why don't you go for a swim? Morag will join you soon."

"Sure, I'd really like that."

"Very good. You go upstairs to the guest room you stayed in before, then unpack and get your bathing suit on, then...Hmmm, excuse us for a moment, Morag."

Wystan drew him a few steps away from her, and then leaned close to whisper in his ear: "Don't forget to lie on your stomach when Morag's dress gets soaking wet."

"I won't forget," whispered Simon as he chuckled.

"What are you two whispering about?" asked Morag.

"Man-talk about yellow water," replied Wystan, grinning.

"Oh! Wystan, you're terrible! Simon would never...Well, he'd never do *that* in the pool!"

"Why, I was just telling him about the Yellow Sea."

"Hah! I doubt that, knowing you. Well, I can see you two will be giggling and laughing again tonight about any little thing. I'll join you soon at the pool, Simon."

"All right," he said, then he and Wystan laughed.

"There you two go again. Oh, well. Tra-la," said Morag.

She shrugged her shoulders before leaving the room, then Wystan winked at him, and followed her. Simon chuckled as he went upstairs to undress while hoping that Wystan would share another marijuana cigarette with him very soon.

Simon quickly unpacked his haversack, then stripped nude, and put on his navy blue, woolen bathing suit, and then he fastened the buckle of the white belt.

After he put on the snug-fitting tank top with the narrow red, white, and navy blue, horizontal stripes, he stood in front of the full-length mirror. Simon decided it was much too warm to wear

the striped bathing shirt, so, he peeled it off, and grinned as he flexed his biceps in the mirror.

He struck a few more poses and he felt pleased that he had developed a better physique than any other youth in school, then he sighed when he thought about Wystan having a much more powerful build. Simon then felt better when he recalled that Morag had complimented him on his physique.

He went back downstairs, poured another glass of lemonade, and then he began walking to the pool, and he stopped on the way to pat Blaze.

Simon took off his bathing suit, hung it over the back of a deck chair, then dove into the pool, and floated on his back while thinking about the very erotic fantasies he'd had when he had smoked marijuana, and he soon had an erection as he imagined seeing Morag in her wet dress after she'd been in the pool.

He got out of the pool, and then after he laid out on his stomach, with his chin on his crossed forearms, he hoped that Morag would be wearing a dress that would become almost transparent when it was wet.

Simon heard her humming, so, he quickly stood up, wrapped a towel around his waist, then just after he sat back down, Morag appeared on the patio, and they agreed that it was a perfect day to swim and bask in the sun.

She dove into the pool, and when she climbed out, Simon's

heart leapt when he saw how her wet dress clung to her body. Morag then asked him to turn around before she removed her dress and wrapped a towel around herself, and then she smiled as she said to him: "I noticed your bathing suit over there."

"Well, I decided against wearing one because we've swam in the nude at other times."

"Does this mean you're going to tan nude, too?"

"No, of course not," said Simon, laughing.

"I told you that I've seen Wystan swimming in the nude, so, it wouldn't shock me if I saw another boy nude."

"Yeah, but you just said that you saw him in the pool, but you probably didn't see him out of the pool."

"All right, so, I *didn't* see him nude. But when he got out of the pool, I would've seen him completely nude if some bushes hadn't been blocking my view," said Morag, then she giggled.

"If the bushes were blocking your view, then for all you know, he might've had on a bathing suit.

"How did you know that he did? Oops!"

"Aha! Then he *wasn't* nude," said Simon as he laughed.

"Well, all right, he *wasn't* nude, but I'll bet he doesn't wear a bathing suit when I'm not here. So, I guess this means that you won't be sunbathing nude with me."

"Sure I will, if you get nude first."

"Not fair because I suggested it," she said.

"Then more reason that you should get nude first."

"Drat! You may have won *this* time, but wait'll we play cards after dinner, *then* you'll be sorry," Morag said, feigning a pout.

"I wouldn't be if we played *strip* poker."

"Oh! You're so naughty!" she exclaimed, laughing.

For the next hour, they talked, laughed, and swam nude in the pool before they strolled back to the house.

"How was your swim?" asked Wystan, winking at Simon.

"Quite nice, thank you," replied Morag, smiling.

"Yes, it was wonderful," said Simon, grinning.

"I'm glad you enjoyed yourselves, and while you two were frolicking in the pool, I prepared a casserole for dinner. Chicken breasts in apricot nectar, with sliced leeks, two types of veggies, and a hint of spices. It'll take just over half an hour to cook, and by that time, the skin of the chicken will be crispy, juicy, and rather tasty, as usual," Wystan said, then he winked and grinned.

"Mmmmm, that sounds sohhhhh delicious," said Simon.

"Yes, it does, and I'll make up a nice, big salad to go with that scrumptious, chicken casserole."

"Your salads are always a delight. I'll fetch a bottle of white wine from the cellar later, and cool it," said Wystan.

"Now that we've planned dinner, I'll leave you two to giggle about nothing while I go upstairs to have a bath, and then work on a drawing I started this morning. While I'm away, I do hope you two will behave yourselves," Morag said, and then she laughed.

"We always do," said Wystan, grinning.

"Yes, we do. Bye, Morag."

They laughed after she left the room, then Simon said: "She was just pretending to be annoyed because I know she doesn't mind the way we act sometimes when we smoke that stuff and start feeling giddy."

"You're right. Morag looks forward to any opportunity she can get to scold us."

"She looks beautiful no matter what expression she has on her face. I'm having another glass of lemonade. I love the way you make it."

"Thanks again. It seems I'm always thanking you for your compliments. Now that Morag's gone upstairs for an hour, let's smoke a marijuana cigarette and go for a stroll around the house."

"Yeah, I'd love that. The effects from it are amazing."

"They certainly are, indeed. We'll be walking around the house with erections."

"I know *I* will, for sure," said Simon, smirking. "I'll run upstairs and change out of this wet bathing suit. I'll be back in less than five minutes, okay?"

"Okay, but I'm timing you. Tick-tock, tick-tock, one — two — three — four — "

"See you in two minutes!" exclaimed Simon as he laughed.

Simon rushed upstairs, took off his bathing suit, and then opened one of the dresser drawers and took out his white shirt with the broad, bright yellow stripes.

He hurried to one of the closets to get his white pants, a yellow belt, and his white tennis shoes, and then he dressed quickly, grinned at his reflection, and then rushed out of the room, along the corridor, and down the staircase.

Wystan saw him rushing toward him, so, he lit a marijuana cigarette, inhaled deeply, and passed it to him when Simon came to a stop in front of him. After they'd smoked it, they began walking through the rooms in the house.

"The sun's given you marvelous color and you look rather good in white with a flash of yellow. Yes, you're quite flash."

"Thanks, that merits you a smile," said Simon, grinning.

"Yikes! The glare from your perfect teeth makes me wince! Spare me!" exclaimed Wystan, cringing away from him.

"Just think of how much wider my smile would've been if you'd said I looked spectacular."

"I've always been a rather curious fellow, so, I'll throw you that particular compliment when I have my sunglasses handy."

"Gee, I can hardly wait. If *I* looked as great as *you* do all the time, then for sure you'd have to wear your sunglasses all the time, because I'd be blinding you with my big smile from the constant compliments you'd be giving me," said Simon.

"Ah, I'm sure you're starting to feel the marijuana's effects."

"Mmmm, yeah, and I feel sohhhhh good."

"So do I, and that's why I prepared dinner in advance. We'll fetch a bottle of wine, later," said Wystan, smiling.

"I didn't know you had a wine cellar."

"Yes, and there are many other rooms in the basement."

"Any bats and huge spiders down there?"

"Yes, and huge, poisonous snakes, and rats bigger than me."

"Now *that*'s big," said Simon, smiling.

"We'll arm ourselves with swords and pistols, then I'll take you on a tour of the downstairs when it's dark and eerie. We'll carry candelabra to light our way through the deeeeeep, darrrrrrk, and ohhhhhh, sohhhhhh dank and ancient basement."

"That'll be fun. Hmmm, there's so many nice oil paintings in these rooms. Lots of portraits, too," said Simon, looking around the room.

"Yes, many portraits of family long gone. In this next room we're coming to, there are paintings in a much lighter vein. Landscapes, seascapes, still life, and such. Unfortunately, there's not one nude, lusty nymph in any of the scenery."

They entered the next large room, and Simon smiled when he saw several paintings of nude women either reclining on a couch or bathing in a stream. Two paintings depicted nude couples embracing on beds and Simon walked closer to look at them.

"A little erotica to add spice to the collection," said Wystan.

"So I see. Have you looked closely at that material laying over his lap? It's poking up like a tent, so, he's got an erection and by the way they're almost lying on the bed, and kissing while he's got

his hand on one of her breasts, it looks like they're just about ready to have sexual intercourse."

"I prefer saying *fucking,* as in fucking them until they're bowlegged, or it's fucking great, and so on," said Wystan, smiling.

"Yeah, I like saying fuck, too. But of course, you can't use that word in certain company, right? Someday, *I'd* like to fuck, but...Hmmm, I like that painting to the left of that seascape."

"Someday you'd like to fuck? Ah, then you're still a virgin?"

"Well, yes," replied Simon, blushing.

"Oh, you'll experience that one day, either before you're married or after. I've had a few experiences, already."

"Yeah? Well, I'm still waiting for *my* first experience. But I almost did it once because there was this girl in school who let some of the lads...Um, *fuck* her, but I didn't want to because she wasn't pretty or attractive in any way. At least *I* didn't think she was, and she got married really young, too, because she was going to have a baby."

"Many very young women throughout the world marry because of that reason, so, you have to be very careful at all times when you're having sex. One way, is to pull it out just before you ejaculate, but even then she can become pregnant."

"She can?" asked Simon, wide-eyed. "So, um, uh...Oh, I didn't know that. Hmmm, so, how...How do *you*, you know, um, take those precautions?"

"I suppose you could say it's part luck and part precaution because I pull out just before orgasm, and I haven't impregnated a

woman, yet. Sometimes when I've pulled out to shoot semen on my lover's breasts and stomach, I've almost shot some on her vagina, but those are rare occasions because usually my partner will stop the fucking when I'm getting close, and then suck me off to orgasm, so that way, all my semen is swallowed. I rather like that, so, I often prefer just fucking a mouth."

"Whew! Thinking of that gets me very...You know, um, so, anyway, you've done it lots of times, huh?"

"Fucking?"

"Yeah, *that*. So? Have you? *Fucked* lots of times?"

"Not as much as I'd like to. I have a very high sex drive, which means I'm sexually aroused all day long, so, my hand has to suffice to quell those urgent needs, but you, as you well know, find that's rather enjoyable, too," said Wystan, grinning.

"Yeah, I *do* know. I...I, uh, I'm aroused quite often, too, so, I do the same thing as you when I feel that way. Um, a lot."

"At your age, it's understandable. However, you'll find that your sex drive decreases as you get older. In fifty years, you'll only be able to do it ten or twenty times a day."

"Ten or twenty times? Hah!" Simon started laughing.

"It's true! I know that because I'm older than you, and I only masturbate forty times a day. Tragic, isn't it? Smoking marijuana always increases my arousal, so, having just smoked some, I feel so sexually...Would you mind walking on ahead? There are some very nice paintings in the next room. I'm going through that door

over there to another room for a few minutes because I have a few papers there I have to attend to. All right?"

"Uh, sure, all right," said Simon, walking away.

He felt sure that Wystan had gone into that room to masturbate, instead of sorting and filing some documents, so, after waiting a couple of minutes, Simon tiptoed back into the room he'd just left, and over to the door of the room that Wystan had gone into.

He pressed his ear against the door, and when he couldn't hear Wystan making any sounds, Simon hurried back to the other room, and went over to a door that he'd seen at the end of that room.

Glancing at his watch, he saw that it had been just over a minute since Wystan had left him, so, Simon decided to do some exploring. He could almost hear his heart pounding in his ears as he slowly turned the doorknob and opened the door.

He saw a very small room with an archway at one end of it, then noticing a banister attached to the wall inside the archway, he realized there was a staircase leading down to the basement.

Simon was just about to leave the small room, when he looked back at the archway and saw a shadow moving down one side of the staircase wall, and he felt sure that it had been Wystan going down the stairs. He immediately decided to follow him, so, he rushed over to the stairs, and hurried down them.

Gas lamps lit the walls of the old, stone staircase, and more of them lit the narrow hall he could see at the bottom of the staircase. Simon was thinking about going back upstairs because it might not have been Wystan he had seen going down the staircase to the

basement, then he caught a glimpse of someone nude, rounding the corner far ahead of him, and he thought it had been Wystan, so, he rushed along the hall, hoping to catch up with him.

The gas lights suddenly began dimming until only two of them remained lit, which made the hall rather dark, but as Simon continued hurrying along the hall, he felt sure that the lights would soon glow brighter again.

He rounded the corner, and wondered where Wystan had gone because the hall ahead of him was empty, and there didn't seem to be any doors for Wystan to have gone through.

He walked back along the hall, and then nearing the end of it, he saw a door that he hadn't noticed before because it didn't have a doorknob, and the door was the same color as the wall.

Simon pushed the door, and found that it opened onto another hall that was poorly lit, and as he started walking down it, he felt certain that Wystan must have walked down this hall, too. Near the end of that hall, he saw a wooden fence-like structure forming a small circle, and he thought that perhaps the fence circled a spiral staircase that led down to another level below the basement.

He reached the circular wooden fence, and saw that it was a barrier to protect people from falling into a deep well. Simon picked up a stone, dropped it in the well, and he counted slowly up to nine before he heard a faint splash.

He was staring into the depths of the well, when he detected a movement near him, then he was just about to turn his head to see

what it was, when he suddenly saw a nude man falling into the well, then disappearing into the total darkness below.

Simon wondered who had sneaked up behind him in the dark hall, then thrown a dummy into the well as a joke to make him think that it had been a real person.

He quickly looked around, but because he'd been watching the dummy falling until it was out of sight, whoever had thrown it in the well had managed to hurry back into the shadows of the hall.

Simon leaned over to look down into the well again, then he looked back up just in time to catch a glimpse of Morag hurrying across the far end of the hall and disappearing into the shadows, so, he grinned and rushed after her.

He neared the area where he'd seen Morag, then after walking through another archway, he saw that he was on another hall. There was just enough light to see a short distance ahead, but when he rounded a curve in the hall, there was so little light that he stumbled over a large, pliant lump on the floor.

Simon almost toppled over, but he was able to quickly regain his balance, and then after taking a few steps backward to see if he could discern what he'd stumbled over, his heel struck another big lump, and he fell backward.

He groaned loudly when he landed on his rump, and he felt relieved that he hadn't hit his head on the stone wall while he'd been falling, then as he stood up, he wished there was more light in the hall so that he could see what he'd tripped over.

He started hurrying down the hall again, then immediately

slowed his pace after he stubbed his toe on another slightly supple, big object in the hall, then after he'd stepped over that large lump, as well as two more similar ones, he walked around the next curve in the hall, and then he lifted a torch off the wall.

Simon carried the torch back to the area where he'd either stepped or tripped over large lumps, and his jaw dropped when he saw four unconscious men sprawled on the floor of the hall.

One of the men let out a long moan as his eyes slowly opened, then Simon squatted, held the torch closer to the man's face, and then he was surprised when he recognized him.

He slowly moved the torch around to light up the faces of the other men, and Simon was startled when he saw that they were all looking at him and moaning, and he suddenly recalled that he had seen them somewhere before.

He stood back up, and as he was stepping over one of them, the man grabbed onto his ankle, so, Simon had to shake his foot loose from the man's weak grasp before he could continue on down the hall.

He struggled free of a few more men who tried to grab onto his ankles, and Simon felt annoyed that they seemed to be trying to hinder his search for Morag.

He felt rather grateful when someone reached out in the dark and started dragging the moaning men back into the shadows. Now that he was free of annoying encumbrances, Simon smiled as he resumed walking down the curving corridor.

Moments later, he saw that he was nearing the deep well he'd

seen before, and he'd completely forgotten about both seeing a dummy being cast into the well, and the moaning men he'd stumbled across on his way through the dark halls.

Simon stood at the wooden fence that surrounded the well, and after he dropped another stone down into its depths, and then waited until he heard the faint splash, he continued on down the hall while wondering when he'd catch sight of Morag again.

He heard rushing footsteps not too far ahead of him, and then a moment later he saw Morag darting across the hall as she giggled. She opened a door and closed it behind her, then Simon broke into a run while hoping to catch up with her.

He was laughing when he reached the door, and saw that it opened into a sparsely furnished room that was sparsely lit by a small torch on one of the walls.

There were no windows or other doors, and only three items of furniture, therefore, Simon felt certain that Morag was seated in the tall wing chair facing away from him across the room.

"Morag?"

When he didn't receive an answer, he laughed and began walking toward the back of the wing chair.

"I know you're in this room because I saw you come in here. Wystan's down here somewhere, too. Morag? Oh, so, you're trying to hide from me, huh?"

Simon grinned as he crept closer to the back of the big wing chair, then he peeked around the side of it, and his jaw slackened when he saw a sleeping, middle-aged man seated in the chair. He

then looked at the other two pieces of furniture in the room, but neither of them were large enough for Morag to hide behind.

Simon looked back at the man in the wing chair, and saw that his eyes were beginning to open at the same time he started mumbling something as he tried to raise his hands, but the effort was too much for the obviously very tired, pale man, so, his hands dropped back onto his thighs.

He leaned closer to hear what the man was mumbling, then Simon recalled seeing *him* somewhere before, too; either in the town near his home, or in another town. He spun around when he heard the door open, and then slam shut, so, he grinned as he ran to the door, opened it, then looked around the empty hall.

On the wall directly across from him, he saw a large tapestry, and it was moving, so, he hurried across the hall, pulled back a side of the tapestry, and saw a narrow, stone staircase. He took one last look in both directions of the hall for any sign of Morag or Wystan, then he stepped behind the tapestry, and went up the stone staircase to the closed door.

Simon opened the door, and walked into the enormous main room in the closed wing of the old house. He couldn't quite recall when he'd been in the room before, but he felt sure it had been sometime when he had smoked marijuana with Wystan.

Among the grand furnishings, there were three large, elegant and very comfortable-looking couches, four tall wing chairs, exquisite paintings, sculptures, and unique objets d'art, and the

flames in the huge fireplace were casting light on the rich colors of the immense oriental carpet.

Simon looked up at the ceiling, which was fifty feet above him, and his heart began beating faster when he saw the colossal, bronze, heavily muscled, male angel suspended from the ceiling.

The nude angel's arms were open wide, holding a lit torch in each hand, and two narrow beams of light shot out from its eyes. The twenty-foot-tall angel had a wingspan of at least twice its height and as Simon gazed up at it, he felt sure that he could hear the faint sound of wind sweeping along the angel's wings because it almost appeared to be gliding across the ceiling.

He sighed, looked around the room, and then seeing the big photo album on a low table in front of one of the couches, he walked over to it, sat down, and began looking through the album.

Simon closed the album, picked up a glass of cognac that he hadn't seen when he'd sat down, and he drank half the glass before getting up off the couch.

He stood at the fireplace, staring into the flames as he drank the rest of the cognac, then he whirled around when he heard laughter. He hurried across the room, and just after he stepped through the two massive, ornately carved wooden doors, he suddenly felt dizzy, and his vision was blurred by rapidly fluttering lights.

Simon blinked a few times, then suddenly found himself standing at the closed door of the room that Wystan had entered to

tend to some documents. When the door began opening, Simon darted away to stand out of sight at the side of an armoire, then he watched Wystan come out of the room, and begin walking away.

Simon rushed to catch up with him, then Wystan turned around when he heard hurrying footsteps behind him.

"Ah, there you are," said Wystan, smiling. "I thought you might've gone on to the next group of rooms while I was busy sorting through papers."

"I, um, I decided to take another look at a few of those sort of erotic paintings in the room we passed through before, so, that's where I was," lied Simon.

"And did you find them just as exciting this time?"

"Well, not too much, really. Do you? I mean, *did* you find them to be exciting?"

"I have to admit they sparked an erotic thought or two."

"I thought they might. So, did they give you enough spark to make you want to have a wank?" asked Simon, grinning.

"Oh, a wank, is it? Hmmm, obviously, it had that effect on *you*, so, I suppose we'd best end the tour very soon so that you can do a bit of that wanking of yours," said Wystan, smiling.

"Uh, no, I was just kidding. Honest. But did *you* just do...Um, finish taking care of those papers?" he asked while blushing.

"Yes, thanks, and I feel much better now."

"Uh-huh. Good," said Simon, looking at a painting.

Wystan smiled and talked about the paintings on the walls around them while they walked slowly back to the living room.

CHAPTER
TWENTY-ONE

Simon felt elated when Morag and Wystan decided to again dress in costume for what he was pleased to find was another gourmet dinner delight, which Wystan had prepared.

By the time he'd finished eating dinner, Simon felt giddy from the effects of the wine and marijuana. After tending to Blaze, he sat in the living room with Morag and Wystan, sipping cognac as they talked, then Simon felt more lightheaded when he smoked a second marijuana cigarette.

Wystan laid his head back on the high-backed couch, then Simon followed suit on the couch across from Wystan. Morag then said it was obvious that he and Wystan wanted to have a nap before playing cards, so, she told them that she was going to have a leisurely bath, and then read a book in her room for an hour. Simon smiled at her, then closed his eyes and fell asleep.

It seemed like only seconds later, when Wystan gently shook Simon's shoulder, and then after Simon opened his eyes, he found that his vision was blurred. He rubbed his eyes and smiled up at Wystan who seemed to be standing in a mist while holding a pair of lit candelabra.

"I have to get a bottle of my favorite wine from the wine cellar, so, how about that tour of the bowels of the house?"

"Mmmmm, sure. Everything looks blurry," said Simon.

"Oh? That's happened to me and a few other people I've known after we've smoked marijuana, but you'll be fine in a little while. Can you see well enough to hold a candelabrum?"

"Yes, I can," replied Simon, reaching out for one.

"Ready?" asked Wystan.

"Ready."

Simon slowly got up off the couch, and then he swayed and almost lost his balance.

"Whoo-oo, I feel a bit woozy."

"Hold onto my arm," said Wystan. "That's it."

They went into a room off the kitchen, and Wystan led him through a door, and they began going down a stone staircase.

"I feel like I'm walking on air. I'm still dizzy, too, but excited at the same time. Really excited," said Simon.

"Yes, it's obvious by that growing bulge in your trousers."

"Oops! Happens a lot, lately," Simon told him as he giggled.

Wystan opened one of the six doors in the hall, then after they were inside a very dark room, he lit three more candelabra on tables, and then Simon saw that they were in the wine cellar.

"Would you take a look at the labels for me, please? See if you can find a bottle with a round, bright blue label. You can't miss it because it's in a row of about a dozen other bottles with blue labels on them," said Wystan. "I'm just going down the hall to one of the other rooms to fetch a painting I meant to hang on one of the walls this afternoon. I'll be back in about a minute."

"Sure, all right," said Simon.

He pulled bottles out of racks, and because his sight was blurred, Simon felt thankful that he didn't have to read the labels to find the particular wine that Wystan wanted. He found an area of the racks that had bottles with round, blue labels on them, so, he took one of them out, carried it over to one of the tables, and waited for Wystan to return.

He felt a tingling sensation rush through his body, and it made him feel more lightheaded. Ten minutes had passed by, and Wystan still hadn't returned, so, Simon decided to go look for him.

He carried a candelabrum as he walked along the hall, trying doorknobs, and looking into unlocked rooms. The hall divided into five smaller halls, and in his vertiginous state, the basement looked like a maze to him. He chose one of the halls and after walking down it for a few moments, he heard faint sounds coming from somewhere ahead of him.

Simon took a few more steps, and realized it had been moaning that he'd heard, then he saw a bit of light coming from a door that hadn't been completely closed.

While walking slowly along the hall, he felt both excited and slightly scared as he looked at the holes in the dark, stone walls as he imagined a rat or some other animal with sharp teeth and claws suddenly leaping out at him from one of those holes.

Nearing the slightly open door that light flowed out from like a slowly moving mist, he heard low voices, and Simon wondered who they could be because Morag was upstairs in her bedroom, and only Wystan had come downstairs to the basement with him.

He blew out the candles on the candelabrum before approaching the door very slowly, then after slowly pushing it open slightly wider, his eyes widened when he saw a nude young woman lying on her back on a long, narrow table.

In the dimly lit room, it almost looked as if she were floating on her back with her arms stretched out as if reaching for whatever items were far from each side of the table.

A single, low-hanging, circular lamp above the table radiated an eerie glow that cast a blue tint on her flesh, and although he could see her clearly, everything else in the rather dark room was out of focus.

The young woman's head rested on a dark green satin, tubular pillow, and most of her facial features were blurred, but Simon could see that her eyes were closed, and he knew that she wasn't asleep because he could hear her muttering something.

He looked at her breasts and pubic area for several moments before looking back at her face, and then over to her left, outstretched arm. The hanging light above the table only lit up her arm as far as her elbow, so, Simon couldn't see what she seemed to be reaching out for in the dark.

When his eyes became more accustomed to the dark, Simon could barely discern someone seated close to the left side of the table, and wearing a long, black cloak with a big hood that hid that person's facial features.

He quickly stepped back against the door when another person, wearing a similar black robe with a big hood, moved out from the

darkness, and sat at the other side of the nude young woman, and then Simon's heart beat faster when he saw what was happening.

One of the hooded figures held a wine glass close to the end of a long, pale yellow, rubber tube attached to what appeared to be a small, narrow, silver tube pressed either against or into the young woman's wrist area.

Simon trembled as he observed dark liquid flowing down through the long, rubber tube and into the wine glass. He then watched the other person whom had moved out from the darkness moments ago, lean over the nude young woman, and hold a similar long, rubber tube to the side of her neck, and then a dark liquid flowed down through that tube, and squirted out into a big wine glass that the hooded figure held.

Simon watched mesmerized as that dark clad person drank the contents of the glass, then both dark-robed people moved slowly away from the young woman on the table, and then blended into the darkness of the room.

Moments later, he realized that he'd been holding his breath while watching the strange ritual, so, he heaved a big sigh, then he ventured slightly past the young woman on the table, and peered into the darkness in the direction that he'd seen those dark robed people seem to fade into.

Simon could vaguely see them crouched over what seemed to be another table, with another nude person lying on it. He caught slight glimpses of more nude people seated on the floor, and leaning back against the walls.

He wondered if he was witnessing some strange ritual being performed by a bizarre religious cult. He walked closer to one of the walls, crouched down in front of two nude men, and there was just enough light coming from the hanging lamp far behind him to enable Simon to see that they were gaping at him.

He shook one man's shoulder, and was surprised when the man fell over onto his side, then Simon stood back up while feeling sure that the marijuana he'd smoked, as well as the shadows being cast by the slowly swaying, hanging lamp were causing him to imagine everything he was seeing in that dark room.

Simon turned around, walked back to the partly open door, and stepped out into the hall. After closing the door, he looked down at the spot where he'd set down the unlit candelabra, and saw that it had disappeared, then he presumed that he'd set the candelabra down on the floor somewhere inside that dark room.

His heart seemed to be pounding in his throat and ears as he walked away down the hall, then after reaching the larger hall, he walked along it until he saw the open door to the wine cellar.

Simon entered the room and saw Wystan blowing out the candelabra on the tables as he held a bottle of wine with a blue label on it. He picked up both lit candelabrum he'd brought downstairs, and then turning to the door, he saw Simon.

"Oh, there you are. I thought you'd gone back upstairs."

"No, I went looking for you. Wystan! I saw something really strange! I saw a girl on a table back there, and two people were standing close to her, and they looked almost like shadows! Then I

saw them drinking wine out of big glasses that they'd filled from...Well, it looked like long, narrow tubes in her neck and her wrists! The girl was just lying there on the table and she was mumbling something while that was happening to her!"

"Are you sure you saw a girl lying on a table?"

"Yes! Honest! She's in a room down one of those halls!"

"*What* halls? There's only this one hall to the storage rooms."

"No, honest! There were at least five other halls and in one of them, there was a really big room with a table that the girl was lying on, and she was nude, too!"

"Nude? Hmmm, Simon," said Wystan, smiling.

"I'll show you!"

"All right, then. Lead on."

Simon began leading him down the hall, but he saw that it ended a short distance away from the wine cellar, and all the walls were solid stone, except where there were two other doors. He opened the doors, and saw that behind each one there was a very shallow storage closet.

"I...Well, I'm sure I saw that big room that the nude girl was in, and I also saw other nude people in there, too, and I'm sure some of them were dead. There were some live ones, too, and they were sitting on the floor, and leaning back against the walls, but I couldn't see them clearly because it was so dark."

"Uh-huh, I see. *More* people besides a naked girl. Simon, do you recall when you first smoked marijuana? The hallucination

you had? Obviously you're having one again, but you're much calmer this time."

"But it looked so...Well, yeah, when I thought I was in a dark room that you said doesn't exist, I thought what I was seeing might be another really strange hallucination I was having from smoking the marijuana. Sorry. I guess I'm still not used to smoking that stuff. I, uh...It really scared me in a way, but I feel much better now."

"Let's get you back upstairs. Now that you're starting to feel better, you'll begin feeling different sensations. Erotic ones."

"Oh, yeah, I remember that happens, too, when I've smoked that marijuana. Mmmmm, I love *those* sensations."

"I know, little satyr. As always," said Wystan as he laughed.

"We're so well-matched in that sense. You know, like having those erotic sensations from the marijuana. I'm glad I feel a lot better now, and I can see a lot better now, too, and I don't feel dizzy anymore, either."

"Good. I'm glad to hear that. Ah, here we are," said Wystan as they reached the basement steps. "I'll put this bottle in the dining room, and then meet you in the living room."

"All right," said Simon, smiling up at him.

CHAPTER
TWENTY-TWO

Simon walked into the living room and stared at the fireplace flames while thinking about that big, dimly lit room near the wine cellar in the basement where he'd apparently only imagined seeing a nude young woman lying on a table, and those dying men who had been sitting on the floor, and leaning back against the walls of that room.

He turned away from the fireplace, then after sitting on one of the three large, comfortable couches, he heaved a big sigh, and then glanced down at the low table in front of him, and saw a note, so, he picked it up and read: *"Dear gigglers, I've gone over to Mrs. Bolton's home for an hour. I made coffee for Laura, then showed her to the pool. I imagine she'll have left before I get back, or at least, I hope she has. If anyone else drops by while I'm away, then for goodness sake don't embarrass yourselves by giggling at the least little thing. Love you both. Behave. Bye, Morag."*

He smiled as he reread the note, and felt pleased that she'd said that she loved them both. Moments later, Wystan walked into the living room, holding two glasses of red wine, and he glanced at the note Simon was holding.

"What's *that* all about?"

"It's a note from Morag to let us know she's gone out for an hour, and she said that Laura dropped by, and after they had

coffee, Morag showed her out to the pool. Oh, and Morag also called us gigglers," said Simon as he grinned.

"Hah! Morag giggles far more often than we do, and not from being under the influence of marijuana, either."

"I love hearing her giggle."

"I'm surprised you do. Mmmm, very nice," said Wystan, tasting his wine. "Ah, wonderful palate with a heady bouquet. Oh, here's your wine."

"Thanks. Mmmmm, yeah, this wine's quite delicious, and it has a very nice aftertaste. By the way, Morag also wrote in her note that she hoped that Laura would be gone before she got back from her visit with a Mrs. Bolton, so, I suppose she and Laura don't get along and that Laura's more of a friend of yours."

"Not really. I'm sure what Morag really meant was that Laura had an invitation to dinner, with cocktails beforehand, and she hoped that Laura would have left here in plenty of time to arrive at the home of her hosts," said Wystan.

"Oh, then I misinterpreted the note."

"But then, Morag might be a bit miffed because about a week ago, Laura and I spent the entire evening alone in my rooms."

"You did? Um, were you working on the cathedral?"

"No, on something else. Try to guess. It's long and hard, and it gets very hot before it shoots off."

"Ohhhhhh, I get it," said Simon as he grinned.

"And that makes me exceedingly happy, little satyr."

"Laura's waiting for you at the pool, so, I'll go to the front of the house and watch for Morag returning from her visit. That'll give you time to be alone with Laura."

"No, please remain here in the living room, and I'll return shortly with Laura because I want her to meet you," said Wystan.

"I just thought that you might want to...Well, you know. Take her upstairs for a while and, uh, do fun things."

"Fun things? Oh, I understand, now. You think that perhaps I'd want to take Laura upstairs to show her the progress I've made on the toy rocket I started building the last time she was here. No, unfortunately, she wasn't interested in combustion-fired missiles, however, she was good enough to help me by drawing various facets of it, and their particular functions."

"Uh, she did drawings for you? You mean, you really *do* have a model of a rocket?" asked Simon.

"Of course. Why would you think I didn't have one?"

"Well, uh, I thought when you told me that it was long and hard, and it got very hot before it shot off, that you were talking about...Well, something else, entirely," said Simon, blushing.

"You did? I can't imagine what else would be shaped like that rocket. Oh, well, I'll be back momentarily with Laura. Incidentally, she's putting on a rather brave front right now because she's been recently widowed."

"Oh, I'm sorry to hear that."

"Yes, so tragic. She's holding up very well, but she must be torn apart inside," said Wystan.

"When did her husband die?"

"A few weeks ago. She was at the cottage at the time of his death, then upon returning to her home in the city, she was told that her mother-in-law had died at almost the same time."

"Oh, no. How awful. Had her mother-in-law been sick for a long time?"

"I don't know because Laura had never mentioned her at anytime, but I think her mother-in-law most likely died of shock when she was told about her son's death. Laura's never spoken much about her marriage, and because she's grieving over the loss of her husband, I certainly wouldn't want to ask her what caused her mother-in-law's death. Incidentally, I'd appreciate it if during Laura's brief visit, you didn't mention her tragic loss."

"Oh, of course, I understand, completely," said Simon.

"Thanks so much. Laura's a rather proper, conservative and very shy young lady, but she does have a charming sense of humor occasionally, and I suppose that's why she can muster up sweet smiles during this trying time for her. Please excuse me."

As Wystan walked away, Simon felt embarrassed for having assumed that Laura had been having sexual relations with Wystan in his bedroom, when she'd actually been working on drawings for the model of a rocket he was building.

He realized that because he'd been so sexually aroused lately, he was presuming there was a sexual connotation to almost anything anyone said.

He'd almost finished drinking his glass of wine when Wystan

returned with Laura, and Simon found her to be rather pretty. Wystan introduced them before he hurried away to fetch her a glass of wine, then on his return, he handed Laura the glass, and stood by the couch where she was seated.

Laura thanked Wystan for the wine, and then after they talked about the pleasant weather, she looked at Simon and smiled when Wystan said: "Simon's been visiting us recently, and we enjoy his company, immensely. He swims with Morag almost every day, and I was surprised when I first saw him at the pool because he's quite muscular, besides being very handsome."

"He *is* very handsome, indeed," said Laura, smiling.

"Uh, I...Well, thank you," Simon said as he blushed.

"Yes, and he told me that he exercises regularly with barbells, so, I'm sure he'll develop his body even more," Wystan told her.

"I certainly don't doubt that because I can tell by the way his clothes fit him that he commands quite a fine physique."

Simon's blush deepened as he smiled at her, then he was about to try changing the subject to draw attention away from himself, when he noticed the shocked expression on Wystan's face as he looked at Laura.

Simon looked at her, and then his eyes widened when he saw that he was now in a different room just as Laura opened a door, closed it, and began walking toward him.

She hadn't noticed him when she'd entered, nor while walking past him, so, Simon realized that he was having another realistic fantasy from the lingering effects of the marijuana.

He watched Laura walk across the large, elegant room to a staircase, then Simon followed her up the stairs, and along a corridor to an open door, and when she entered a large room, he saw a man seated at a desk, writing in a ledger.

The only light in the room was coming from the desk lamp in front of the man, and he had his back to the door, so, he wasn't aware that Laura had entered the room.

She remained in the shadows while taking off her shoes, and when she opened her long coat, Simon was surprised to see that Laura was nude, so, he assumed that she wanted to sexually excite the man.

He then realized that the man at the desk was her husband after Simon had glanced at one of the walls, and seen the framed photo of the man and Laura on their wedding day.

She stepped quickly to her left when her husband looked up from the ledger to look to his right for a moment, then he lowered his head again, and resumed writing.

Laura withdrew a boning knife from her large handbag, then Simon watched her creep up behind her husband, and then begin stabbing him repeatedly in the neck and back as spurts of blood shot up onto her face, shoulders, arms and breasts.

Her husband fell sideways off his chair, then Laura knocked over a few pieces of furniture before opening cabinet drawers, taking out items, and throwing them around the room.

She took off her husband's wristwatch and cufflinks, removed the billfold from the inside pocket of his suit jacket that he'd

draped over the back of his chair, then she wrapped those items in a handkerchief, and put them into her handbag.

Laura then hurried out of the room and Simon followed her along the hall, around a corner, and after walking to the end of another hall, she slowly opened a door to a large bedroom.

A woman whom Simon estimated to be sixty to sixty-five years old was reclining in bed, propped up by several pillows, and she'd fallen asleep with a book in her lap.

Simon watched Laura creep over to the side of the bed, then he winced when she began repeatedly plunging the boning knife into the older woman's neck and chest. He watched more blood splattering on Laura, then she hurried to a dressing table, and took two boxes of jewellery out of the top drawer before rushing out of the room, and then she returned to her husband's room.

As Simon watched her emptying the contents of the jewellery boxes into her large handbag, he realized that Laura wanted the police to think that her husband and her mother-in-law had been murdered during a robbery.

She then wrapped the boning knife in a silk scarf, and put it in her handbag before rushing out of the room. When she returned, Simon saw that she'd washed the blood off her face and body.

She folded the damp towel she'd used, shoved it down inside her now bulging handbag, and then after putting on her shoes, she looked into a mirror while smoothing out her hair.

Laura smiled while putting on her coat, then she hurried out of the room, and down the stairs, with Simon close behind her. The

downstairs area of Laura's home began rippling and fading until suddenly, Simon found himself standing beside Wystan in the bright, sunny living room, and looking at Laura as she sat on a couch, drinking wine and smiling at them.

"So, how often do you exercise, Simon?" she asked him.

"Huh?" he gasped.

Simon's thoughts tumbled in confusion as he hoped that they hadn't noticed that he might have been acting out of the ordinary.

"I asked you how often you exercised," said Laura.

"Oh, I, uh, you...Uh...Well, not as often as Wystan, obviously."

"He said you're quite muscular, so, I'm sure you look rather impressive in a bathing suit," she said while smiling.

"Um, I guess so," Simon said, feeling slightly uncomfortable.

"We should let you compare our bodies. Why not take off your shirt, Simon, and let Laura see your torso?" asked Wystan.

"Oh, I, um...I...." Simon stammered while blushing.

"I'm removing *my* shirt," said Wystan, then he began taking off his shirt as Laura and Simon watched.

Wystan laid his shirt over the back of an armchair, then smiled as he undid his trousers, let them drop to the floor, and then after stepping out of them, he leaned over, picked them up, and laid his trousers neatly beside his shirt.

"Simon? Come on, don't be so shy," said Wystan, smiling.

"Uh, I...Well, it's just that I..."

"Now you're embarrassing me because I've already undressed. I don't know why you're being so shy."

"I don't know, either," said Laura as she frowned. "Maybe he thinks there's something odd about our request."

"No, it's just that I...I was thinking about something and I didn't realize Wystan had already taken off his shirt and pants."

Simon certainly didn't want to appear naive by making it seem that there was something unusual about comparing physiques with Wystan, therefore, he took off his shirt and pants, then he smiled and stood beside Wystan as Laura looked at them.

"Oh, yes, now I see what you mean, Wystan. His physique is quite wonderful, indeed. Mmmm, yes, *and* he's very handsome."

"Yes, he certainly is."

"Awww, c'mon. I'm not really *that* good-looking," said Simon, blushing deeper.

"And modest, too. That's a rare trait in a person one would compare to a demigod," said Laura.

"Wystan's far better-looking than I am."

"No, you're just as handsome as him, but in a different way."

"Simon's genital endowment is quite impressive, too."

"Really? How *very* interesting," she said.

"Huh? Why did you tell her that?" Simon asked wide-eyed.

"Because she likes knowing everything a man has to offer."

"Yes, indeed. I find those...Well, *statistics* about a man, *particularly* interesting," Laura said with a slight smile.

"I'm sure his penis will be as big as mine in a year or so. Look at the size of mine now, and see how big Simon's is."

He gaped while watching Wystan take off his undershorts, and then Simon looked quickly back and forth from Wystan's hardening penis to Laura, whom was leaning forward to examine the growth of Wystan's penis.

When his penis had hardened completely, Wystan stood close in front of her, leaned over, and as he kissed her, he pushed her back in the couch and Laura started moaning while helping him take off her clothes. Simon realized that they wanted to be alone, so, he started walking out of the living room.

"He's leaving! I hope it wasn't something I said!" cried Laura.

"Where are you going?" Wystan asked him.

"For a walk until you're finished," replied Simon.

"I'd rather you stayed."

"Why? You and Laura are going to have..."

"Take off your underwear," interjected Wystan. "Simon? Why are you acting like that? And don't try telling me you're shy."

"No, of course I'm not shy. It's just that I don't want to do anything sexual with her because she's a...."

"Aw, stop that bullshit," said Wystan. "It's rare that you'd ever pass up a fuck unless you were bound hand and foot, and even then, you'd find some way not to miss out on any of the fucking action. Now lose the underwear and join the party."

"Hmmm, well, okay," said Simon.

He took off his underwear, tossed them across the room, and then he began stroking his penis while watching Laura caressing and licking Wystan's erection.

"Oh, my. Simon's erection *is* rather impressive. Mmmm, yes, nothing to ever be ashamed of," said Laura.

"Nothing at all," said Wystan, smiling.

"Uh, your erection's bigger than mine."

"Both of you lads've got equipment that'd be the envy of many a man in this world. Ohhh, Wystan. *Please* fuck me. *Please*. Oh, God, I want it so much. Oh, yes. Yes, yes, yes!"

Laura fell onto her back, lifted and spread her legs, then she began screaming and begging Wystan to start making love to her.

"Hey! Stop all that fucking noise!" shouted Wystan. "I like loud moans and groans from somebody I'm fucking, but hell! Your horrible, high-pitched shrieks cut through my brain like a jagged knife! It's so fucking irritating!"

"I'm sorry. Please forgive me. Oh! Oh, God! No, I'll try not to shout. Just fuck me. Fuck me now. Please."

"Hmmm, all right, but keep your hands over your mouth so that I don't have to listen to your awful screeching. Simon?"

"Yeah?"

"Don't ejaculate before things get interesting."

"No, I definitely won't do that."

"Good man. Now I'll fuck her for a little while, then you come over here and show her how well you fuck."

"What does *she* think about that?" asked Simon.

"She wants you to fuck her senseless. Don't you, Laura?"

"Yes! Both of you! Oh, God, yes!"

"Oooo, yeah, mmmmm, your cunt is surprisingly tight

considering that you're such an overly used slut. Mmmmnfff. Awwww, yeah, so fucking great."

"Uhhh-uh-uh! Mmmmm, oh, Wystan," she moaned.

"Simon?"

"Yeah?"

Wystan grinned as he withdrew from her, then he stood up, walked over to Simon, grabbed his arm, and led him to the couch, and Simon glared at him for a moment before he began having sex with Laura.

Simon scowled each time Laura told him to fuck her harder and deeper, and when he was close to orgasm, he quickly moved away from her, walked over to the other couch, sat down, and glowered at her as Wystan sat down beside her.

Wystan laid on his back, then Laura crawled on top of him, and after she very slowly lowered herself onto his erection, she started shouting out in her high-pitched, squeaky voice that she'd never been so sexually excited in her entire life.

Simon lifted her off Wystan's erection, then she cried out in shock when he raised her high in the air, then dropped her, and she fell onto her back on the couch, and then she grinned while looking up at him, waiting for him to make love to her again.

Laura mistakenly assumed that Simon was looking at her with intense sexual desire, however, he was really glaring at her while thinking about how much he hated her for killing her husband and her mother-in-law.

Simon then sat beside her as Laura smiled while watching

Wystan slowly masturbating as he stepped closer to her, then as he began bending his knees, Laura reached up and held his erection, and began masturbating Wystan while Simon licked and caressed her breasts and sucked on her nipples.

Wystan slid some of his erection into her mouth, then as Laura began fellating him, Simon sneered at her before turning his head so that he wouldn't have to look at any part of her.

He glanced down at the low table near the couch, then he frowned when he saw a small, rectangular object that he hadn't noticed before.

Simon become intrigued by the gleaming, navy blue metal object that was outlined by a thin, silver trim, and because it was approximately one and a half inches wide by about three inches long, and about an inch thick, he presumed it was an elegant cigarette case that held about six cigarettes.

He leaned forward, picked up the small, rectangular, navy blue case, then holding it in his left hand, he slid the tip of his right, index finger along the edge of silver-trimmed case to the tiny nub at the middle of it.

When he pressed that tiny, silver nub, the case sprung open, then Simon saw two stainless steel tubes that could be assembled into one, long, narrow syringe.

He admired the excellent craftsmanship of the two pieces that fit perfectly into the dark red velvet lining of the case, then after picking them up, he assembled the syringe.

Simon then picked up the navy blue metal case again, after

noticing another tiny silver nub on the side at one end of the case, then he pressed that other nub, and the inside bottom of the case sprung open.

He saw a long, narrow rubber tube wound to fit neatly inside the lower compartment of the case, then Simon lifted the tubing out of the case, and saw that there was a stainless steel tip at each end of the four-foot-long rubber tubing.

The insides of the steel tips were threaded, then he attached an end of the rubber tubing to the stainless steel syringe, and then after setting it down beside the open rectangular blue metal case, he was startled when both the case and the syringe vanished.

He gaped down at the spot where both the blue metal case and the stainless steel syringe had suddenly disappeared, then he turned his attention back to Wystan and Laura when she moaned and yawned, then moments later, she fell asleep.

When Laura awoke approximately twenty minutes later, she smiled while seeing Wystan and Simon smiling at her as they raised their glasses of wine and toasted her, then Wystan told her that she was an almost adequate lover.

After drinking their fifth glasses of wine, Simon picked up Laura, and began carrying her out of the room and he noticed that she was asleep and smiling.

Simon felt certain that this time he hadn't been hallucinating from the effects of the marijuana because the conversation and sexual acts with Laura had been quite realistic.

CHAPTER
TWENTY-THREE

Simon began opening his eyes, then he gasped when he saw that he was in the wine cellar, leaning back against the edge of the table, and holding a bottle of wine in his right hand.

Wystan then entered the room, and asked: "Did you find one of those blue-labeled bottles yet?"

"Huh?" asked Simon while staring wide-eyed at him.

"Never mind, I'll look for one. I started to walk down the hall, and saw the painting on the floor, leaning against the wall, then I remembered I'd set it there, earlier. Saves me searching high and low for it. Hmmm, now which rack are those bottles in? So many bottles here," said Wystan as he examined rows of dusty bottles.

Simon's thoughts whirled in confusion when he realized that he'd only imagined Laura, and that the sexual acts he'd participated in with her and Wystan were merely a figment of his overactive imagination.

He now understood that only brief moments had passed by since they'd come downstairs to the wine cellar, and then Wystan had gone down the hall to fetch a painting. Simon gaped at the bottle of wine he was holding in his hand, and he saw that it had a round, bright blue label on it. He was trembling as he held up the bottle while thinking about his most recent sexual hallucination.

"I...Uh...Wystan?"

"Yes? Oh, let me see that," then he walked over to Simon for a closer look at the bottle, and said: "Yes, this is the wine. Good man. Let's get back upstairs. Simon? Are you all right?"

"Hmmm? I...Oh, uh, yeah, I'm fine, thanks."

"Still have a problem seeing?" Wystan asked him.

Simon felt quite bewildered as he looked down at the bottle, then up at Wystan's smiling face.

"No, everything's fine. I'm all right."

"I'm sure you'll like this wine because it has a splendid bouquet as well as being quite delicious. I save it for very special occasions, and your visits are always one of those. I should've thought of this wine before, but it somehow slipped my mind."

"Um, you go on ahead, and I'll blow out the other candles."

"But aren't...Oh, well. Thanks, Simon. I'll meet you upstairs. I understand how erotic feelings flow hotly when you smoke marijuana, so, enjoy yourself," he said, then he winked and smiled at Simon before he started to leave the room.

"Wystan? I *am* going to...Oh, now I feel *so* embarrassed."

"Why feel embarrassed? After all, it's perfectly natural to masturbate when the urge strikes, so, enjoy yourself and I'll see you upstairs," Wystan told him as he grinned.

"Uh, okay."

Wystan left the wine cellar, then Simon realized he couldn't masturbate because Morag would wonder why he'd decided to stay in the basement, instead of coming back upstairs with Wystan.

He picked up his candelabrum and began walking to the

basement staircase, then he stopped when he saw two figures rushing across the hall. He felt sure that he'd just seen Morag and Laura turning the corner of the hall, and he thought that if it had indeed been Laura, then that meant she really existed.

He hurried after them, then after rounding a corner of the dark corridor, Simon saw that he was in the same area where he had looked into that dimly lit room and seen two, black-robed figures seated close to a nude young woman lying on a table.

He presumed that because it was so dark in the basement, Wystan hadn't noticed that there was another hall not far from the basement steps, and that at the end of that second hall was the room in which Simon had seen that strange bloodletting ritual.

He walked down the hall until he again saw a slight amount of light coming from the partly open door. His heart began pounding faster as he slowly opened the door a bit wider so that he could peer into the dimly lit room.

Simon was quite surprised when he saw Laura nude and lying on her back on the table, and Morag, also nude, standing beside it, and drinking a glass of red wine. He then knew that he really had met Laura, but he'd forgotten when and where he'd been introduced to her.

When Morag leaned over and began very slowly sliding the fingertips of her right hand up and down the left side of Laura's neck, then Simon decided it wouldn't be polite to watch them having a very intimate time together, so, he smiled as he turned around and began heading for the basement staircase.

He reached the top of the basement stairs, opened the door, and gaped when he saw Morag fully clothed and smiling at him as she exclaimed: "Oh! You startled me! I was just reaching for the doorknob when you opened the door. I was about to go downstairs to see what was taking you so long. Wystan should've gone with you, or he should've looked for that wine himself, but I don't know why you insisted on going alone. Oh, you brought up *two* bottles. Good idea."

Simon saw that he was now holding the necks of two bottles of wine in his right hand, which meant that he'd only imagined that Wystan had accompanied him downstairs to the wine cellar.

"I...Uh, I thought it was a good idea, too. I was so sure I saw you down...Uh, so, you look very pretty in that dress. I like your hairstyle, too."

"Why, thank you, Simon. When you didn't come back upstairs after almost ten minutes, I thought your candles had gone out, and you couldn't find your way back to this old basement staircase."

"I'm glad you didn't come downstairs because I...Uh, I was just looking at wine bottles."

"I rarely go down there because it's so smelly and dank, and the dust makes me cough. I'll give these to Wystan, and after he pours us a glass of this wine he calls his favorite, are you ready to lose at cards again?" asked Morag, then she giggled.

"Aw, we just let you win," replied Simon, grinning.

"A likely story, indeed," she said, smiling.

As he walked back to the living room with her, Simon was

astonished by the astounding effects that the marijuana induced.

A few minutes later, Wystan entered the living room, carrying a small, round tray with three glasses of wine on it, and he smiled as he served them, then asked Simon: "Did you have a difficult time finding the wine cellar?"

"No, I didn't. It wasn't far from the basement staircase."

"I still think *you* should have gone instead of Simon. He could've tripped on the stairs because it's so dark down there."

"Never argue with a guest. Policy," Wystan told her, smiling.

"Mmmmm, this tastes so wonderful," said Simon.

"Thanks. I'd hoped you'd like it. Let's have a toast. To a warm, wonderful, and close friendship," said Wystan, then he raised his glass and grinned at Simon and Morag.

"Yes. To the three of us," said Morag as she raised her glass.

"Here's to you and Wystan with much thanks to both of you."

They sipped their wine, laughed and talked, then Morag suggested that they begin playing cards.

"Did you enjoy your visit with your friend?" asked Simon.

"Visit? With whom?" Morag asked him.

"You went to visit a friend. A Mrs. Bolton, I believe."

"I don't know anyone called Mrs. Bolton."

"Oh, sorry, my mistake," said Simon, blushing.

He felt embarrassed because he'd only imagined the note Morag had left, in which she'd written about Laura whom had been part of his fantasy, or perhaps his hallucination.

"Not to worry, Simon," said Morag, smiling. "It's happened to

me before, too. You know, mixing up one friend with another one. By the way, after I went upstairs to have a bath, then read for an hour or so while you and Wystan napped, I hope you slept well."

"Yeah, I *did,*and I had some very nice dreams," said Simon.

"I'm glad you did, instead of having another bad reaction to the marijuana you smoked with Wystan."

"I made sure he'd sleep comfortably because we only smoked one marijuana cigarette," Wystan told her.

"Good, because it causes people to giggle at nothing, and often lose their concentration on what they're doing, so, if we bet money on the card games, I'd be a multimillionaire in two or three days if you two got any giddier," she said, smiling.

"Naw, you'd be a pauper. Right, Wystan?"

"Most definitely," he replied with a grin.

They played cards while listening to music on the radio until they agreed that it was time to go to bed. They went upstairs, then Simon said goodnight to them before entering his bedroom.

After undressing, he put on a robe and went to the bathroom to draw a bath, then just over half an hour later, he returned to his room, and got into bed feeling pleasantly tired, and then he drifted off to sleep.

CHAPTER
TWENTY-FOUR

Simon awoke during the night when he heard a rapidly patting sound, then after sitting up in bed, he saw a white bird fluttering its wings as it hovered outside his window for a few seconds before it alit on the sill.

He smiled as he walked over to the window to look at the white bird, then it suddenly flew away and he watched it slowly flying toward the horizon to his left.

Simon looked at the moon close to the horizon, and he felt certain that it was slowly rising. He watched it rising higher in a great arc across the sky, then it slowly sank behind the horizon to his right. The horizon shimmered with silver and pink light for a moment before suddenly flickering with brilliant gold light, startling him, and making him wince.

He blinked a few times, and saw that it was very dark out, then he looked up at the full moon that was directly above him. Bright moonlight lit his room as Simon began walking back to his bed, then he stopped when his room was suddenly cast into darkness.

He went back over to the window and frowned when he saw the moon was again low to the horizon to his left. Simon stared mesmerized, as the moon repeated the same arcing route it had taken before, then after it sank out of sight, he saw the horizon on the right side of the landscape brighten, and then flash again.

He looked up at the full moon that was again directly above him, then he looked down and it was suddenly daylight again, and he was sitting at the dining room table, looking at his father folding the newspaper, then suddenly throwing it across the dining room before scowling and saying: "Ken told me you stole some coins from his coin collection, and that you spent them."

"That's a lie!" Simon shouted at his elder brother, then the lights on the horizon flashed again and he was standing outside the amusement park near the train station. His mother opened her change purse, gave him a dollar and told him not to wander away from the park while she was at the bank for about an hour.

Simon looked to his left and watched the sun rising, then moments later, he, Colin and Jennifer were on horseback at the top of a hill as they agreed to take separate routes through the forest.

Suddenly, he was far from the top of the hill, waving at Jennifer and Colin, then after they waved back at him, they began riding into the trees at the same time Simon began riding his horse into the trees to follow the stream.

The sun plunged beyond the horizon, and Simon looked up at the moon while realizing that his game was ending. He heaved a big sigh, turned away from the window, got back into bed, and then hugging his pillow, he fell back asleep.

CHAPTER
TWENTY-FIVE

He awoke in the morning, feeling well-rested, then Simon put on his robe and walked to the bathroom. He lolled in the soapy water, recalling the erotic hallucination of Laura nude and sexually aroused while letting both him and Wystan have sex with her.

He then realized that if he lolled in the bathtub much longer, he'd miss having breakfast with Morag and Wystan, so, he got out of the tub, dried off while the tub was draining, and then he hurried back to his room to dress.

He entered the dining room and when he saw Morag looking so beautiful, he hoped to have another realistic, marijuana-induced fantasy of making love to her.

"Good morning, Morag," said Simon, smiling.

"Oh, good morning. Did you sleep well?"

"Yes, I did, thanks. And you?"

"As if I'd been lying on a big, soft cloud."

"That sounds very nice. Is Wystan up, yet?"

"Yes, he's out talking to Blaze. Wystan's been taking care of him while you were sleeping, and he took him for a walk, earlier. He probably rode him for a while, too."

"Blaze must've liked that," said Simon.

"I'm sure he *did*. Oh, and about twenty minutes ago, Wystan made you some coffee."

"That was very nice of him. I'll get it."

"He also baked fresh, blueberry muffins for you, and he'll be in shortly to prepare breakfast," Morag told him as she smiled.

"This is like staying at a posh hotel with a gourmet chef preparing every delicious meal. Wystan sure has so much energy in the mornings."

"He has so much energy all day long. I'm the lazy type. I love lounging about and ringing a bell to have my servant wait on my every need. Why not have one of those blueberry muffins with your coffee while we're waiting for our breakfast? They're in the oven with a tray of bacon."

"Mmmm, I will. Thank you."

Simon took a muffin from the oven, poured a coffee, added cream and sugar, then walked back to sit at the table with her.

"He makes such good coffee. Muffins, too," said Simon.

"As a chef, he's flawless. Absolute perfection. It may take me many more years than I'd originally thought to reach the point where I can cook just a few of the scrumptious meals that he can prepare with what seems to be a simple wave of his hand. Oh, well, onward I struggle. Hmmm, it looks like it may rain today, and if it does, we'll find something to do inside."

"If it *does* rain, I'll put Blaze in the stable."

"Wystan's still building that model of a cathedral out of little sticks, so, we could help him with it while it's raining."

"Oh, right, he told me about it. Sure, I'd like doing that."

"It's in the room adjoining his bedroom, and that room has

many windows in it, but if it becomes too dark outside because of heavy clouds, there's many lamps in the room that we can turn on. I hope it doesn't rain for long, though."

"It usually doesn't at this time of year."

"Oh, here he comes now," said Morag, waving at Wystan.

"Hi, Simon! Sleep well?" Wystan asked him, smiling.

"Yes, thanks. Did *you*?"

"Like a well-fed, contented baby. I see you have a coffee. Good. I'll start breakfast."

"Is there something I can do to help? I'd like to," said Simon.

"All right," said Wystan. "You can prepare eggs the way you'd like them while I take care of the fish. Thanks."

"Good idea. You two go toil in the kitchen, and I'll sit here and look through this magazine," said Morag.

"Fine. Shout if you want tea," Wystan told her.

They were just finishing breakfast when the room darkened, then a flash of lightning preceded a very loud clap of thunder, and that was followed by deep rumbling that seemed to almost vibrate through the house as the thunder abated.

"Wow! It's going to be really big storm!" exclaimed Simon.

"Yes, I'm sure it will be. It was getting very dark in the west before I came in, so, I took Blaze to the stable," said Wystan.

"Oh, thanks. That was very nice of you. Wow! Another one! *That* bolt of lightning was as bright as the last one. Really loud

thunder, too. We won't be going outside for a while today by the looks of that pending storm," said Simon.

They sat at the table, sipping on their hot beverages, and looking across the room at the windows whenever there was another huge bolt of lightning, and then a crash of thunder.

"During times like these, when people are stuck inside the house, they sometimes work on a big jigsaw puzzle, or some project or other. Oh, and speaking of projects, Morag told me you're still working on that model of a cathedral, so, I bet it's very intricate and really big, too," said Simon.

"Yes, it's quite large," Wystan told him. "If this storm doesn't pass for another hour or two, we could all work on it together."

"I'd really like that."

"I'll cut the sticks to the length you ask for," said Morag.

"Everyone seems eager, so, we'll start after I make another pot of tea. I'll make fresh coffee for you, Simon."

"No, please don't bother. I'll have tea with you."

"And we'll have some of those biscuits you brought me. I'll be careful not to get chocolate on the little sticks," said Morag.

"I certainly hope you won't, so, sit in the bathtub to cut them. Either that, or I'll keep a bucket of water handy to pour over you when your fingers get sticky," said Wystan, smiling.

"Oh, yeah? Then if you do that, I'll push you in the pool with all your clothes on," Morag told him, then she giggled.

"Hmmm, brat. Go upstairs and start cutting wooden sticks to the same length as the ones I have on the yellow sheet of paper on

the table by the window. Please? Oh, and there's a small bundle of sticks on that table. too."

"All right. When are you and Simon coming up?"

"Whenever the tea is ready and I've put some biscuits on a plate. Would you mind helping me, Simon?"

"No, not at all. I'll gather the breakfast dishes and bring them to the kitchen, and I'll wash them, too."

"Oh, just leave them for the maid."

"You have a maid?" asked Simon.

"Morag," replied Wystan, grinning.

"I scrub the floors, too. Tra-la!" cried Morag, hurrying away.

"I'll give you a hand with those dishes, Simon," said Wystan.

Simon was impressed by Wystan's model of a cathedral, and he enjoyed spending the next few hours helping to work on it as Morag busied herself with the very thin wooden sticks, cutting them to the size Wystan requested.

Wystan prepared lunch, then as they were dining, the sun began to shine, and within an hour, it became very warm outside.

"Suntan time!" cried Morag.

"You'll soon look African," said Wystan.

"That'll be fun. I'm going to the stable to bring Blaze out. Are you coming with me, Simon?"

"I'll meet up with you in about ten minutes," he replied. "I want to clear the table. Oh, and thanks for taking care of Blaze."

"I love doing that," said Morag. "Tra-la!"

She hurried to the stable as Simon helped cleare the dining room table while hoping that Wystan would want to smoke some marijuana with him.

They carried the lunch dishes into the kitchen, and Wystan filled the sink as he told Simon to let the dishes soak until later in the day.

"It's getting rather warm out, so, I think I'll make up a big pitcher of lemonade," said Wystan.

"Are you coming out to the patio?"

"Hmmm, perhaps later. How do you feel?"

"Just fine, thanks," replied Simon. "I'm a little thirsty, so, I'll have some lemonade when it's ready."

"Oh? Why not have a glass of the wine that you were good enough to bring up from the cellar for me?"

"I really liked it, so, sure, thanks," said Simon, smiling.

"I'll have a glass of it, too. Get down two glasses from the cupboard, please. No, that one to your left. Thanks."

Wystan poured the wine, clicked Simon's glass, and then they sipped on the wine as Wystan cut lemons for the lemonade.

"This is very nice wine. I feel rather honored that you wanted to share your favorite wine with me," said Simon.

"Hmmm? Oh, yes. I'm pleased you like it as much as I do. Pour me another would you, please?"

"Sure."

"Thanks. Let's have a toast. To another wonderful day."

"Yes, and to you, and Morag, too," said Simon.

"You know, marijuana goes very well with this. Feel like sharing a cigarette with me?" asked Wystan, smiling.

"Sure, I'd love to. Thanks."

He lit a marijuana cigarette, and handed it to Simon who inhaled the smoke deeply before passing the cigarette back to him. They talked as they smoked and drank wine, and Wystan refilled their glasses each time they were empty.

Simon's spirits lifted higher as he felt the effects of the marijuana slipping through his system, although by the time they'd drank most of the wine, he was feeling drowsy.

When Wystan noticed him yawning and often trying to keep his eyes open, he suggested he have a nap for an hour. Simon agreed with him, and walked slowly upstairs, laid on the bed, and fell asleep.

CHAPTER
TWENTY-SIX

Simon dreamed that he was sharing a marijuana cigarette with Wystan while they watched Morag lying on a bed, nude and masturbating as she urged them to have sex with her.

He slowly awoke when Wystan nudged him gently, then Simon smiled up at him before sitting up in bed.

"Good nap?"

"Yeah, I feel great now," replied Simon, smiling.

"I came upstairs to tell you that dinner is ready."

"Really? I slept that long?"

"Uh-huh. I'll meet you downstairs."

After Wystan left the room, Simon went to the bathroom, and as he splashed water on his face, he felt surprised at having slept for so long. He left the bathroom, and went downstairs and saw Morag and Wystan sitting at the dining room table.

"I slept right through the afternoon," said Simon.

"It was the combination of the marijuana and wine. Morag, would you pour the wine, please?"

"Certainly. You still look slightly tired, Simon."

"Yeah, I feel a bit groggy, but I'm very hungry."

"Oh? Then you'll most likely enjoy the dinner I've prepared. Stuffed roast pork, oven browned potatoes with asparagus and fresh mixed vegetables," Wystan told him.

"Mmmmm, that sounds absolutely wonderful. You always cook something I love," said Simon.

Morag poured wine for Simon, handed him the glass, then she smiled and winked at him.

"Thanks, Morag. Mmmmm, this is the same wine. I don't want you to use up all your favorite wine on me."

"Not to worry. There are many bottles down in the wine cellar. At least another four dozen, so, it'll take us quite some time to go through all that," said Wystan, smiling.

After dinner, Morag and Simon sat on a couch, drinking coffee while listening to Wystan play the piano. Simon was surprised at both his talent and the beautiful music Wystan chose to play.

Morag put her finger to her lips as she got up slowly and tiptoed out of the room, then she returned a few minutes later carrying a small, round tray with three glasses of liqueur on it.

Wystan continued playing music, changing to a jazz piece, then back to classical, and then half an hour later, Simon felt tired again. He laid his head back on the couch, and Wystan smiled as he glanced over at Simon trying to stay awake.

Morag got up off the couch, then after sitting beside Wystan, she started playing the piano as he stopped. Wystan walked over to the couch, and saw that Simon was sound asleep, so, he picked him up and carried him upstairs. He laid Simon down on the bed, covered him with a light blanket, and left the room.

Simon opened his eyes immediately after Wystan closed the door, then he got off the bed, walked over to the door, and opened it before he started to get undressed.

He hummed as he laid out the clothes he had selected while listening to faint sounds from the piano that Morag was playing downstairs, and then he walked slowly across the room and stood in front of the full-length mirror.

He grinned as he looked at his erection while thinking about how sexually aroused he felt almost all day long, every day, then he turned away from the mirror and walked over to the window, and looked out at the gardens below as he waited for Wystan to finish his bath.

He turned away from the window when Wystan opened the door, then much later, he grinned as he started to leave the room. Simon yawned, turned over in bed, and after heaving a sigh, he dismissed his recent, very erotic illusion, then fell asleep.

CHAPTER
TWENTY-SEVEN

Simon awoke in the morning, and squinted because of the bright sunlight. He felt so disappointed at having slept for almost the entire day before, and now he had to leave for home.

He had wanted to be awake for most of his visit so that he could enjoy Morag and Wystan's company, but he had either slept or experienced quite erotic, marijuana-induced hallucinations that had seemed to last for hours each time.

He walked down the hall to the bathroom, and after entering it, he saw Wystan turning off the taps of the bathtub.

"Good morning," said Wystan, smiling.

"Good morning. I'll take a bath after you have yours."

"I already had one. This is for you."

"Oh? Great. Thanks a lot. It was very nice of you to do this."

"I'm planning an early dinner. Four o'clock, so you can dine with us before returning home. All right? Oh, and Morag wants to speak to you after you have your bath. She's in her room."

"Sure, okay," said Simon as he removed his robe.

"I'll see you later. Enjoy your bath."

"Thanks, I will," said Simon while stepping into the tub, then his smile broadened as he lowered himself down into the water, and then as he slowly bathed, he wondered what Morag wanted to talk to him about.

Just as he was getting out of the tub, the door opened and Wystan entered. He held out a bath towel for him, and after Simon had dried off, Wystan helped him put on his robe, then asked Simon to accompany him to Morag's bedroom.

Simon looked up at him and frowned when they stopped outside her door.

"She didn't tell you what she wanted to talk to me about?"

"Yes, she did. She accepted an invitation to visit with some friends for a couple of weeks."

"Oh? I'm going to miss her," said Simon.

"I gathered that because you've become very good friends, but please don't let her absence keep you from visiting. You're always welcome here," Wystan said as he smiled.

"Thanks. I like you just as much as I like her."

"Well, go in and have a chat with her, and I'll go downstairs and make a pot of coffee for you."

"Thanks, Wystan."

Simon watched him walk to the staircase, then he opened Morag's bedroom door and saw that she was still in her dressing robe as she sat at a desk, painting a scene of the garden.

"Good morning, Morag."

"Good morning."

"Wystan told me you were leaving for two weeks."

"Yes. Please sit down."

He sat in an armchair as Morag rinsed out her paintbrush in a jar of water before she stood up and walked over to the floor-to-

ceiling windows of her bedroom. Simon sensed that it was best for her to begin speaking, so, he sat watching her as she stood looking out the window.

Morag stood at the window, looking down at the gardens, as she said: "I've really liked the fun we've been having recently."

"I really like it, too," said Simon.

She slowly turned around and smiled at him, then she began unfastening her robe while saying: "We've had fun, but I'd like a little more attention."

"More attention?" asked Simon.

"Yes. Don't you think I deserve it?"

"But we've been together so much lately."

"*Here*, yes, but I'm never included when you and Wystan go out carousing at night, then after you wake up, you start joking with each other almost all day," said Morag.

"What gave you that idea? Most of the time I've been getting tired early, then going up to bed for the night. Maybe Wystan's been staying out 'til late every night, but *I* haven't."

"Oh, stop joking!"

"Okay, I'll try. Now what's on your mind?"

"I've been hoping to get a rather nice thank you from you before I leave tomorrow morning. I'm going out soon and I'm sure I won't see you when I get back, so, now is the ideal time for you to thank me by fucking me," she said while opening her robe to display her nudity, then she said: "I want to make love with only you for a change."

"What do you mean? Hmmm, this must be another dream."

"Damn it! You know you're not dreaming this!"

"Well, I...Oh, all right."

Simon slowly stood up and grinned while removing his robe, then after walking to the bed, he held out his hand to her, and then he suddenly fell over onto his back after Morag had run to him, and thrown herself on him while shouting in excitement.

Over an hour later, he lay on his back, panting heavily while Morag licked and sucked on his testicles. She got off the bed, put on her robe, and left the room, after telling him that she was going to have a bath.

Simon got off the bed, put on his robe, left the room, and began walking slowly downstairs, then after reaching the bottom of the long staircase, Wystan appeared, and winked and grinned before leading him through to the living room, and then he sat beside him on one of the couches.

"Did you leave her panting and begging for more, as usual?"

"Huh? You know I had sex with her?" asked Simon.

"I knew she wanted more than just a little chat with you."

"Oh, uh, yeah, she did."

"You yawned, which means you didn't get enough sleep last night, so, I'll bring you a glass of wine, then after you drink it, go back upstairs and have a nap."

"I can't believe that Morag really let me have sex with her, so, I know I'm dreaming all this," said Simon. "Everything. Like the sex with her, and sitting here talking with you."

"*Are* you dreaming? You've been telling me that you can't tell whether you are or not."

"Not this time. I'm sure I'm having another one of those sexual fantasies from smoking marijuana."

"Oh? Maybe it *was* real and not a fantasy. Let me know when you decide what it really was," said Wystan, with a crooked smile.

Wystan left, and returned with a glass of wine for him, which Simon drank, then he held out the empty glass for Wystan to refill, and then after drinking half of it, he grinned.

Wystan then held out his hand to him, and Simon, feeling lightheaded, gripped it as he got up off the couch.

"I've got things to do, so, go back to bed for a while."

"Mmmmm, yeah, okay," said Simon. "I'm always having so many erotic dreams recently."

"You certainly love those dreams."

"Yeah, they're...Well, they're almost beyond description. But then, you should know that because you're a major part of them."

"Gee, thanks. I greatly enjoy being a part of anyone's sexual fantasies. Now off you go to dream some more."

"Yeah, okay. See you later."

-✖-

CHAPTER
TWENTY-EIGHT

He awoke feeling refreshed, then Simon went downstairs, smiling while recalling the sexual fantasy he'd had of Morag.

"Hi, Wystan," said Simon as he smiled.

"How was your nap?"

"Wonderful, thanks."

"Good. I'm pleased you slept well," said Wystan.

"I planned to leave for home in half an hour, so, it's a good thing I woke up when I did."

"Yes, I suppose so. Oh, and you won't be able to say goodbye to Morag because while you were having a nap, Mr. Bolton dropped by to ask her if she'd take care of their two young children for the afternoon because his wife had her baby sometime around seven this morning."

"Oh, I see. That's great news about the baby," said Simon.

"You can well imagine the excitement in the Bolton home."

"Yeah, I sure can, and it's lucky that the baby wasn't born yesterday if they're at all superstitious because there's that old rhyme about Saturday's child works hard for a living, but a child born on a Sabbath day, is bonny and blithe, and good and gay."

"Yes, a few hours earlier, and it would've been a Saturday baby, unless of course, a child happened to be Jewish, then his Sabbath would be Saturday, so, I guess that'd mean he *wouldn't*

have to work hard for a living," said Wystan, smiling.

"I never thought about that, but I guess you're right."

"I sincerely hope that the Bolton baby will be healthy and happy even if it wasn't born on a Sunday. So, when will we see you again, Simon? Can you make it for lunch on Tuesday?"

"Sure, thanks, I'd really like that."

"Good. I'll look forward to seeing you, then. Have you time for a glass of wine?"

"Yes, thank you. Oh, but first, I'll get Blaze ready."

"I've already taken care of that for you," said Wystan.

"It seems I'm always thanking you. It's a very nice day. What are your plans for the rest of the afternoon?"

"I'm going into the village, then on my way back, I'll drop in to see how Morag is coping with the Bolton children."

"I'm sure she has them under control," said Simon, laughing.

"Yes, she can be quite the little mother when she wants to be, can't she? Oh, and knowing what a long ride it is to your home, may I suggest something to keep you amused and your thoughts occupied on the way?"

"Such as?" asked Simon, smiling.

"Such as sharing a marijuana cigarette with me while we're drinking wine."

"Ah, that'd be perfect," said Simon, then they both laughed.

"I knew you'd agree to that. Here we are, one glass of wine for the gentleman, and...Oh, what's this in my shirt pocket? Hmmm,

why, it's a cigarette," Wystan said, grinning, then he lit it, and passed it to Simon.

"Now I know I'll enjoy my ride home."

"I'll bet you won't be aware of that ride, considering the erotic fantasies you have when you smoke marijuana."

"Smoking this stuff *does* give me very hot fantasies. You told me it often has the same effect on you."

"Yes, it does, and I'm certain my fantasies are just as erotic as yours. Hmmm, speaking of those effects makes me recall a few sensational images of my fantasies."

"I keep recalling many of mine, and so often, too, because they're so realistic and slightly unusual."

"Oh? How so?" asked Wystan, then he laughed.

"They involve almost anything and everything."

"Not unlike mine. Some would shock you, I'm sure, because they often involve more than one person, and it doesn't matter who they are as long as I find them very, very attractive and very willing to have sex with me. In a fantasy, you don't have to have any inhibitions, therefore, you can do so many exciting things that'd shock the rest of society," said Wystan, smiling.

"Yeah, I know, because I've had fantasies that included both women and...And, uh, well, they're extremely erotic."

"Simon, I know what you were about to say. Both women and men, right? They're just fantasies in your, and nothing's wrong with that because no one ever knows the depths of their thoughts. I've often had fantasies about making love with both genders, and

I simply give in to the pleasure of them. No one can control where their imagination might take them, so, I'd advise you to discard your socially conditioned guilt and inhibitions and just enjoy every erotic dream you have. Okay? Incidentally, if by chance I happened to be in one of your sexual fantasies, then I do hope I was a great lover," he said, then he winked at him.

Simon grinned and said: "Yes, and you *were* a great lover."

"Wonderful! I'm so relieved!" exclaimed Wystan, laughing.

"So am I because I thought you would've been shocked to know that you were in some of my sex fantasies."

Wystan passed the cigarette back to him, then he grinned and said: "Next time you have a fantasy with me in it, then tell me all the details because I'm quite certain that they'll be fodder for *my* erotic fantasies. In fact, I insist that on your next visit, you tell me every detail of *all* your past fantasies where I've been a participant. Hmmm, I do hope you fellated me in your sex fantasies because I rather enjoy that."

"So do I, and, uh, yeah, I *did*." Simon blushed as he laughed.

"Good! Then I *must* have enjoyed your fantasy!"

Simon then felt free to tell him anything he wanted to, and he decided that he would indeed relate a few of his erotic fantasies to him sometime during his next visit.

He picked up his backpack as he said: "Thanks so much for your fine hospitality. You're a wonderful cook, too."

"*And* lover, apparently," said Wystan, smiling.

"I'm relieved that I haven't shocked you."

"Oh, nonsense. I'll tell you a few of *my* fantasies on your next visit, and then *I* may shock *you*. To be honest with you, I did have two or three fantasies of us involved in a rather raunchy orgy."

"You did? Then my next visit should prove quite revealing. We'll compare notes on sexual positions," said Simon, grinning.

"It'll be fun. No inhibitions in our conversation. I'll walk you to the stream, and then...Oh, just a moment, I'll be right back."

Wystan hurried away and returned carrying a leather bag with long straps.

"I packed you a lunch with a few bottles of soft drinks."

"Oh, thanks. Wystan, you're super."

"And there are apples in there, so, Blaze will have a treat."

"Thanks again. I'll definitely come to lunch on Tuesday."

"Very good. I'll prepare a very nice lunch for us on your return, and we can have it on the patio."

"You treat me like royalty," said Simon, then he laughed.

"Hmmm, when you think about it, I suppose we *are* royalty."

Wystan accompanied him to the road, then Simon waved goodbye to him as he rode off.

He smiled at people he passed on the road while he thought about the wonderful visit he'd had with Morag and Wystan. Slightly over an hour later, Simon led Blaze off the road, then he dismounted, sat on a grassy incline overlooking the road, and opened the leather pouch that Wystan had packed for him.

He was pleased to find sandwiches made of thickly sliced chicken on buttered bread, with a delicious sauce, and Wystan had also wrapped four large cookies, a slice of cake, and an assortment of fresh fruit wrapped in waxed paper.

Simon reclined, propped up on one elbow, eating a sandwich and looking at the road, smiling and nodding at passersby. His thoughts swept back to the conversation he'd had with Wystan just before he'd set out for home. Simon felt pleasantly relieved that he had been able to tell Wystan that he'd had sexual fantasies that had included him.

He eagerly looked forward to his next visit when they would discuss their fantasies, and then Simon wondered if sometime in the future, he'd really become sexually intimate with both Morag and Wystan.

He knew that he could tell his mother and stepfather about his sex fantasies, but definitely not his friends because bisexuality and particularly homosexuality were held in contempt by the majority of the society he lived in.

Wystan, however, had told him that he wouldn't be shocked or disgusted by stories of sexual variations, and that made Simon feel greatly relieved to know he could confide his innermost sexual thoughts to Wystan, and still be accepted as a close friend.

He fed an apple to Blaze, then laid on the grass, looking up at the clouds while luxuriating in the effects of the marijuana. He felt certain that after he smoked more marijuana with Wystan, he wouldn't experience any more strange hallucinations, however, he

knew from what Wystan had confided in him, that his highly pleasurable sexual fantasies would continue.

He got back on Blaze, and then as he rode home, he concentrated on his past erotic dreams. Simon led Blaze into the stable, then after entering the house, he saw a note from his mother on the kitchen table.

He read that she and Noel had gone into town to shop for groceries, so, he went upstairs to his bedroom, laid on his bed, and smiled as he thought about his visit with Morag and Wystan until he fell asleep.

PART FIVE

Simon's Jubilee Game Ends

CHAPTER
TWENTY-NINE

He awoke from his nap, then just after he walked over to the window, Simon saw the car driving up to the house, so, he went downstairs to greet his mother and stepfather.

"Hi, I'm home!" exclaimed Simon.

"So I see," said Miranda, smiling.

"Where's dad?"

"He went over to Mr. Blake's."

"I'll help you put away the groceries."

"Thanks, honey. Oh, and Simon? Take those things on the table with you when you leave. I packed some fruit and a box of assorted fancy biscuits as a gift for them."

"Again? Thanks, mom. You always wrap things so nice. Morag loves those biscuits," said Simon, looking at the parcels.

"Did you pack your toothbrush?"

"Yes, I told you I did," he replied, smiling.

"It was nice of them to invite you to visit for a few days, and I'm sure you'll have a wonderful time. I thought you'd be gone before we got back, so, you'd better get on your way, dear, and I suppose you'll be back home sometime Sunday evening."

"Huh? What do you mean?"

"Well, you *did* say you were staying with them for a few days, so, I presumed you'd be back home Sunday evening, but if you're staying over another night, then I suppose we won't be seeing you 'til sometime Monday. Right? I know Morag will love the watercolor paints and brushes you'll be giving to her, and I'm sure Wystan will like whatever magazines you decide to buy for him. Oh, and don't bother going over to Mr. Blake's because Noel's driving him to the garage in town to get that new part he ordered for his car."

"I don't understand," said Simon, as his thoughts swirled.

"Neither do I. I know very little about what makes a car run. That car part was supposed to be in by last Saturday, and here it is Thursday. It's a wonder that car is running as well as it is. He's lucky it hasn't gone kaput. Oh, well, as long as he can keep replacing parts for it, I suppose it could last him another five or ten years. You know, Simon, for someone who was so excited and impatient about going off for a three-day visit with your friends, you're certainly taking your time about it."

"I, uh...I'm...I..."

"I'll bet you've checked everything at least five times, so, I'm sure you haven't forgotten anything. Now you get on your way because you don't want to keep a lady waiting. Besides, you've got to stop in town to buy gifts for them," said Miranda, smiling.

"Today is Thursday?" asked Simon.

"It *has* been all day. What's gotten into you?"

"I don't know. Um, sorry."

"So? Off you go."

"Huh? Oh, sure. Um, I'm going. Right now."

Simon felt confused as he kissed her cheek, then Miranda picked up the box of assorted biscuits that she'd wrapped in very nice, colored paper, and then put ribbons and a bow on it.

She smiled while handing the gift to him while Simon's heart was pounding faster as he turned to walk out the door.

He walked slowly down the porch steps and over to the stables, and then with his thoughts whirling, Simon held onto the saddle while leaning against his horse.

He'd left home on Thursday to visit Morag and Wystan for three days, but now he was at home on the same day that he had left. Simon knew that he couldn't tell his mother that he'd already visited Wystan and Morag because he wouldn't be able to explain how the days had shifted forward, and then back to this time.

He rode slowly away from the stables, looked over at the house, and waved at his mother as he headed for the road. He felt his fingers and toes tingling as he rode along the road, then he began feeling thirsty.

He reached into the leather bag that Wystan had given to him, withdrew a soft drink bottle, unscrewed the cap, and drank almost the entire bottle at once.

Moments later, Simon pictured Wystan standing by the stream, grinning and waving to him. Morag appeared, standing by the

opening to the garden, smiling and waving at him before she picked up a suitcase and began fading as she walked away.

Simon looked back to wave at his mother again, but because he'd started riding his horse around the bend in the road, he couldn't see his home anymore.

He looked back at the road ahead of him, and it was becoming blurred at the same time everything around him began shimmering and changing shape.

He then saw that he was riding over the stone bridge and he could see a small part of the roof of Wystan's summer home above the trees.

Simon turned off the road near the old, cobblestone pathway that was almost hidden amidst huge bushes and trees at the front of Wystan's property, then he dismounted, leaned his bicycle against a tree, and began walking along the pathway at the side of the house to the back gardens.

He laughed when he started thinking about how his jubilee game had been telepathically manipulated a few times, but now he planned to confuse that prankster by pretending he was still deep in his jubilee game.

When he reached the flowered arbor that was the entrance to the back garden, he saw Wystan sitting in a deck chair, shaded by a big sun umbrella as he read a magazine and occasionally took a drink of lemonade from the tall glass he held in his right hand.

Simon suppressed a grin as he slowly walked over to him, then Wystan looked up from the magazine, and smiled as he said: "Hi. Did you enjoy your bike ride?"

"Bike? No, I rode here on Blaze, like I always do."

"Oh? Oh, of course. Your horse and not your bicycle."

"It sure is another great day, isn't it? Sunny and with refreshing breezes. I left Blaze by the stream so that he could have a drink of cool water whenever he feels like it, and I never have to worry about him wandering off somewhere," said Simon as he smiled.

"Hmmm, yes, I've noticed that."

Wystan tried to read Simon's thoughts, however, they were being blocked because Simon was concentrating very hard on one of his favorite memories.

He felt sure that Simon was pretending to be still in his game, so, Wystan decided to continue playing along with him until he could persuade Simon to admit that the game had ended.

"Oh, I just noticed that the wall's been repaired."

"What wall?" asked Wystan.

"That broken part of the high stone wall where I used to come through every time I arrived here by leading Blaze along the side of the stream."

"Yes, I felt it was time that I had it repaired, so, yesterday, I hired a few men from town. They used some of the broken pieces of the wall, as well as all the huge fieldstone blocks they brought here on their truck."

"They sure did a great job because the repaired part of the wall

looks just like the rest of the old wall," said Simon. "Yeah, those workmen did an excellent job on that wall, and I'm very surprised that they could do all that work so fast."

"Yes, I was just as surprised as you because I'd thought it would've taken them much longer than five minutes to do all that work. Let's go into the house and have a glass of my favorite wine and a marijuana cigarette, shall we? While we're doing that, you must tell me about a few of your sexual fantasies because they sound rather intriguing," said Wystan, smiling.

Simon smiled and talked with him as Wystan opened a bottle of his favorite wine, and filled two glasses, then he lit a joint, took a long toke, and then handed the joint to Simon.

He tried to read Simon's thoughts again, but they were still whirling with memories of his past, however, Wystan felt sure it wouldn't take him long to penetrate Simon's thoughts.

He decided to test Simon by seeing his reaction to some truths about himself, and then he might admit that he was only pretending to be lost in his jubilee game.

Wystan took another long toke from the joint, then held the smoke in for a few moments before slowly exhaling as he passed the joint back to Simon.

"Thanks. I sure like the effects of marijuana, and besides the very erotic fantasies I have when I smoke it, I also sometimes lose all track of time," said Simon, smiling."

"Ahhh, time," said Wystan. "It has as little meaning as guilt. Guilt is like a cloak that one puts on to temporarily appease the society we are momentarily in. Don't you agree?"

"Yes, of course."

"And do you understand that the marijuana has absolutely nothing to do with your fantasies?"

"Oh? But I thought it did."

"It doesn't," said Wystan, smirking. "Oh, granted marijuana gives pleasurable effects, but not in the least as pleasurable as a pertinent life-giving nectar."

"Oh, yeah? I'd love to have a drink of that type of nectar next time you have a bottle of it open. Man, this marijuana is already starting to make me a bit dizzy."

"The effects of it still hit you so fast," said Wystan.

"Yeah, they sure do, and I love the sensations I'm getting."

"Erotic sensations, no doubt. I've drawn you a bath so that you can freshen up and relax."

"You've already run a bath for me? Oh, then you must've been at the front of the house, and you looked out a window and saw me riding toward the house."

"Hmmm, sure, okay, that's what I did. Now go have your bath. I'll wait down here 'til you're ready."

"Thanks, Wystan. My whole body feels very, very sensitive, and I...That's because I'm, uh...I'm very sexually aroused."

"Then you'll enjoy your bath. Ahhh, yes, you lie in the tub, caressing your body so slowly and sensually, then your breath

deepens as you grasp your erection. Mmmmm, you think about hot, nude flesh pressed against you as your lust begins soaring higher and higher. Ohhhhhhh, yes, and you begin striving to lick, suck, kiss and caress every part of your lover. Uh! Uh! Uh, mmmmmmm, so close! Just a few more thrusts! So hot! Now, enjoy your bath and I'll have a glass of my favorite wine waiting for you when you come back downstairs."

"Thanks, Wystan. I, uh...I'm going to enjoy my bath, so much. And now, I feel even more aroused than I did when I arrived here."

"Hah! You *should* be after that ridiculous spiel of mine."

"You mean that talk about me in the bathtub? I thought it was great. Very sexy. Like a lot of other things you say that always make me so horny, and then every time I...Hmmm, every time I what? Was I talking about sex again? Man! It seems that's all I like talking about. And doing it, and ohhhhh, yeah. I'd better start trying to think about something else, like having a bath, and then...Well, after that, I'll...Oh! Right. I was going to take a bath, right? Yeah, okay. I'll do that right now."

Wystan started laughing while Simon walked to the staircase, and then he was halfway up the stairs, when he saw Wystan smiling at him as he walked down the stairs toward him.

He turned his head to watch Wystan descend the stairs, then a few minutes later, as he stepped back out into the corridor after undressing in the bedroom, he saw Wystan standing on his hands, grinning at him.

Simon laughed while walking past him on the way to the

bathroom, then he laughed again when, just as he was about to step into the bathtub, Wystan suddenly appeared at his side to help him into the tub.

Wystan left the bathroom, and then Simon grinned as he leaned back in the tub, loving the feel of the hot, soapy water. He began laughing as he thought about how successfully he'd fooled Wystan into thinking that he was still playing his jubilee game.

Simon's thoughts whirled, and then he was riding Blaze slowly around the kitchen while telling his mother and stepfather that Blaze had stumbled a few times while coming downstairs.

He then looked at the kitchen door and wondered why it was now much narrower than it had been when he'd ridden Blaze into the house.

Simon then decided to ride his horse back upstairs, then lead Blaze out of his bedroom window, and then his thoughts whirled again, and he was back in the bathtub.

He resumed bathing, then moments later, he laughed when he thought about the fun he was going to have teasing Morag by pretending he was still playing his jubilee game.

Simon then thought about how pleasant and calm she'd been during the game, but he knew that Stasius and Wystan were planning to exterminate Morag before she went completely insane and became much more vicious than she already was.

He wouldn't be able to playfully tease her when he went downstairs after his bath because Simon was still trying to erase

remnants of his game, therefore, he wasn't aware that Morag had left early that morning for a two-week vacation in America, after which she'd be returning to her home near Hathersage.

Last night, Morag had traveled swiftly seven kilometers over the moors to a wooded area to greet the two men whom she'd been assigned to study for a few weeks.

She planned to blatantly defy Wystan again by inviting those two men to Wystan's summer house for what she knew would be a very satisfying experience for her.

CHAPTER THIRTY

The four men had agreed to place higher bets for their last poker game of the night, which is why Jason's heart had leapt when he'd been dealt four aces, then after scooping up all the money, he grinned as he got up from the table.

"Don't go now. How about one more game to let us win back some of our money?" asked Charles.

"Sorry, but I've got to get on my way home."

"So do I," said Luke, smiling.

"You got lucky *this* time, but next Wednesday night, be prepared to lose all your money to *me*."

"You're such a dreamer, Barry," said Jason, laughing.

They talked and laughed while walking to the front door, then Barry, Luke, and Jason said goodnight to Charles and began walking to their cars. Jason got into Luke's car, then Luke took a small bottle of whiskey out of his jacket pocket, and then after taking the lid off it, he said: "Here. Have a swig."

"Thanks. Make sure you drive slow if you're going to have more than a few drinks of whiskey."

"I never worry about that because there's always only about three or four cars on the streets at this hour, and definitely no cop cars cruising around," said Luke.

"Hmmm, speaking of cops, I didn't like the way Charles looked at me a few times. It was like he suspected something."

"Naaaa, you're just a bit paranoid because he's a cop, okay? Whenever he stared at you, I'm sure he was just studying the expression on your face while he was trying to guess what cards you were holding."

"Yeah, maybe you're right."

"I *am*," said Luke. "We're just two, regular working guys like everyone else, right? And close friends with Charles, right? So, neither he nor anyone else would ever suspect that we have a little kinky sex now and then."

"I just hope nobody sees the two spades in the boot of your car, then ask why you have even one spade in there."

"Fuck, Jason! Even if somebody *did* see them in the boot, I've told you that I'd just say that I put the spades in there because I'm giving them to a couple of friends who were planning to buy new spades. Okay?"

"Yeah, I know."

"And we always bury bodies where there's no chance that anyone'll start digging for some reason, so, change the fucking subject and let's talk about finding some sex tonight."

"Yeah, okay. Hand the bottle back to me. Thanks. Mmmm, aaaaaaa, thank fuck I've got lots of breath mints on me. Hmmm, sorry about going on like I did about the spades, okay? And for thinking Charles suspected something when we were playing cards. But I still think we should roll some big boulders over that spot out back of McClelland's. Someone's dog around his neighborhood might sniff something and start digging."

"You really *are* getting paranoid. Okay, if it'll make you feel any better, we'll put some boulders over it on Wednesday night when McLelland goes to his lodge meeting, okay?"

"Yeah, I'd feel a lot better doing that," replied Jason.

"Hah! That's exactly what you said a few days ago just before we fucked little Emmy. You and I both were so sure it'd feel so great fucking a ten-year-old, and we were right. Right?"

"Right. Mmmmm, it felt so great strangling her while you were fucking her, and then watching her trying to scream when you began stabbing her."

"Yeah, that *was* hot," said Luke, grinning, then he glanced at his wristwatch, and said: "It's almost eleven, so, let's try our luck at the end of Alcorn Road again. Who knows? Maybe this time, we'll see a few sweet teen nymphs roaming through the trees while hoping to find some great sex. Remember last week when we saw Doreen there, with her bare boobs jiggling around?"

"Oh, fuck, yeah. I never thought she cheated on Hank, so, I was very surprised when we saw her there, and it was lucky that we saw her before she saw us. It's a great place to meet and fuck, but because it's so dark there in some places, you've got to get close to someone to see what they look like, otherwise, you might end up fucking someone's mother."

"Right," said Luke, laughing. "One can't get a reputation as a mother fucker. By the way, I've gone by there a few times in the late afternoon, and I've seen some of the kids going off into the

bushes. I'd love to get it on with one of them. Mmmm, so young and ripe for the picking."

"I seem to have a winning streak tonight, so, maybe we might meet some pretty young thing to fuck."

"Yeah, some teenaged girls like guys in their thirties."

"I feel so old since I hit thirty last year," said Jason.

"Aw, c'mon. I'm thirty-two, and I sure as fuck don't feel old. Guys don't hit their peak 'til they're thirty-five. I read up on that, and I believe it because I'm horny all the time. If I had the...Pass me the bottle again. Thanks. So, as I was saying, if I had the chance, I'd be fucking ten times a day, but Sue's not in the mood that much. Only once a week, if I'm lucky."

"You do okay without her, right? So, if there's nothing in the woods tonight, then..."

"Tell me later," said Luke. "We're close to the end of Alcorn, so, I'll slow down and turn off the headlights."

Luke drove very slowly along the road with the lights off, then he turned onto an unpaved path, drove past some high bushes, and then turned off the ignition. They got out of the car, and began walking slowly through the trees, then Jason grabbed his arm, held his finger to his lips, and nodded his head to the left.

"What?" asked Luke.

"Look over there. See? Just walking off the road."

"Oh, yeah. She looks really young," said Luke.

"Yeah, and it's a bit late at night for someone her age to be out walking around here, instead of being at home, so, I bet I know the reason she's here, man."

"You don't know that for sure, though. She might've gone to spend the night at another girl's home, then changed her mind for some reason, and now she's taking a shortcut home through the woods. But on the other hand, you might be right," said Luke.

"I'm sure I am, because why else would she be wandering around here at this hour? Don't tell me that most teenagers aren't fucking each other because *we* sure were when we were their age, right? Shhhhh, she's walking this way," whispered Jason.

"What're you doing?"

"Undoing my pants. My white undershorts'll make her look down and if she's interested, well, we'll see."

"You're taking a big chance, man," said Luke. "She might run away because she'll think you want to rape her. Well, we *both* want to rape her, *and* kill her, but first we've got to get her to talk to us."

"So? My open pants might be just the thing to get her to start talking to us."

"Hmmm, well, you might be right about that," said Jason.

The girl stopped walking when she saw them, then she smiled while waving at them.

"She sees us!" Luke excitedly whispered.

"Stay cool. She looks gorgeous."

"Hi! Bobby? Is that you?" she asked, walking toward them.

"That's what I heard," she said. "Maybe you men would show me how you have sex with a girl, unless you think I'm too young to have sex with."

"Not at all, kid," said Luke, grinning. "I'd love to show you all about sex with a man."

"So would I," Jason eagerly agreed.

"Oh, wow! Can we do it now? You see, my parents left this morning to visit my grandparents and they won't be back 'til after supper tomorrow, so, would you like to come back with me to my place and show me how you have sex?"

"We sure would, kid. Where do you live?"

"It's a bit far from here. My best friend, Linda, invited me to her birthday party, and her father came to my home and he drove me to his home, but I was at the party for about an hour when I got into a tiff with Linda. That's when I decided to leave and I didn't care how long it'd take me to walk all the way back home. Now I feel so lucky that I've met you two, nice men because you can drive me home, and then we can have lots of fun while you show me how experienced you are at doing sex."

"We'll gladly do that, kid," said Luke grinning.

Luke was just as sexually excited as Jason as he followed the girl's directions while driving to her home, which he then could barely discern in the dark because there were many trees and high bushes in front of it.

She then told Luke that she was worried that the neighbors would see his car and tell her parents that she'd had some guests in the house late at night, therefore, she asked him to drive the car off the road, and then park it of sight amid high bushes.

After getting out of the car and following Gwen past more high bushes to the side of the house, Jason and Luke were able to see most of the side of it because that part of the house was lit by moonlight, and they whispered to one another that she must have wealthy parents, considering that the house was enormous.

She led them through a door at the side of the house, then Luke and Jason stood in total darkness until the girl lit candles on a candelabrum, which lit up a narrow stone staircase leading down into the lower part of the house. She lit candled wall sconces on the way down the stairs to light more of the stone staircase.

After reaching the bottom of the stone stairs, Luke and Jason followed her along winding, lowly lit halls, then Jason laughed and said: "This is the biggest fruit cellar I've ever been in. Is there some sort of downstairs living room or some bedrooms near the end of these halls?"

"Oh, then you've been in other houses like this?" she asked.

"No, but I was just sure you were taking us to some sort of rooms around here."

"Yes, just a little farther along, there's a big, very nice lounge area, with a big, big living room and some other rooms and a big kitchen. It's our downstairs apartment where we often have guests

stay if all the other guest rooms on the second floor of the house are occupied."

"I see," said Luke. "Must be nice to have lots of money."

Less than a minute later, she led them through another door, and then her candelabrum lit up what Luke and Jason could see was a rather nice, large, expensively furnished living room, then she hurried around the room, turning on lamps.

"Please sit wherever you feel most comfortable, and I'll be back in a minute," she said, smiling.

After she hurried away, Jason and Luke sat on one of the big couches and began remarking on the expensive furnishings, then they grinned while talking about having sex with Gwen, then killing her, and then burying her body behind big bushes at the side of her home.

Moments after they'd discussed their murderous plans, the girl hurried back into the room, smiling and carrying a small, carved wooden box, then she knelt close to the low table in front of the couch that Luke and Jason were seated on.

She opened the box, took out five joints, and then she giggled as she lit one and passed it to them.

"This is great. I haven't smoked marijuana for over a month. Mmmmm, here, Luke," said Jason, passing him the joint. Luke inhaled some smoke, then passed the joint to Gwen, but she declined, and said: "No thank you. I never smoke marijuana, but I keep it hidden in my bedroom for my uncle. He has two really big bags of it, so, he won't miss some of it."

"Oh, yeah? Thanks, kid. This is so smooth," said Jason.

"Really," said Luke. "Great stuff. Thanks, mmmmmm."

"I know you'll really like getting high because I heard that sex is even better that way," she said before laughing.

They chatted while Luke and Jason began feeling high from the marijuana, and by the time they'd finished smoking the joint, they were quite lightheaded.

"I feel so-ohhhhh high, man," said Luke, then he giggled.

"Whew! My body feels like it's made of jelly."

"I hope not *all* of your body does," said Gwen, smiling.

"Not to worry, sweetheart. I feel really horny," Luke told her.

"Let's take our clothes off, okay?" she suggested.

"Oh, yeah, great," replied Jason, grinning.

They got up off the couch, and as they undressed, Luke and Jason stared at Gwen undressing, then they felt very excited when she was nude and fondling her vagina and breasts.

They sat back down on the couch, and then Gwen knelt in front of them and played with their erections. Luke and Jason felt rather high from the marijuana, and their thoughts were swirling as she ran her fingers slowly up and down their erections.

"Mmmmm, your erections feel so nice. Let's lie on the carpet and...Well, then you men can show me what it is that you do that makes you have more experience than Bobby when he has sex with me."

"Oh, yeah, that'll be so great," said Jason, grinning.

"This'll be an experience you won't forget, kid."

"Oh, yes, I'm sure it will," she excitedly replied.

Luke and Jason began exploring her body with their hands and mouths as she gasped and cried out in pleasure, then moments later she began groaning loudly while Jason and Luke were showing her how wonderful oral sex felt.

Several minutes later, Luke began moaning as he slid his erection into her, then soon both he and Jason were taking turns fucking her and often kissing and sucking tongues with her.

Luke and Jason's thoughts began swirling faster while they looked into her eyes, and felt strange sensations emanating from them, but those sensations seemed to make both men become much more sexually excited.

Jason groaned and shouted when he reached orgasm, then after he withdrew from her, Luke began thrusting his erection into her, and when he eventually had an orgasm, he felt sure it had been the most intense orgasm of his life.

Both men found it difficult to believe that they still had erections after their orgasms, and Gwen seemed almost delirious with sexual excitement as she crawled all over them, straddling and riding one erection, then the next.

Their frenzied lovemaking suddenly stopped when she pulled away from them, and began rushing out of the room while telling them that she wanted to heighten their sexual fun even more, then

Jason and Luke wondered what other very erotic sexual acts they'd be participating in.

She returned with a big plastic sheet draped over her left forearm, and she was holding a bottle of baby oil in her right hand while she grinned and suggested that they all lie on the sheet and cover themselves with baby oil, then grapple and slide their bodies all around on one another.

Luke and Jason eagerly complied, and then as they laid on their backs on the plastic sheet, she squirted baby oil on most of their bodies. She threw herself on top of them, and they began grappling with one another's oil and sweat-slicked bodies.

She then took turns straddling their erections and riding them until both Jason and Luke had thrilled to another intense orgasm. The men then laid on their backs, with their chests heaving as they gasped for air.

"Man, I'm gonna be in deep shit with my wife because it must be getting near two in the morning," said Luke, then he chuckled.

"You? Fuck, Sue'll kill me for staying out this late. Hmmm, but it sure as fuck was worth it."

"Yeah, it sure was. Well, we can think up some great excuse while we're driving back home," Luke said.

"Did you like the marijuana?" asked Gwen.

"Oh, fuck, yeah. Amazing high," replied Luke.

"Amazing high and amazing sex. I'm wiped," said Jason.

"Yes, you men do look a bit tired out, so, I bet you find it very difficult to get another erection to have more sex with me."

"Hmmm, you may be right," said Jason as he giggled.

"I mightn't be able to fuck you anymore, either, but you're one great fuck, Gwen."

"Why, thank you. *You* look as though you might be able to fuck me one more time."

"Yeah, maybe I might," replied Luke, grinning.

"Go ahead and try it," Jason urged him. "We're already late getting home, so, another hour won't matter."

"More than an hour because don't forget that we've got some digging to do before we head home."

"Oh? Are you both gardeners?" she asked.

"Huh? Oh, yeah, gardeners. Yeah, that's what we are, kid, and Jason and I have to do a bit of gardening at a client's home so that the ground'll be ready to plant flowers tomorrow morning. That shouldn't take too long to do, but before we do that, I'm hoping my dick gets hard enough so I can fuck you one more time."

"You will? Oh, that's wonderful! Thanks, Luke! You just lie there on your back, and I'll get on top of you and we'll do it again *that* way! Okay?"

"Yeah, great idea, kid. Hey, Jason, start rolling some joints we can take with us, okay?"

"I sure will," he replied, smirking, then he began rolling a joint as Luke watched, then he began telling Jason to hold the paper differently in his hands, and to put more marijuana on the paper before rolling a joint.

The cigarette paper slipped out of Jason's fingers, then after picking it up, Luke began telling him again how to hold the paper to begin rolling a joint.

While he was looking at Jason trying to roll a joint correctly, the girl whom had introduced herself to them as Gwen, took that opportunity to lean sideways as she straddled Luke's hips.

She then lifted the small couch cushion that she'd placed beside them on the carpet before she had straddled Luke. Neither of the men had noticed that when she'd picked up that small cushion off the couch, she had also pulled out a boning knife that she had previously stuffed down between two of the much bigger couch cushions.

She gripped the handle of the boning knife, leaned back up, then while straddling Luke's hips, she raised the knife high, and then thrust the blade down into his neck, piercing a carotid artery.

Jason was looking down at his hands while trying to roll a joint properly, so, he thought that Luke was moaning in pleasure. Luke's legs and arms were shaking while spurting blood was being sucked out of the deep wound in his neck.

She then pulled her mouth off his neck and began cutting open his stomach with the boning knife, and then she shoved her hands inside the gory gash, gripped his intestines and began yanking them out.

Jason turned his head to look at them, and his eyes widened when he saw the crazed expression on her face, then he shouted in terror when she suddenly threw herself on top of him, stabbing

him repeatedly before pressing her mouth against a deep gash in his neck, and then she began sucking his squirting blood.

She screamed and giggled as she kept stabbing them, then she ran to the kitchen, grabbed a meat cleaver, ran back, and began hacking their bodies.

She laughed wildly while hacking off their hands, feet and arms before flinging herself on top of their ravaged bodies, then moaning loudly as she sucked and lapped up blood pumping out of Luke and Jason who were dying as they gaped up at the ceiling.

Satiated, she threw back her head and began screaming and laughing hysterically. Morag was splattered with blood as she reached for the meat cleaver, then chopped off their heads.

She began picking up body parts and stuffing them into a big, canvas bag that dripped a slight amount of blood after she picked it up with her right hand, and began carrying it out of the room.

For the past few years, it was becoming increasingly difficult for Morag to control her heightening, insane bloodlust, and now her eyes were almost bulging out of their sockets as she hummed and grinned while carrying the bloodstained canvas bag of body parts along dark halls.

After dropping the bag into the very deep well that was surrounded by a centuries-old, wooden fence, she began laughing hysterically again as she hurried away.

Morag drove Luke's car back to where he'd parked it before he and Jason had started walking through the trees, looking for a very young female whom they could rape and kill.

She then took several lightning-fast leaps over the seven kilometers back to Wystan's sumer house, then moments later, she was upstairs in the bathroom of her guest room, taking a shower to rinse all the blood off herself.

Morag dressed, lit a joint, and began smoking it while sitting in an armchair near the fireplace, glaring at the flames as she clenched her teeth because of the rage she felt from having to obey the law of only preying on murderers like Luke and Jason.

She then giggled while thinking about how she'd been able to again secretly slaughter her victims, instead of either slashing a vital vein with her hooked ring, or withdrawing blood with a syringe as decreed by Great Stasius whom had wielded total power for the past thousand years.

Wystan had assigned her to kill Jason and Luke, then before Morag had left the house, she'd felt quite pleased that Wystan had been concentrating most of his thoughts on Simon whom was near the end of his game.

Wystan had told her that he was quite worried because Simon was almost finished playing his game, which meant that his thoughts might suddenly veer into the horrific tragedy he had witnessed at that point in his past.

Morag had then known that because of his great concern for Simon, Wystan wouldn't be concentrating on what she'd be doing with Luke and Jason, because if he'd been aware of the way she had killed them, Wystan would have used his telepathic powers to cause her excruciating pain in mind and body for several hours.

She finished smoking the joint, then flicked it into the fireplace before picking up her suitcases while eagerly anticipating her vacation in New York City.

Morag hummed while carrying her suitcase downstairs, and then she put on her best smile to pay a brief homage to Wystan whose powers were almost equal to those of Great Stasius.

While driving away from the house, Morag hoped that after she left her car in a parking lot in the town near the airport, and then took a cab two kilometers to the airport, that her plane would be leaving on schedule.

※

CHAPTER
THIRTY-ONE

Simon got out of the bathtub, pulled the plug, then dried off, put on his robe, and looked forward to the fun he planned to have by teasing both Morag and Wystan.

He started whistling as he walked downstairs, wondering if Morag was at the pool, and then as he entered the living room, he grinned when he saw Wystan seated on one of the couches.

"How was your bath?" asked Wystan, smiling.

"Wonderful, thanks. I didn't see you when I came in, earlier. Were you upstairs working on your model of the cathedral?"

"Simon! What the fuck are you...Never mind. I'm sure you're faking being confused, but I'll indulge you a little while longer. Hmmm, okay, tell me what happened when you arrived here before you went upstairs to have a bath."

"Yeah, sure. Now, let's see. I rode here. I saw Morag. Said hello to her. She asked me if I'd like to take a bath to freshen up, which I just did, and now here I am."

"Uh-huh, I see. Interesting. Here's your wine."

"Thanks," said Simon, taking the glass from him.

"You're welcome. Now tell me about the last fantasy you had that involved me."

"Well, um, I...you...I, uh, it had something to do with a young woman named Laura. She dropped by to visit you and...and uh,

you started telling her about my physique. Yeah, then we took off our clothes so that she could compare our bodies. After that, you and I talked about the various exercises we did to build up our muscles, then Laura talked about exercises *she* did every day, and then we talked about the usual things. You know, like the latest news reports and the weather, and so on."

"And?" asked Wystan.

"I just told you."

"Hmmm, one often never knows if you're pretending to be confused or if you're just teasing. Now we'll see. I want to hear what else happened with Laura, and in detail this time, Simon."

"Um, you and I did sexual things with her."

"You're still toying with me. What happened after that?"

"I don't remember. I woke up, I think. Yes, I woke up, and then I realized I'd only been having a sexual fantasy, and that the woman called Laura never really existed."

"Oh? Well, I'm sure Laura would tell you that it hadn't been one of your sexual fantasies, but if you want to keep telling me it *was*, then fine. Fuck ya," said Wystan, feigning a scowl.

"Aw, c'mon. Smile. Please? I hate it when your upset."

"I'm not. It's just that I think this bit of fun of yours is getting out of hand."

"Huh? What fun do you mean? I don't know what you're talking about," said Simon, wide-eyed.

"Oh, of course not. More bullshit. All right, I'll play along a bit more. I'll start by asking you again if you recall exactly what you

did from the time you arrived here less than an hour ago. Can you recall that?"

"Yes, clearly."

"Clearly. I see. Hmmm, then tell me, little satyr, what's that in front of you on the table?"

Simon looked down at the low table, and saw the small, navy blue metal case, with a thin silver trim around the edges of it. He then frowned as he leaned forward in the armchair to take a closer look at it.

"Hmmm, you know, now that I'm looking at it closer, I seem to have seen it before," said Simon, suppressing a smile.

"Indubitably. The miracles of modern medical science."

"Oh? Really. Hmmm, how very interesting."

"Hah! You find it very interesting, do you? Ah, Simon, you just love to play, don't you?"

"Play at what?"

"Man, you can be so fucking devious at times. Okay, let's see what you'll tell me next. In this *supposed* sexual fantasy you had about Laura and me, I want you to stop trying to fuck with my mind, and tell me what happened about an hour before we fucked her. That was when you reminded me again for about the fiftieth time what you wanted most from me for our anniversary. Now *that* should stop this game of yours."

"I was so sexually aroused, that I really don't remember."

"Oh? Still want to play your game, do you? You can't have forgotten what you wanted most of all for *this* anniversary. I

understand you're still a bit confused from your game, but I don't believe you're unable to recall that very special request. Now stop all this bullshit, and start telling me what you want. Don't look at me with that sohhhhh confused expression because I'm sure you're pretending not to know what I'm talking about."

Simon wanted to continue confusing him by making him think he was still deep in his jubilee game, so, he did his best to continue looking bewildered while staring at Wystan.

"I'm waiting, Simon."

"Waiting? I don't understand. Waiting for what?"

"You know God damned well *what*."

"Huh?"

"My blood. You were so excited when I agreed to strengthen you much more on our anniversary this year."

"Oh? Hmmm, sorry, Wystan, but I don't understand what you mean. Anniversary? Blood? Strengthen what?"

"Aw, fuck ya. C'mon, little satyr. Stop the fucking pretense."

"I...Oh, well, okay, then."

Simon set his glass of wine down on the table, slid the small, oblong case closer, and then after opening it, he sucked in his breath while looking at the gleaming, stainless steel objects.

He picked up both pieces, quickly assembled them to form the beautifully crafted syringe, then he smiled while unscrewing the bottom part of it to expose the inner threading so that a metal tip at the end of a narrow rubber tube could be attached to the syringe.

Simon held the syringe in his right hand before reaching out

with his left hand to pick up the intricately carved, silver ring that fitted snugly into one end of the small oblong case. He slid the silver ring onto the second finger of his right hand, then after making a fist, the long, sharp, curved hook part of the ring arced out from his finger.

He often used that sharp hook part of the ring to slash open a vein to either begin sucking blood, or to let the blood flow into a glass which he could keep refilling while drinking and savoring that sweet flavor he so often craved.

Simon slipped the ring off his finger, then pushed it back down into the satin lining, and then he smiled at Wystan as he set the syringe down beside the small, navy blue case on the low table.

He stood up, took off his robe, then picked up the syringe again before sitting close beside Wystan whom then bent back his head to laugh, and then he closed his eyes slightly, and smiled.

Simon smiled when Wystan didn't wince as a vein in his wrist was pricked by the tip of the syringe. He filled the syringe, emptied it into a finely carved crystal wine glass that Wystan had brought to the table, then Simon set the syringe down on the low table, and lifted the wine glass to his lips.

He thrilled to the tingling sensations as he drank, and he felt himself becoming much more sexually aroused. Simon set the empty glass down on the table, then he sat back and laughed.

"Any Laura left?" asked Simon, then he winked and grinned.

"Hah! You ought to know. Incidentally, I wanted her dead moments after I fucked her, so, I hope to fuck you did it before

you went into town to look for a savory wench to fuck bowlegged. You've been doing that a lot lately, considering that you're always telling me you're well-satisfied here at home."

"But you know I occasionally take a fancy to particularly pretty playthings, although they're only quite fleeting flings."

"You're impossible, *and* insatiable," said Wystan, laughing.

"Plus totally loyal, as you know so well, oh, great one. I'll always worship you."

"And Morag *always* lusts for you, but you're such a tease. You know she'll do anything for you, so, she agreed to play your little jubilee game with you. I thought she played that part very well, didn't you? Considering how disgustingly decadent she is. Rather vicious little thing, too, at times, however, I'm pleased that when she arrived, you didn't fuck with her head, and instead, you agreed to let her have a bit of sex with us. Morag's not a bad fuck, although, after a few hundred years of practice with countless men, she still isn't as good as you," Wystan said, grinning.

"Nor you, stud. Where is she at the moment?"

"She decided to accept that invitation to a party in New York, so, she's on her way there. It's the opening of the new World Trade Center, and they feel sure that this one is structurally safer than the previous one. Terrorists are like vile, implacable gnats."

"Terrorists could never pester me for more than a moment because I have a much deeper bite than a gnat."

"Uh-uh-uh, Simon. We mustn't cling to the past, and that's why I gave you that syringe," said Wystan, smirking.

"By the way, in case you're interested, I disposed of Laura's body minutes before my game began ending."

"I would expect you'd have done that. After all, it's the least you can do, because I do all the fucking cooking."

"That's why I bonded with you about eighty years ago, and it's forever because of your culinary skills."

"Nothing else?" asked Wystan, pretending to pout.

"Well, besides the amazing sex, and my eternal love for you."

"Thanks so very much. I know you wanted a complex game, but next time, devise one that doesn't take almost two days to play because most of the time you were in your game, I was left trying to placate Stasius. Ilona told me that he was slightly miffed because we were supposed to arrive at his estate, yesterday. She said he went to quite some bother arranging a party for our anniversary, so, by the time we get to..."

"He's having a party for us?" asked Simon.

"Oops! It was supposed to be a surprise."

"Hey, you know me, man. I can act really surprised."

"Yes, I know that, but he'll read right through you, then know I accidentally told you about his surprise party for us. Aw, he'll get over it, although I was worried about you when you devised that memory game as part of our anniversary celebrations because it meant bringing your mother and stepfather into play, as well as your two closest friends at the time."

"Yeah, Colin and Jennifer. They were my best friends, although I spent much more time with Colin."

"Unfortunately, I never had the privilege of meeting them, but I'll never forget how terribly distraught you were after your parents and friends were brutally and senselessly murdered. I'm sorry I didn't sense the horror 'til you were in mortal danger, so, by the time I got to you, it was too late for them."

"You've apologized thousands of times, Wystan, but there's nothing you could've done. But you blocked them from attacking me any further, and I'll be eternally grateful you were able to get to me before they killed *me*. Well, they almost killed me because I was dying when you got to me," said Simon, smiling.

"You were enraged when you took a vow of revenge, but thankfully, after we bonded, you replaced your rage with cool determination, then hunted them down *our* way. But it must've been very difficult for you to've seen and heard your family and friends with such clarity, and know of their eventual fate."

"Oh, I was okay, because I put myself far into my game just before I recalled them in vivitime, and besides, I've always got you here to comfort me whenever I think about them and grieve."

"So, what did you think of the way I occasionally spun your thoughts to confuse your game?" asked Wystan as he grinned.

"It was great because I had some wild fantasies, and I forgot that I'd brought Laura here to the summer house. Hey, and I loved the story you thought up about a local legend called The Moors Bull. You'd based a bit of that story on my experience before and after we bonded, as well as a little about yourself."

"That Moors Bull legend wasn't too inventive because, after all, we actually do dispose of murderers. Never an innocent."

"Yeah, like that foul, disgusting Laura. I don't know why you gave that murdering bitch a last fuck."

"It sure as hell didn't fuck up your game because you helped yourself to a piece of the action," Wystan said as he laughed.

"Oh, c'mon, I had just a very small piece of the action, okay? I may have fucked her, but you set up that part of my game."

"Okay, so I set it up, but if she hadn't been the person she was, you would've jumped on her so fast, and I would've had to pry you off her with a crowbar."

"Bollocks! I'm no longer *that* naive about women! If I hadn't been sidetracked by your mind-fuck, then I never would've fucked her! But you blocked my thoughts almost completely, and I only began hating her just before the fucking started. You like fucking around with my head, don't ya? Huh? Yeah, you do! I'm going to toss you across the room!"

"Stop! Damn it, Simon! Okay, you asked for it!"

They laughed and wrestled for a few minutes, and then they grinned as they sat back up on the couch.

"You can be rather generous at times because since the time you met Morag about forty years ago, she's had the hots for you, but you've rarely been able to stand her because she's almost insanely bloodthirsty, so, she was rather pleased when you invited her to play a part in your game."

"Yeah, I could tell that she loved playing a supposed virgin and my first love interest, that gorgeous Brenda Wilkinson who had already lost her virginity over a hundred years before I met her."

"Yes, she *is* quite beautiful, although as violent as Morag. But of course, you were too infatuated with Brenda at the time to ever believe how heartless she was. A vicious, maniacal, little bitch."

"Yeah, I sure as fuck got over her fast after I realized what Brenda was really like. But then you always kept a close watch on us to make sure she didn't feast on me like a ravenous jungle cat. I needed you then, *and* now. You know I'll always love you."

"And that pleases me greatly," said Wystan, smiling. "Well, your game lasted slightly more than a day and a half, and that's too long to visit your past, regardless if you didn't relive how close you came to being murdered, or seeing the murders of your mother and stepfather, and your two closest friends."

"Yeah, but if I had started to relive that horror, then I knew that you would've stopped the game."

"True," said Wystan. "And I loved how you put yourself so deep into your game at times, that you really believed we were meeting for the first time and that was wonderful because it was rather hot reintroducing you to sex."

"My mind's still swirling a bit, but it'll take awhile 'til the remnants of the game disappear."

"You love devising wonderfully fun games, although sometimes they can be somewhat confusing, little satyr."

"Oh, yeah? Just wait. On our next jubilee, I'll devise a game even more confusing," said Simon, then he laughed.

"Maybe while you're playing it, I'll throw you a few more curves than I did *this* time."

"Would you throw lots of sex into the game, too?"

"I'd have to, because you're constantly horny."

"Yeah, I know. Just like you," said Simon, smiling.

"Great, huh? Okay, c'mon. Let's get ready, because we have a party to attend."

"Are we traveling conventionally?"

"Of course. I occasionally enjoy taking in the scenery at my leisure, and as you said, your mind still hasn't completely cleared from your game. Hmmm, which I rather enjoyed at times."

The End